THE WARRIOR KING

Recent Titles by Brenda Clarke from Severn House

ALL THROUGH THE DAY
THE FAR MORNING

LAST OF THE BARONS
RICHARD PLANTAGENET

THE
WARRIOR KING

Brenda Clarke

This title first published in Great Britain 1998 by
SEVERN HOUSE PUBLISHERS LTD of
9–15 High Street, Sutton, Surrey SM1 1DF.
Originally published 1971 in Great Britain under
the title *Harry the King* and pseudonym *Brenda Honeyman*.
First published in the USA 1998 by
SEVERN HOUSE PUBLISHERS INC., of
595 Madison Avenue, New York, NY 10022.

British Library Cataloguing in Publication Data

Clarke, Brenda, 1926-
         The warrior king
         1.   Henry V, King of England - Fiction
         2.   Great Britain - History - Henry V, 1413-1422 - Fiction
         3.   Historical fiction
         1.   Title II. Harry the King
         823.9'14 [F]

         ISBN 0-7278-5376-7

Printed and bound in Great Britain by
MPG Books Ltd, Bodmin, Cornwall.

CONTENTS

PART ONE

THE GREEN YEARS, 1399–1413

Page 7

PART TWO

THE GOLDEN YEARS, 1413–1420

Page 99

PART THREE

THE END OF THE RAINBOW, 1420–1422

Page 195

LIST OF BOOKS CONSULTED

The Hollow Crown. Harold F. Hutchison.
Henry V. Harold F. Hutchison.
England in the Late Middle Ages. A. R. Myers.
Six Medieval Men and Women. H. S. Bennett.
The Plantagenets. John Harvey.
The Popes. Edited by Eric John.
Renaissance and Reformation. G. R. Elton.
The Fifteenth Century. E. F. Jacob.
A History of Medieval Ireland. A. J. Otway-Ruthven.
English Social History. G. M. Trevelyan.
A History of Everyday Things in England. M. & C. H. B.
  Quennell.
Life in Ireland. L. M. Cullen.
How They Lived—55 B.C.–1485. W. O. Hassall.
Dictionary of National Biography.

PART ONE

THE GREEN YEARS, 1399–1413

1

THE two young men were closely related, the father of the younger boy being first-cousin to the elder, and their mothers having been sisters. This fact, however, was not immediately apparent, for whereas Humphrey of Gloucester had the golden colouring of the Plantagenets and the sickly constitution of the de Bohuns, Henry of Monmouth had inherited the almost midnight colouring of his mother's family and the magnificent physique of his Angevin forefathers. But a second, closer look, revealing as it did the arrogant set of the two youthful heads, the thin flaring of the nostrils and the proud sneer of the long, full lips, indicated not only the boys' kinship to one another, but also to the man who sat his horse a little ahead of them in the pouring rain and whose blazons and quarterings proclaimed him no less a personage than the King of England.

Henry of Monmouth wore black, for, on the first of June, 1399, it was a mere five months since the death of his grandfather, John of Gaunt, and sable clothes were still requisite for one so recently bereaved.

Humphrey of Gloucester also wore black, although his bereavement was of longer standing: it was two years now since his father, the King's uncle, had died mysteriously at Calais. But the mourning was a constant reminder to his cousin, Richard, of the rumours, current throughout the past twenty-four months, that the late Duke of Gloucester had been murdered on the orders of his nephew.

Humphrey's hatred of King Richard went deep and he had done his best to fan the spark of his cousin Henry's resentment into a flame as bright as his own. Last night, as the ships had lurched and heaved towards Waterford, Humphrey had told the younger boy: "Now that your father has been exiled for good and his estates and titles all seized by the crown, his life won't be worth a candle. What Richard did to his uncle he can easily do to his cousin. While your grandfather was alive, matters were very different. The King was fond of Uncle Gaunt; trusted him; relied on him for support. But now that your grandfather's dead . . ."

He had broken off, peering through the gloom of the cabin for some trace of emotion on that immobile face, with its almond eyes and heavy jaw, but had gone unrewarded. Not quite twelve years of age, Henry of Monmouth had learned how to dissemble his feelings. Since March, when the vast Lancastrian estates had all been confiscated by the King, Henry had not been heard to pass comment upon it; not even to his half-uncle and tutor, who sat his horse beside him now, in the rain on Waterford quay.

Henry Beaufort, thin, with a sharp, clever face, was also attired in black, for John of Gaunt had been his father. And of those three sombrely clad figures, he alone had reason to feel grateful towards the King, for it was Richard who, three years earlier, had sanctioned Gaunt's marriage to his mistress, Lady Katherine Swynford, and granted a patent of legitimacy to their four bastard children, of whom Henry Beaufort was the second. Henry's aspirations, unlike those of his two martial brothers, lay in the Church, and at twenty-four he had already achieved the Bishopric of Lincoln. But to one as inordinately ambitious as Beaufort, this was a mere stepping-stone: in the secret places of his heart, Henry's desires encompassed a cardinal's hat.

His vaunting ambitions, however, had recently received two serious setbacks. Nine months ago, after the fateful Lists of Coventry, his half-brother, Henry of Bolingbroke, Earl of Derby, had been exiled for six years, deeply in disgrace with the King. But Gaunt had remained high in his nephew's favour and had been able, therefore, to protect in some measure his other sons from their share of Richard's displeasure. Then, a brief four months later, John of Gaunt was dead, his duchy and his enormous wealth all seized by the crown. Henry Beaufort, quitting his post as Chancellor of an Oxford college, had hastened to Kenilworth to take the advice of that worldly-wise and still-beautiful woman, his mother.

Katherine, formerly Lady Swynford, now Dowager Duchess of Lancaster and second only in importance to the Queen, had been born the daughter of a Picardy herald; one, Payn de Roet. Her elder sister, Phillipa, had married the squire, Geoffrey Chaucer, whose employment by John of Gaunt had drawn his sister-in-law within the orbit of that somewhat choleric prince. Gaunt, entranced first by Katherine's dazzling beauty and, later, by her sympathetic personality, had taken her as his mistress after the death of his first wife, Blanche of Lancaster. Katherine had borne him three sons, John, Henry and Thomas, and a daughter, Joan, all of whom had been given the surname of Beaufort after their birth-place in France. And it was one of the Dowager Duchess's greatest pleasures in life that these handsome and talented children still turned to her for counsel.

To Henry, the cleverest of them all, she had said : "Stand by Richard for the present. You can do no good—and may do much harm—by declaring too openly your sympathy for your half-brother. Keep in touch with Bolingbroke, however. He's too much his father's son to accept quietly the King's injustice. I have already sent Roger Smart to him with the news."

Katherine had seen her son's mobile eyebrows shoot up at the word "injustice" and had promptly made him free of some more of her advice.

"There are times, Henry, for seeing both sides of a question, but this is not one of them. There is an odd temper abroad in the country and I recommend you to make up your mind just whose side you are on; Richard's or Henry's. If the King's, then you will of course admit that Henry of Bolingbroke was, ten years ago, one of the Lords Appellant, responsible for the judicial murder of Burley, the exiling of de Vere and the fall of Michael de la Pole. You will admit that,

11

unlike your father, Henry was always the King's enemy and that for a hostile cousin to hold the massive palatinate of Lancaster is a very different proposition for King Richard than to have it in the hands of a loyal and friendly uncle. And you will not, therefore, use the word 'injustice'.

"If, on the other hand, you see in Richard's action a dangerous precedent which can be used in the future against any man who owns property and who hopes to pass it safely to his sons; and if you see your half-brother as a strong man with much support among the magnates of this country, who will not sit tamely in exile while his inheritance is squandered by the crown, then you will admit yourself to be Henry of Bolingbroke's man. And you will talk, although quietly, of 'injustice'."

These words of wisdom were still echoing through Henry Beaufort's head as he watched all the panoply of kingship—the beds, the coffers, the tapestries, the horses—being unloaded from ships to quayside. He watched, also, the long, arrogant face of the King as he leant, smiling, towards the Frenchman, Creton, who had come to court in the train of the eight-year-old Queen Isabella. And Henry Beaufort wondered uneasily why Richard had insisted on bringing to Ireland Bolingbroke's eldest son, young Henry of Monmouth.

Did Richard expect trouble from his cousin and was the boy to be a hostage? Henry Beaufort dashed the rain from his eyes and shivered. An unstable man, King Richard, or so he had always appeared to the youthful Bishop; a man given to sudden outbursts of rage or grief, as when he had ordered the destruction of that part of Sheen palace where his first, beloved wife, Anne of Bohemia, had died. But, conversely, a patient, secretive man; one who could bide his time for ten years if necessary—as he had done in the case of the Lords Appellant—before striking in revenge. Altogether a dangerous man, thought Henry Beaufort, as the procession at last moved off into the heart of Waterford town.

No such thoughts troubled the head of Henry of Monmouth. He was more interested in looking about him; listening to Creton's exclamations of horror at the general poverty and squalor to be found on every side. Never before, it transpired, had the Frenchman beheld such wretched people, such filth, such miserable houses.

"Why, some of them do not even have a covering over their heads!" he exclaimed, his indignant finger pointing in the direction of various hovels whose roofs had been utterly destroyed.

"Oh, as to that," came in a slow, drawling voice from Creton's other side, "many thatched roofs were pulled down in order to lessen the fire hazard. My cousin—" a fair head nodded towards the King—"made an ordinance to that effect some years ago."

The speaker was a fat young gentleman, perhaps two years senior to Henry Beaufort, and his red-gold colouring, if nothing else, would have proclaimed him a Plantagenet. There was in addition, however, an indefinable likeness between the plump Edward, Duke of Albemarle, and the lean, taut figure of the King, his cousin. Their fathers had been brothers and Albemarle's sire, the weak and vacillating Edmund of Langley, Duke of York, was acting as Regent of England during his nephew's absence.

In his bumbling and indecisive way, the Duke of York had done his best to deter the King from setting forth upon this Irish expedition.

"To go now, just when you have confiscated all young Bolingbroke's estates," he had muttered, "is not very wise."

But neither had been his choice of words. "Young" Bolingbroke was the same age as Richard, thirty-three, and although his nephews might remain perennially youthful in York's ageing eyes, it was not an attitude of mind which commended itself to the King, who had, throughout his life, suffered from over-weening elders. And York's next words had only served to exacerbate the situation.

"Your father would not have gone in the circumstances."

"Well, I am not my father," the King had shouted, flustering his one remaining uncle into a flurry of nervous apologies. "Surely the murder of my heir—the heir to the throne of

13

England—is of sufficient importance to warrant my personal investigation!"

York had been forced to agree, but his misgivings had prompted him to one further effort.

"But it is now nearly a year since Roger Mortimer died. And we know how; in battle, at Kelliston."

"I should have gone before," the King had answered coldly, "had I been able. My uncle Gaunt advised it at the time. He, at least, was concerned about the fate of his great-nephew, even if you are not. This Art McMurrough cannot be allowed to plunder and kill as he pleases, particularly when it involves the death of my Lieutenant and heir."

"You may have a son of your own," York had said, but without any great optimism. Like many other people, he had found his nephew's choice of an eight-year-old child for his second wife a puzzling one. It was almost as though, having had no children by Anne of Bohemia, Richard did not wish to beget them by any other woman.

"Perhaps so," the King had replied, off-handedly. "But in the meantime, I shall have Roger's son, Edmund Mortimer, proclaimed my heir."

"A baby," York had grumbled, more to himself than to the King.

"Seven years old!" Richard had responded tartly. "Your elder brother's great-grandchild and, if I die childless, un-doubted King of England by the law of primogeniture."

York had again been forced to agree. It would have looked odd had he not done so, for his younger son, Richard, was betrothed to Anne Mortimer, Edmund's elder sister.

Nevertheless, York had wished fervently that the King had not chosen to leave England so soon after the sequestration of the Lancastrian estates. He knew that his sister-in-law, the former Lady Swynford, had already sent the Constable of Kenilworth Castle to her step-son with the news and, knowing his nephew as he did, York had not supposed that Henry of Bolingbroke would meekly accept the situation. And if he broke his exile and returned to England, York did not know that he could resist him. He was not even sure that he wanted

14

to, for what Richard had done to the estates of one relation, he could do to those of another.

Some of these feelings York had communicated to his eldest son before the Duke of Albemarle had left for Ireland with the King. And Edward Plantagenet, mentally slothful, had been forced to stir himself out of his normal apathy and consider his cousin Richard, of whom he was fond, as a potential enemy; a man who might one day be capable of debarring him from his rightful inheritance. In the end, Albemarle had, in his usual fashion, shelved the problem and hoped for the best. And, as he rode into Waterford, discussing with the Frenchman Giraldus Cabrensis's theory that the high proportion of physical defects among the Irish was due to their inordinate sexual depravity, Edward Plantagent sent up a small prayer that he would never have to choose between either his cousin, King Richard, or his cousin, Henry of Bolingbroke. Life was very well as it was.

In Dublin Castle, where the court had established itself after leaving Waterford, King Richard laid down his pen and smiled across at his half-nephew, Thomas Holland.

"I have just written to my uncle York," he said, "telling him of your success against McMurrough. One hundred and sixty-two men killed, as well as a vast herd of cattle captured."

"It would have been more to the point," Thomas Holland answered bitterly, "if I could have captured McMurrough or O'Brien."

"We mustn't be greedy," the King replied, rising to his feet as his squire, Henry Castides, entered the room. "Is everything ready for the investiture, Henry?"

Castides passed his hand fussily across his thinning hair.

"I hope so, Your Grace! I sincerely hope so! Oh, it's not that I fear your two young cousins or any of the other young men to be honoured will disgrace you. No, no! It's the four Irish kings whom Your Highness also wishes to honour with the accolade of knighthood. The Irish are charming people— as Your Highness knows, I am married to one of them—but they are also—how shall I say?—very natural!"

Thomas Holland began to laugh. "You mean they have shocking table manners," he said.

"Well—yes, I'm afraid so." Castides fidgeted from one foot to the other, his brow creased with the cares of office. "They will encourage their servants to join them at mealtimes, all eating and drinking from the same dish. The Irish have no sense of . . . of . . . of *place*! They have this absurd idea that all men are equal. And then, of course, there is the matter of their clothes. They insist on dressing in those dreadful smocks and half of them absolutely refuse to wear breeches underneath. They say—"

"Yes, we can imagine what they say, Henry," the King interposed hurriedly. "However, I trust that you have ensured that they are all wearing breeches tonight."

"Indeed, yes, Your Grace! I made certain that a plentiful supply of linen trews were laid by in readiness for their arrival. It will not be my fault if the ceremony does not go without a hitch."

Castides's faith in himself was not misplaced, and the four Irish kings, as well as Henry of Monmouth, Humphrey of Gloucester and their companions, were knighted without any untoward incident occurring. As Richard drew his youngest cousin to his feet, kissing him on both cheeks, he said: "My dearest Henry, from now on be brave and chivalrous, for unless you win, you will have very little name for courage."

Henry of Monmouth, looking up into his cousin's face, realised for the first time something of the dilemma which had always beset this unhappy king; the man of peace and culture whose inheritance had been one of martial glory— Crecy, Poitiers, Najera—handed on to him by his warlike sire and grandsire.

Then Humphrey was stepping forward to take his cousin's place and the moment of understanding slipped away, to be replaced in Henry's mind by the more immediate and practical thought that Humphrey was looking ill; thin and wasted by his racking cough. That consideration, too, faded before the realisation that he was now a knight with his spurs at his heels and his sword by his side. After that, he gave himself

16

up to the pleasures of the evening, for he had inherited from his father a deep love of music, and the Irish were an extremely musical race. (Giraldus Cambrensis, in his day, had remarked nastily that music was the only thing to which the Irish would apply themselves with any diligence.)

In July, the news that Art McMurrough had issued forth once more from his woods and his bogs and was now claiming to be the rightful King of Ireland, had the effect of ensuring the royal party's departure from Dublin as Richard moved hurriedly south.

"Art McMurrough," he told Thomas Holland, "must be taught a salutary lesson. If he thinks to obtain French aid, he will be disappointed. My marriage to Isabella and his alliance with England means more to King Charles than any confederation with the wild Irish."

Thomas Holland nodded. "We'll give the 'King of Ireland' something to think about," he promised.

But, in the event, it was not Art McMurrough who was brought face to face with Nemesis: it was the King. As he approached Kilkenny, Sir William Bagot, sent by the Regent, York, urged his beaten horse out of the town to meet him.

Henry of Bolingbroke had broken his exile. He had landed at Ravenspur on the fourth of July.

2

THE castle of Trim in Meath was very cold. The pale October sunlight, filtering through the window of the solar disturbed Humphrey of Gloucester, lying full-length on a day-bed. He was too weak now to stand and Henry, observing him closely from his seat in the embrasure, wondered in panic if his cousin were going to die. He was not particularly fond of Humphrey, but in Henry's present predicament, his fellow prisoner was the only person to whom he could turn for comfort.

As soon as Richard had heard of Bolingbroke's landing, he had sent for Bolingbroke's son. At Kilkenny, the eleven-year-old boy had faced the infuriated King, and it was at that moment that Henry of Monmouth had discovered in himself an immense depth of physical courage when confronted by immediate danger. He had never been aware of it before—circumstances had not been such as to bring it to his notice—but he had found that he was able to listen to Richard's maddened diatribe against the whole House of Lancaster without experiencing the slightest fear (although, when the interview was over, he shook and sobbed with terror for half-an-hour or more).

In reply to Richard's accusations and threats of condign punishment, he had said calmly: "My lord and cousin, I am as greatly distressed as you are by this news. I assure you of my total ignorance of my father's intentions."

Henry Beaufort, standing nearby, had let out his breath on a great gust of approval and relief. If there was one thing that the King admired more than another, it was courage.

Moreover, he was very fond of young Henry and eager to accept the boy's protestations of innocence. He had, however, refused to take either Henry or Humphrey with him when he returned to England, and had consigned them both to house-arrest in the castle of Trim until the rebellion was resolved.

Henry Beaufort, had he been so minded, could have told Richard that he was making a grave mistake in leaving his cousin behind. The thought of his eldest son in the hands of a royalist army might have done much to deter Boling-broke from militant action; but it was not a part of the Bishop's policy to advise the King. And so Richard had gone, sailing from Waterford to Milford Haven, taking Beaufort, Albemarle and the rest of his entourage, but leaving Henry of Monmouth and Humphrey of Gloucester mewed up in Meath.

Humphrey half turned his head and his cousin noticed a film of dried blood along his upper lip. Henry recalled uneasily that the de Bohuns were not a robust family and thought of his youngest brother, Humphrey, called, as was this cousin, after their de Bohun grandfather; a thin, active boy of eight, but perpetually plagued by minor ailments. And Thomas, the brother next to Henry in age, was much the same, although nine-year-old John was a sturdy, healthy child. His two sisters, Phillipa and Blanche, were also inclined to be delicate. No; the de Bohun constitution was not good and Henry wondered if he might have inherited any of its weaknesses.

"No!" he exclaimed aloud, startling his cousin out of his doze. He, Henry of Monmouth, had inherited no weaknesses of any kind : he was sure of it.

Humphrey raised his inimical gaze to Henry's face. How he disliked this self-contained, self-sufficient, self-confident boy! Had his cousin been a loud-mouthed braggart, Humphrey could have tolerated him more easily, for Humphrey had sense enough to know that bombast was often a cloak for uncertainty. But it was obvious that no feelings of inferiority troubled Henry of Monmouth's mind. His quiet conviction that he was always right, his priggish air of self-righteousness had always irritated Humphrey beyond endurance. He knew that he was dying and his one hope now was to receive tidings of Bolingbroke's downfall, thus making Henry the son of a defeated and attainted rebel. That he should wish success to his cousin Richard, whom he regarded as his father's murderer, was the measure of Humphrey's hatred of Henry of Monmouth.

Humphrey was racked by a spasm of coughing. When the fit had subsided, he asked: "No news, I suppose? From England?"

"No, nothing. I should have wakened you if anyone had come." Henry spoke impatiently, considering the question stupid.

"What do you think will happen to you if your father is defeated?" the elder boy asked slyly.

Henry turned to stare at him, his eyes blank with surprise. "Why, what should happen to me?" he enquired. "I'm not my father's keeper. Richard has accepted my innocence."

Humphrey felt as though he had been douched with cold water. "You wouldn't be sorry? For your father, I mean."

Henry thought about this. Then, after a pause, he said: "I don't know him very well, you see. He has been abroad so much of my life. After my mother's death, he travelled in Hungary and went on pilgrimage to Jerusalem. This last year he has been in exile in France."

"You wouldn't hate Richard if he executed your father?"

"It would be the law."

Humphrey struggled on to his elbow, staring incredulously. "The law?" he queried in an awed voice. Somewhere at the back of his not very retentive memory there stirred the remembrance of a story he had once heard, of a Roman Emperor who had condemned his own son to death for treason. Henry could quite well turn into just such a man.

"And if your father wins?" Humphrey persisted, and Henry shrugged.

"I imagine that the King will then have no option but to restore my father's estates and titles and to make the best of things."

Humphrey's eyes narrowed. "You don't envisage . . . any other outcome?"

"What other outcome could there be?" Henry's tone was pettish : he was tired of this catechism.

"What *do* you think will happen?" The insistent voice grated on Henry's nerves.

He snapped : "How can I say? I don't even know what support my father can command in the country. And the King has an army with him; Beaufort, Albemarle—"

Humphrey's crack of laughter made Henry break off with an enquiring lift of his eyebrows.

"Henry Beaufort," his cousin said contemptuously, "is your father's half-brother. There's little doubt where his loyalties will lie. As for Albemarle . . ." He let the sentence go with a sneer.

"I don't know what you mean," Henry said defiantly. "I'm very fond of Edward."

"Oh, we're all fond of Edward," Humphrey answered, smiling. "He's a likeable fellow, but not one I'd care to have with me in a crisis of conscience." He lay back on his pillows, a further spasm of coughing once more flecking his chin with blood and putting an end to further conversation.

And perhaps it was just as well, Humphrey reflected. It would be too difficult, trying to explain to a boy who had only just celebrated his twelfth birthday that although some men could be physically courageous, mentally they could be cowards. Edward Plantagenet, Duke of Albemarle, was like that. Tell him to attack some impregnable fortress and he would hurl his fat carcass into the fray without a second's thought; but ask him to decide between black and white, right and wrong, one man and another, then he would instantly become a weak, irresolute creature, always putting off the moment of decision in the hope that someone else would eventually make up his mind for him.

Humphrey began to drop once more into a doze and Henry stared through the narrow window slit into the distance.. He was, by now, as much bored as afraid and wished that something might happen to break the monotony of the days.

In answer to his wish, he heard the drawbridge groan in protest as it was lowered across the moat and, a moment later, the rattle of harness and the thud of hooves came to his ears as a party of mounted men clattered into the courtyard. The arrivals were outside his range of vision and he waited, tense with expectation, his heart hammering in his chest.

"Humphrey!" he exclaimed in a restricted voice, rising and shaking his cousin by the shoulder. But Humphrey had already awakened, his eyes very bright in his emaciated face.

Voices sounded, a long way off at first, then nearer as mailed feet echoed against the stone stairs leading to the solar. Humphrey, glancing at his cousin, was at last gratified by a glimpse of fear, which momentarily contorted the handsome young face.

Then the door burst open and Henry was betrayed into giving a gasp of relief. For, on the threshold, stood his half-uncle, Thomas Beaufort, Earl of Dorset.

Henry's face was set and closed; closed against something, some fact, which he could not as yet accept.

Thomas Beaufort, that uncomplicated and hearty young man, was thankful that his brother, the wily Bishop Henry, had forewarned, and also forearmed, him against this particular contingency.

"Our half-nephew," Henry had told Thomas, as they had strolled together beneath the walls of Bristol Castle, where, six weeks earlier, King Richard's three favourites, Bushy, Green and Scrope, had been summarily executed by the victorious Lancastrians, "our nephew, if he is to be a worthy heir to his father, must be convinced that his claim to the throne is just. No; not merely just. Let me see . . . that it is . . . right! Right in the sight of God! Young Henry, my dear Thomas, is a precisian. Indeed, I have often felt that with the wrong encouragement his religious zeal might well turn to fanaticism. However, that for the future!

"When you recount to him the events of the past two months, it will do no good to dwell on Richard's bad government . . . or injustice . . . or his father's popular acclaim.

You must stress what our half-brother, himself, will stress to his son; that Henry of Bolingbroke is rightful King of England." He had seen his brother's sceptical look and laughed. "Oh, no one will believe it, of course—except perhaps those most closely concerned."

So now, the bluff soldier had the unsavoury task of convincing his perspicacious young half-nephew of something in which he did not himself believe. The first part of his story had been easy. Both Henry and Humphrey had listened goggle-eyed to his narrative of events, starting with Bolingbroke's landing at Ravenspur in July and ending with his claim to the throne of the now deposed Richard at the end of September. They had heard how Bolingbroke had been met by a great muster of his retainers; how, at Pontefract, he had been joined by the mighty Earl of Northumberland and his son, Henry Percy, and, at Doncaster, by his half-sister's husband, Ralph Neville of Raby; how the Regent, York, moving half-heartedly against the rebels and, finally, meeting them midway between Bristol and Berkeley, had thrown in his lot with the obviously stronger side; and how, as Humphrey had predicted, Albemarle, accompanying his King to Conway in a desperate effort to rouse the loyal Welsh and Cheshire archers, had been unable to make up his mind what to do until he had, at last, weakly obeyed York's summons and joined his father at Bolingbroke's side.

Humphrey had jeered and gestured knowingly at this final piece of information, but even he was not totally prepared for what was to follow.

Making his voice as unemotional as possble, Thomas Beaufort recounted subsequent events. He skimmed as lightly as he could over the trickery which had been employed to lure Richard from Conway Castle; over his humiliation at Chester where Bolingbroke had been waiting with the ex-Archbishop Arundel, who had also broken his exile and returned to England; and over the way in which Richard had been carried as a prisoner to London and thrown into the Tower. But then came the most difficult part of all; explaining to the stern young moralist, who sat watching him so intently, how a crowned and anointed King had been forced to abdicate in order that his cousin might step into his shoes—an act which had not only deposed the reigning monarch, but also set aside the claims of his heir, the seven-year-old Edmund Mortimer.

Thomas Beaufort saw Henry's heavy brows descend over the almond-shaped eyes; the thick lips compress beneath the sharp, jutting point of the nose. After a long silence, the boy said "You cannot depose a lawfully consecrated King. It is against the law of God."

His half-uncle was prepared. "Your father," he told Henry hastily, "has laid lawful claim to the crown through his mother, Blanche of Lancaster."

Both boys stared at him and the Earl cleared his throat awkwardly. "Your father's claim," he said, as though reciting a lesson learned by heart, "goes back some hundred and thirty years. It is said—" a nicely anonymous phrase, that— "that Edmund Crouchback, the ancestor of the Duchess Blanche, was really the eldest son of King Henry the third and should have inherited the throne when his father died. But because of his deformity, he was put aside in favour of his brother, the first Edward."

Humphrey gave a most unseemly hoot of laughter. "You can't be serious," he gasped, "not really serious! For if that's true, it makes a usurper not only of Richard, but of the first three Edwards as well."

Thomas Beaufort bit his lip. He had anticipated incredulity but not open derision and he did not know what to say. But his main concern was with the reactions of his half-nephew, not with those of his cousin. He noticed that Henry's face had lost some of the disapprobation of a few moments earlier; that there was that same gleam in his eyes, compound of disbelief and self-interest, which Thomas had often noted on the faces of those whose intuition was at war with their inclinations. Gently, he prompted the boy's thoughts in the right direction.

"It is a story that I have heard now and again," he lied.

Humphrey snorted. "Tell me," he invited, "how many

times in all the fullness of your—twenty-two years, is it? How many times have you heard that story repeated?"

Thomas judged it wise to remind his cousin of the fact which he seemed as yet unable to grasp. "You are talking to the half-brother of the King," he said coldly.

But Humphrey, with the licence of a dying man, merely sniggered and Thomas glanced anxiously at Henry.

His half-nephew, however, had not attended to this verbal passage-at-arms : he had been busy with his own thoughts. In some ways, Henry was old for his age, but in others he had all the simple, uncluttered instincts of his twelve years. His highly developed religious sense had given him a keen feeling for right and wrong (too keen, as Humphrey had not scrupled to tell him). But when something he wanted could be justified, he was young enough not to question the justification; indeed, he was capable of embellishing it, as he did now.

"It is God's will," he pronounced, startling both his listeners.

"God's will!" Humphrey exclaimed scathingly. He might have laughed again, but he did not. There was nothing amusing about the grim, almost fanatical look on Henry's face.

But Thomas Beaufort was relieved. The prospect of returning to his half-brother a recalcitrant and conscience-ridden son was not one which he could contemplate with any pleasure. Now, however, he was able to make plans for their immediate departure. The coronation date was fixed for October the thirteenth, and if the new heir to the throne were to be present, speed was essential. Arrangements had to be made, also, for Humphrey's transportation, but, as it turned out, these were unnecessary. When his attendants went to rouse him the following morning, they found that he had died in his sleep.

25

3

HENRY's first thought on seeing his father again was that exile had agreed with Bolingbroke. Although only thirty-three years of age, the King's figure was beginning to thicken : gone was the lean, hard body honed to fine proportions by crusading with the Teutonic knights. The face, too, had started to coarsen, losing its handsome contours in a flabby jaw-line and a broadening nose; and young Henry surreptitiously felt his own features, as though to reassure himself that his own good looks would last for ever.

A second glance, however, showed him that his first impression had been wrong; his father's increasing bulk stemmed not from good health, but from bad. And it did not take the boy long to realise that Bolingbroke, having attained to the dizziest of heights and achieved his ambitions to the full, was already finding the price which he had had to pay too high. Trouble was stirring both abroad and at home. Charles the sixth of France, whose daughter had been brutally deprived of her Queenship by the usurpation, had closed the Somme at Abbeville and was assembling an invasion fleet under the command of the Comte de St Pol. Anti-Henrician feeling was rife, also, in Scotland and the Netherlands, while the Welsh, never slow to take advantage of the internal upheavals of their neighbours, were already beginning to chant the ancient cry of "Freedom!"

In Westminster itself, disaffection had raised its head in the person of Thomas Merke, the Bishop of Carlisle, who now languished in prison for daring to speak out openly in defence of the deposed King. More subtle, but none the less audible, were mutterings amongst certain of the barons who had helped Bolingbroke along the road to success, but who had been unprepared for the final step. A few were satisfied, naturally; the exiled Thomas Beauchamp, who had been recalled and restored to his title of Earl of Warwick; Arundel, re-instated as Archbishop of Canterbury in place of Roger Walden; his nephew, now restored to his father's earldom of Arundel. But in the Tower, lay the biggest problem of all; Sir Richard of Bordeaux, whose very existence had become an embarrassment and a continuing source of danger to his cousin.

Money was also a headache. Many of Richard's debts, as well as his own, had to be honoured by a King anxious to ingratiate himself with the City of London. Henry even felt obliged to repay that extremely wealthy man, Richard Whittington, the hundred marks which King Richard owed him. The ex-Mayor, in his blunt way and with that trace of a Gloucestershire accent which never left him, had said : "Your Grace can forget it," but Henry had preferred not to do so.

When her husband had expatiated upon the King's generosity, Mistress Whittington, the former Alice Fitzwarren, had smiled. "That, my dear," she had remarked sapiently, "is because he will one day wish to borrow from you again; bigger sums which he won't be quite so eager to repay. This coronation will cost a pretty penny, mark my words!"

Her words were marked. And it was not only the coronation which proved to be expensive. The day before, on October the twelfth, the King knighted his four sons, along with a number of other young men, in a ceremony the more lavish because he wished people to forget that his eldest son and heir had been knighted, and only recently, by King Richard in Ireland.

Young Henry accepted this as being necessary, having by now quite convinced himself that his cousin had never truly been the King and, therefore, had been unable to bestow the accolade of knighthood. He also had another reason. Between himself and Thomas, the brother nearest him in age, there existed an animosity, the reason for which was buried deep in

27

their childhood and long since forgotten. But they never missed an opportunity to needle each other, and Thomas's constant references to Henry as a 'bog-knight' had convinced the latter of the necessity for the new ceremony.

"What is more," he told his brother coldly, "I shall be Prince of Wales. My father has promised me, and before Christmas! And I shall carry Curtana in the coronation procession." Before Thomas could open his sulky mouth in a suitable retort, Henry's eye had alighted on his youngest brother, Humphrey. "Get that child in from the garden," he commanded, outraged. "He really is disgusting!"

The ten-year-old Prince John rolled his placid eyes towards the door and suppressed a giggle. Humphrey, lying full-length on his stomach, was peering beneath the skirts of a group of ladies gossiping in the courtyard. At eight, Humphrey's blatant preoccupation with the opposite sex was indicative of what was to be one of the main interests of his life.

"I like women," he protested as John good-naturedly hauled him indoors. "Well, I do," he added defiantly, braving the icy glare of his eldest brother. "They're different!" And he grinned, brazenly.

"You're nauseating," Henry informed him.

"At least he's not revoltingly conceited," Thomas shouted and slammed out of the room. But all his anger could not alter the fact that it was Henry who carried the pointless sword of mercy at their father's coronation.

In places of honour at this event were the Earl of Northumberland and his son, a large, swarthy man of thirty-seven, whose personal valour and explosive temperament had earned for him the nickname "Hotspur". Both the Percys had played a prominent part in helping Bolingbroke to a throne, but it occurred to Henry Beaufort, as he watched from his place in the Bishops' ranks, that Hotspur's wife was Elizabeth Mortimer and that the younger Percy was, therefore, uncle-by-marriage to King Richard's disinherited heir. Henry Beaufort reflected that his half-brother should tread warily in his dealings with the Percys.

The Bishop's eyes continued to roam over the brilliant

congregation. He saw his mother as she stopped to speak to her brother-in-law, Geoffrey Chaucer, her beauty in startling contrast to his pale, tired face. Behind Katherine, Henry Beaufort noted his other, and less prepossessing half-brother, Thomas Swynford, whom the King had recently made Constable of Pontefract Castle. Now why? mused the Bishop thoughtfully. And there was the Duke of York, the last of Edward the third's six sons; a weak creature, who had gone over to the winning side without striking a blow in defence of his King. Yet he was not so deserving of contempt as his eldest son, for in his position as uncle to the King, York had probably felt as much loyalty to one nephew as to the other.

But Albemarle's case was different. He had been a close friend of the deposed King, and Richard had trusted him utterly. A spineless creature, Edward Plantagenet, in matters of conscience, and yet, for all that, a thoroughly likeable fellow. There was no real vice in Albemarle, which was more than Henry Beaufort could say for the Duke's younger brother, the Earl of Cambridge. Now there, thought the Bishop, was a discontented young man, if ever he had seen one; and much stronger-minded, too, than his elder brother. And as Cambridge leaned across to whisper something in Hotspur's ear, Henry Beaufort was reminded of the fact that Cambridge was also about to make an alliance with the Mortimer family; to Anne, sister of the child Edmund, whom many still secretly regarded as rightful heir to the throne.

As the Bishop glanced in the direction of the central figure in the day's ceremonies, he considered that it behoved the new King, Henry the fourth, to be constantly on his guard. What had been done once, the enforced abdication of a King by a powerful baronial faction, could be done again.

On the night of December the seventeenth, the candles burned very late in the office of the Privy Seal. Huddled over the green cloth of the table, steadily writing, sat Thomas Hoccleve, his nose almost touching the paper before him. He refused to wear spectacles even though, after eleven years in the kingdom's busiest office, his sight was beginning to fail. This was not altogether the fault of his job, for Hoccleve, like his friend, Geoffrey Chaucer, wrote poetry in his spare time which added to the strain on his already overburdened eyes. But, as he remarked acidly to his fellow clerks, one had to do something to alleviate the boredom of working for the crown.

In his late thirties, he looked older; again, as he was fond of pointing out, the result of his job. Long hours huddled over warrants, writs and summonses, licences, grants and safe-conducts was conducive to nothing but ill-health : he suffered constantly from stomach-cramps and backaches, and for what? The pay was niggardly; ten pounds per year after ten years' service. Hoccleve, himself, had had to wait eleven years for his rise, which had been awarded him by the new King just over a month ago. All in all, it was hardly surprising that he drank heavily in every Cheapside tavern and indulged in a riotous bachelor existence which was the envy of all his married friends. Occasionally small emoluments came his way, the forfeited goods of some pirate or outlaw, but as his notions of largesse were extremely grand, it was the taverners and boatmen, the brothel-keepers and cooks who eventually benefited.

His work, this late December evening, was a labour of love —if one could call anything he did in the course of his duty by that name. But writing a book of precedents and formu-laries for the junior clerks' instruction was certainly preferable to wrestling with some knotty legal problem not yet resolved.

After a time, however, even the pleasures of the pedagogue began to pall, and he realised that his toes were numb, his fingers stiff and the candle almost gutted. He became aware, too, of the unaccustomed emptiness of the room, normally filled with seven or eight other bodies all jammed in close proximity to one another. Hoccleve rose to his feet with difficulty, easing his cramped limbs, stowed his paper and pens away in one of the chests, locked it carefully and blew out the candle. Then, feeling his way slowly, he inched around the calculating table and let himself out into the cold night air.

It was his habit in winter to go by water to his lodgings in the Strand, as the unpaved road between there and Westminster was often ankle-deep in mud. Seeing a boat already moored by the water-stairs, he was about to hail it when something furtive in the demeanour of the men who were at present disembarking made him draw back into the shadows.

The muffled figures advanced hurriedly, and in the flickering light of their solitary torch Hoccleve had a fleeting glimpse of several faces that he knew; John and Thomas Holland, King Richard's half-brother and nephew, followed by Thomas Merke, Bishop of Carlisle, only recently released from imprisonment. They failed to notice the clerk, and so intent were they upon their own business that he was able to trail them quite easily. Not that he had far to go. Outside the Abbot of Westminster's house they stopped and there, after a moment or two, they were joined by a man in clerical robes. Again, Hoccleve was able to see the face quite distinctly before the torch was doused and he recognised Roger Walden, the deposed Archbishop of Canterbury. Together the four men passed indoors, after which, at irregular intervals, other dark and less identifiable shapes glided along the frosty street and disappeared inside the Abbot's lodging.

Then, for a long time, no one else came and Hoccleve turned to make his extremely thoughtful way back to the water-stairs. As he did so, he collided with a thick, burly young man who looked as startled as Hoccleve himself.

"I—I beg your pardon! You're not hurt?" The voice trembled uneasily and a heavily beringed hand jerked up to pull the hood more closely about the face.

Hoccleve, whose wits were sharpened by his unusually long abstinence from sack—he had had nothing to drink since the previous night—pretended to be drunk. It might be safer, in case the young man had seen him spying. He hiccupped loudly and said: "Thash—thash very kind of you to ashk—but, no!" And he lurched around the corner.

A few seconds later, however, he cautiously reappeared

31

and was rewarded by seeing his quarry vanish into the darkened cavity of the Abbot's doorway. Hoccleve smiled to himself. If the Duke of Albemarle thought that he had passed unrecognised, he was wrong. But whatever was going on in that house—and Hoccleve had no wish at all to know what it was—he could not help feeling that the other men would be better off without Edward Plantagenet. For a more frightened young man the clerk thought that he had never seen.

Henry was enjoying his first Christmas as Prince of Wales. The twelve-day feast, held at Windsor, had been slightly marred by an outbreak of food-poisoning, but such occurrences were too common to be of much importance, particularly as none of the royal family had suffered.

The King himself was feeling easier in his mind. Sir Richard of Bordeaux was safely locked up in Pontefract Castle, in the charge of Sir Thomas Swynford. (Odd, reflected the King, looking down the long boards to where his step-mother sat, that such a beautiful woman could have mothered such a brutish son.)

But if the King felt happier, the Duke of York did not: he was worried about his eldest son. He had noted the signs of mental conflict on Albemarle's florid face and guessed that some mischief was brewing. He could neither enjoy himself at the banqueting table nor concentrate at the Council table, where the King was planning his first campaign, against the Scots. Hotspur's rough Northumbrian accent grated on York's ears and set his teeth on edge; Northumberland was over-bearing; Arundel unctuous. No one escaped York's private censure, but he recognised the true cause of his irritation.

He tried approching his younger son, Cambridge, but that young man merely shrugged his elegant shoulders and recommended his father to consult the culprit himself.

"Whatever it is, Edward won't be enjoying it," Cambridge sneered. "How he gets inveigled into these affairs I can't imagine. He has no stomach for anything except a plain, straightforward fight. So English!" And the Earl sneered

32

again, conscious that his mother, the Spanish Infanta, Isabella, had passed on to him not only her Latin features, but her southern temperament as well.

Still waters, there, thought York as he looked after his son's retreating figure. Just as the foppish clothes hid a body of immense Plantagenet strength, so the long sallow face in its frame of dark hair hid a brain of Castilian subtlety. York recalled that his father-in-law had been known as Pedro the Cruel, while his sister-in-law, Constanza, his brother Gaunt's second wife, had been a cold, hard woman whose piety had been oddly at variance with her iron will and bloodthirsty desire for revenge. Well, Isabella had not been like that, thank God! But he felt uneasy sometimes about his sons' Spanish heritage. Coupled with their hot Plantagenet tempers, it led them into devious paths.

This reflection had the effect of sending him off, hot-foot, to find his eldest son, whom he eventually discovered standing moodily in a corner of the tilt-yard, watching the apprentice-knights attack the quintaine with more enthusiasm than skill.

"I want you, Edward," said York, and Albemarle jumped guiltily at the sound of his father's voice.

It was bitterly cold on this fourth of January and York's long, thin face peered out at his son from the massive fur collar of his cloak—for all the world, thought Albemarle, like an anxious mother-hen with ruffled feathers. At any other time, the sight would have made him smile, but he was in no mood for humour. He felt sick with apprehension and uncertainty and the need to tell his father of his troubles had suddenly become overwhelming.

Half-an-hour later, York burst unceremoniously into his nephew's private solar, dragging Albemarle with him. The King looked up in amazement at the intrusion, but his uncle, forgetting himself in his agitation, commanded Henry's silence with a peremptory wave of his hand.

"My son has something to tell Your Grace," he said, his voice cracking with strain. "And I trust that in view of his confession, Your Highness will deal mercifully with him."

33

"That will depend," Henry answered, his bloodshot eyes fixed upon Albemarle.

The Duke wetted his lips, hesitated and then, in response to a prodding finger from his sire, brought the words rushing out in torrents.

"Your Grace must leave here immediately! There is a plot to assassinate you and all your children tonight. King Richard is to be restored to his throne. You must go! Now! At once, or it may be too late."

"And you are—were—one of the conspirators," the King stated with contempt, not wasting his time by asking foolish questions. Albemarle nodded tragically.

Then, seized once more by the urgency of the situation now that he had decided to throw in his lot with Henry, the Duke reached out and gripped his cousin's arm.

"There is no time to lose," he whispered impressively. "Even now it may be too late for you to reach London and the safety of the Tower."

4

THAT wild night ride from Windsor to London remained alive in young Henry's memory long after many other events of his childhood had faded into insignificant shadow-play. The smell of the cold air, the thud of the horses' hooves as they struck sparks from the frostbitten earth, the disjointed utterances of the grooms and the squires, the furtive turning of heads to peer for pursuit; all these things, ever after, brought back that ignominious flight with agonising clarity.

No sooner had the gates of London slammed behind them, than the royal children were hustled to the Tower. Henry said nothing, his face closed against the prying interest of others, but his burgeoning confidence of the past months severely shaken. It appeared that not everyone accepted his father's claim to the English crown as valid; that there were still people loyal to King Richard.

The same thought was in King Henry's mind as, together with the Mayor and Aldermen, he roused the city's levies to his assistance. And the news that Windsor Castle had been taken and sacked with comparative ease—indicative of treachery within—not an hour after he had quit its roof, lacerated still more his overwrought nerves. Moreover, Albemarle had revealed that John Holland, a man whom King Henry had done his best to placate by giving him his sister in marriage, was one of the chief conspirators. It seemed that Holland still preferred half-brother Richard to brother-in-law Henry.

Others involved in the plot, besides Albemarle and ex-Archbishop Roger Walden, included Richard's nephew,

Thomas Holland; his clerk, Maudelyn; the Earl of Salisbury; Bishop Merke and the Despensers; Sir Thomas Blount and Sir Benedict Cely; and even Richard's French doctor who had been allowed to stay on in England in the retinue of the deposed Queen Isabella at Sonning. Worse than all, John Ferrour, who had saved King Henry's life nineteen years earlier during the great revolt of the peasants, had now joined his enemies.

Inside the Tower, young Henry and his brothers and sisters waited in suspense to know their fate; royal children or penniless fugitives. They refused to go to bed, but sat huddled around a fire hastily lit in one of the rooms in the Lantern Tower. The two girls, Blanche and Phillipa, held each other's hands and started at every sound that reached their straining ears. John sat still, outwardly composed as always, but the frequent dilation of his eyes betrayed the fear within : even Henry and Thomas forbore to quarrel. Only Humphrey was truly indifferent, having buried his nose in a book. Reading was Humphrey's passion and the fact that he had so easily mastered this difficult art made him a butt for his brothers' ill-will as well as for their envy.

He rolled on to his back amongst the rushes on the floor and enquired: "What's aut . . ." He hesitated, then enunciated carefully : "Aut-on-o-my?"

One of the two men guarding the door stirred and answered : "Self-government." He looked surprised as he said it, and indeed Sir John Fastolfe, who was attached to Prince Thomas's household, was a man of action, not of words. He wondered vaguely how he had known this fact.

Humphrey digested this information. Then: "This man," he announced, waving his folio, "says that we all ought to be aut . . . autonomous and not sub . . . sub . . . oh ! subsomething to the Pope. I don't understand a word of it !" and sitting up, he threw the book from him in disgust.

His eldest brother, momentarily diverted from the serious business of the night, snatched the folio from the floor. "What are you reading?" he demanded angrily. "Who's this Marsiglio de Padua?"

The second man standing watch by the door showed a sudden animation, looking upon Humphrey with an interest hitherto lacking. "I can lend your lordship a better book than that," he said eagerly. "A contemporary work by a man called Hus. Jan Hus! He's a preacher in Bohemia . . ."

He broke off as Sir John Fastolfe rounded on him. "For God's sake shut your mouth, Oldcastle," Fastolfe whispered wrathfully. "We want none of your Lollard heresy here."

Sir John Oldcastle laughed, but, noting that the outraged eyes of young Henry were upon him, he wisely obeyed Fastolfe's behest. Humphrey importuned him to tell him more, but Oldcastle realised in time that the youngest boy's interest lay not in free-thought but in stirring up trouble.

Towards dawn, the children were persuaded into their beds, for it was felt that as the rebels had not attacked under cover of darkness, they would scarcely do so in broad daylight. But as he watched the youthful Lancasters file wearily away, Sir John Oldcastle could not help reflecting how ironic it was that the men who were now stigmatised as rebels would, a year ago, have been faithful defenders of the crown.

By morning it was known that, far from attacking London, the insurgents had withdrawn westward; whether on account of Albemarle's failure to join them at Colnbrook as arranged, or because the Hollands felt that the westcountry might be more favourable to their cause, no one could say. But as the January days wore on, one thing became abundantly clear. Whatever second thoughts some of the nobility might have had, the commoners were not yet disillusioned enough with Henry of Bolingbroke to support his enemies.

At Cirencester, the revolt came to a bloody and barbarous end when the populace dragged several of the rebel leaders to their deaths in the town market-place; while those who managed to escape that particular slaughter, were taken and executed in places as far apart as Bristol and Pleshey. By early February, the insurrection was crushed and Henry the fourth's usurpation of his cousin's throne amply vindicated.

But the most important result of the Earls' revolt, as it came to be known, was the sudden death of Sir Richard of

Bordeaux, whose body was brought by easy stages from Pontefract to London and, in its simple lead coffin, put on display outside St Paul's. Afterwards, it was buried in the Dominican friary at King's Langley.

The rebellion over, King Henry was able to turn his attention once more to his projected invasion of Scotland; George Dunbar, the Scottish Earl of March, having offered himself as an ally of the English. The Scots, too, had internal troubles—"although when did they not?" shrugged Henry Beaufort to his brother, Thomas. The saintly but ineffectual King Robert the third was contending for his throne with a refractory eldest son and two predatory brothers, the Duke of Albany and Alexander, known as the Wolf of Badenoch. All in all, it seemed a propitious moment for the English to attack.

At a meeting of the Common Council, Alderman Whittington, generally held to be one of the two richest men in England, was given a seat of honour. Mistress Whittington had predicted correctly when she had prophesied that King Henry would need further loans from her husband. The representative of the Coleman street ward was not complaining, however, for Whittington was an easy-going man who liked to devote his vast wealth to the public good—and what could be better than his beloved country's military prestige?

"A splendid thing if we give those children of the Devil a trouncing," he remarked to his neighbour, Thomas Chaucer, who sat in Parliament for Oxfordshire.

Chaucer nodded, his face pale above the mourning clothes which he wore for the death of his father, Geoffrey.

In looks, Thomas Chaucer was not unlike his cousin, Thomas Beaufort, for both men had the heavy Flemish features of their mothers' father, the Picardy herald, Payn de Roet. Henry Beaufort, on the other hand, was more of a Plantagenet and it was easy to see in him a resemblance to his royal half-brother, who sat at the head of the table issuing peremptory orders.

All parts of the country were to raise levies and various gentlemen present were entrusted with Commissions of Array. Those absent would receive theirs by messenger, or, if more convenient, by a neighbour's hand.

"You," grunted the King to Lord Grey of Ruthyn, "can take our summons to Glendower when you return home to Wales." He saw the expression on the other man's face and gave his snort of laughter. "No love lost between you, I know, but you won your case with my backing. The land is yours now. You can take satisfaction from the fact that together we outwitted a man trained in law in the Westminster courts."

"Perhaps," said Henry Beaufort thoughtfully, "Glendower won't obey Your Grace's summons. The Welsh are known to be vindictive."

"And to have very clean teeth," murmured Whittington absentmindedly. Then, seeing everyone staring at him, he became covered in confusion. "The Welsh have very clean teeth," he explained awkwardly, conscious of the King's raised eyebrows. "They were always known for it . . . in Gloucestershire . . . when I was a boy. They use green hazel and a woollen cloth. . . ." The Alderman floundered into silence and King Henry, after staring at him for a moment or two, and reflecting upon the inadvisability of offending a very rich man, merely shrugged and turned back to his half-brother.

"I think it unlikely that Glendower would fail to obey me," he answered. "He is not the man who would wish to be branded as a coward; as a man who had failed in his feudal duty."

Lord Grey, who had pocketed his neighbour's Commission of Array with a very ill grace, suddenly stopped biting his fingernails and sat extremely still. After a while, he started to grin and Henry Beaufort, noting it, smiled inwardly. Later, he remarked to his eldest brother, John, Earl of Somerset : "I shall be exceedingly surprised if you see Owen Glendower on this Scottish expedition."

John, like his half-brother, King Henry, scoffed at the notion. Glendower was recognised as a man scrupulous in all matters of honour. "He won't risk contravening the code of chivalry," the Earl replied, tossing his little daughter, Joanna, in his arms, "out of petty spite. Not just to revenge himself because the King backed Ruthyn in that land dispute."

"I daresay you're right," smiled the Bishop. "However, we shall see."

And see they did, for in the summer campaign against Scotland—which achieved nothing more spectacular than a forced march to Edinburgh and an ignominious retreat when the English found their lines of communication cut by the Scots guerrilla forces—Owen Glendower was conspicuous only by his absence.

Furious, the King issued a proclamation condemning the Welshman as a traitor. To Owen's protestations that he had never received the royal summons, Henry turned a deaf ear. Equally furious that his attempts at explanation should be so spurned—"tantamount," he snarled, "to calling me a liar" —Owen Glendower, descendant of the Princes of Powys, retaliated in the only way he knew how when his honour was impugned.

By the time King Henry reached Chester on his homeward march from Scotland, Glendower and the whole of north Wales were in arms.

Shortly after his thirteenth birthday in the late September of that same year, Henry of Monmouth had his first taste of warfare. Together with his father, Hotspur and an avenging English army, he endured the rigours of an autumn campaign as far as the Menai Straits.

Hotspur, who earlier in the year had suffered a humiliating defeat by the Scots at Cocksburnpath, was in a wild mood and prayed daily for the appearance of Glendower. But the Welshman, knowing himself not yet ready to face the English in open battle, vanished with all his forces into the mists of Snowdonia.

"We've seen the last of him," King Henry remarked with satisfaction to Thomas Beaufort as they beat their way back to Chester before the snows of winter severed their lines of

40

communication. "All the same, it's time that these Welshmen knew who is the master. It's time that the Prince of Wales became just that."

It was a consideration which fully occupied the King's mind for the next few months and made him preoccupied, even during the Christmas season, when he entertained with lavish splendour—which he could ill-afford—the Greek Emperor, Manuel the second.

The Greek delegation had come seeking English help to defend Constantinople against the advancing Turkish hordes; but although they were given many expensive presents and expressions of goodwill, no promise of military aid was forthcoming from Henry of Bolingbroke. His subjects proffered no assistance, either, merely pouring ridicule on these outlandish foreigners.

"God's teeth, have you seen them?" Cambridge demanded of his brother, Albemarle, pirouetting before his mirror of polished metal and admiring the extravagances of his huge, padded sleeves. "They wear nothing but those hideous white robes; the Emperor as well as his men." And he noted with obvious satisfaction the deep border of fur on the skirt of his blue velvet doublet.

Albemarle smiled uneasily. He could never quite fathom this younger brother of his, whose dandyism, he felt sure, was nothing more than a pose.

"Perhaps the Greeks don't care for *our* clothes," he suggested—and was perfectly correct.

Manuel and the member of his entourage thought that the diversity in English dress was absurd and did not hesitate to say so. They also commented unfavourably on the shop-keepers' habit of hanging a red cloth over their lanterns—a protection against the smallpox it was said, but in reality, as the Greeks were quick to appreciate, to make the inspection of their goods more difficult; all of which in no way endeared the visitors to their hosts. The Greeks had yet to learn that while it was quite in order for the English to criticise other nations, the reverse could only give offence.

And it was not merely the differences in English fashion

which came under the Greeks' verbal fire, but also the many divergences of English opinion concerning religion. The extent of the Lollard movement amazed them, as did the fact that the Earl of Salisbury, executed for his part in the Earls' revolt, had become something of a folk-hero because of his refusal to accept the ministrations of a priest on the scaffold. This follower of Wycliffe had stood firm in his beliefs even in the moment of death and, because of it, the English, even the most orthodox, accorded him a grudging respect.

King Henry, however, was less tolerant towards the growing heresy in his kingdom. His throne was as yet insufficiently secure to risk offending the other Christian countries of Europe. It was bad enough that, for the past twenty-two years, there had been two Popes, one at Rome, the other at Avignon and that there was still little hope of the schism being ended. He allowed himself, therefore, to be persuaded by the fanatical Archbishop Arundel into sanctioning a statute, *De Heritico Comburendo*, which authorised the burning of heretics.

In the spring of 1401, the new King made his first dynastic alliance when his daughter, Blanche, was married to Lewis of Bavaria.

"And it is high time," the King told his half-brother, Henry Beaufort, "that the Prince of Wales was thinking of settling down."

The Bishop agreed. "There's always Isabella de Valois," he suggested. "And it would save us having to refund her dowry when we return her to France."

But the King was a realist. "She wouldn't have him," he said, "without being forced. They tell me that she wears nothing but black and spends her time snivelling for Richard. There's no sense in saddling the boy with a wife who hates him. Moreover, there's the father . . ." He broke off with a significant look, and Henry Beaufort nodded. He, too, had heard the rumours that Charles the sixth of France was subject to violent fits of madness. There seemed little point in tainting good Plantagenet blood with the bitter inheritance of the de Valois.

"The mother, also . . ." he murmured, and once again silence spoke more eloquently than words.

Not that there was any sign of insanity in the brilliant and astute Isabeau of Bavaria, but her lechery was a by-word, while her liaison with her brother-in-law, the Duke of Orleans, was one of the great scandals of Europe. Hardly the mother-in-law, reflected the Bishop, for his pious and priggish young nephew. "We must think again," Henry Beaufort conceded.

But before either the King or the Bishop could give their matrimonial schemes any further consideration, their thoughts were diverted by the news of uprisings in Wales; and the seriousness of these outbreaks could be measured by the fact that the Welsh students were leaving the universities and hurrying home to take up arms. Glendower had raised his standard and was proclaiming himself rightful Prince of Wales. And if his claim to be descended from Llewellyn the Great was received with a certain amount of scepticism by some of his compatriots, these doubting Thomases kept their misgivings to themselves. Owen's personal magnetism was hard fact and the cause of Welsh independence had long needed such a man as its focal point. "Freedom from the Saxon yoke!" was the Welsh battle-cry; a cry which had always ignored the fact that it had been the Norman, not the Saxon, kings who had been so determined to subdue them.

The King made up his mind. It was more than time that his eldest son, who, since the previous autumn, had been holding his own court at Chester, became Prince of Wales in deed as well as name. He had Hotspur with him as his mentor and chief adviser, and surely no boy could ask for more than to be under the direction of the greatest soldier of his age. It was time indeed for both the eldest sons of Lancaster to be making their marks in the world.

Prince Thomas should be appointed Lieutenant of Ireland. Prince Henry should prove once and for all that Wales was a mere appanage of the English crown.

5

HENRY OF MONMOUTH was finding the process of growing up less painful than many other boys of his age. For this, his elementary sense of right and wrong was largely responsible, simplifying life for him in a way which some of his elders found terrifying. When Hotspur announced his intention of resigning from the Prince's Council because of lack of payment for his labours, Henry, fond as he was of the younger Percy, had no hesitation in condemning his action as reprehensible.

"You cannot refuse to do your duty simply through want of money," he said coldly.

"My men can refuse to do their duty, though," roared Hotspur, furious at being taken to task by this sententious thirteen-year-old boy; he, a man in his forties! "And small blame to them, either," he spluttered on. "It's time, my lord, that your father opened his purse strings."

"He cannot give you what he has not got," replied the Prince tartly, and Hotspur snorted.

Henry Percy's disenchantment with the House of Lancaster, which he and his father had done more than most to enthrone, was growing apace. The elder Henry, from whom they had hoped so much, appeared now as an ungrateful miser, unwilling to recompense his most faithful servants; whilst the younger Henry, the inheritor of that crown which Hotspur and Northumberland had helped to bestow, seemed little better. Hotspur was mollified, however, by the Prince's avowed intention of going to London to see his parent for himself, but would have been less appeased had he known that the Percys' arrears of pay would figure but negligibly in Henry's consultations with his father.

In the February Parliament, the Commons had warned the King and his Councillors, that the state of affairs in Wales was grave; that the present series of minor rebellions could escalate into a full-scale war. The King and his magnates chose to ignore the warning, dismissing the Welsh as "bare-footed churls with a poor reputation for fighting". The Prince knew better, for whatever else might be said of Henry of Monmouth, not even his enemies denied the boy's possession of a military sense which, in the opinion of Hotspur, amounted almost to genius. And Henry felt it his bounden duty to convey to the King the seriousness of the Welsh situation and to convince his father that the capture of Conway Castle by Rhys and Gwillim ap Tudor was no easily remedied fluke.

Henry's arrival in London coincided with the departure of Isabella de Valois for France. The usurpation had at last been accepted by the French, who realised that with Richard's death, continued hostility was pointless. The true heir, Edmund Mortimer, was nothing to them and, in April, representatives of the two countries met at Calais; with the result that the English had agreed to refund a part of the ex-Queen's dowry if the French would arrange to fetch her from London.

In the new and friendlier atmosphere between the two countries, King Henry felt it incumbent upon him to take a personal farewell of the French Princess and, accompanied by his eldest son, travelled in state to Billingsgate. He was unprepared, however, for the sight which greeted him.

Isabella, emerging with her attendants from her overnight lodgings, was dressed in unrelieved mourning from head to foot, her face, hands and feet totally obscured by a clinging black veil. Whatever her countrymen might have decided, Isabella de Valois had every intention of keeping fresh in people's minds the reason for her departure from England.

King Henry was enraged. "We'll soon put an end to this ridiculous farce," he muttered, and signed to one of the Princess's attendants to put back the veil from the child's face.

45

It was a false move. Isabella of France might only be twelve years of age, but, being the daughter of Isabeau of Bavaria, she knew how to love and to hate. She had loved Richard with all the intensity of a child for her idol : he had captured her heart so completely that throughout her short life there was never to be room for anyone else within it. In her mind's eye now, she saw him as he had been at their last meeting, just before he had left for Ireland, sitting on the floor of her room and talking to her about her dolls. For Richard of Bordeaux had had the rare faculty of being able to commune with children; had found them spiritually akin in a way in which he had never found his coevals or his elders. And at the memory, tears welled up in Isabella's great blue eyes, spilling unheeded down her pale cheeks, as she stared, rigid with hate, at her husband's murderer.

Suddenly, gathering the spittle in her mouth, she expectorated violently in King Henry's direction. The French envoys were horrified and prayed that it would never come to Queen Isabeau's ears. However much she might understand, she would never forgive her daughter's insult to her newly acquired ally, the King of England.

Isabella was hustled on board the French ship which rocked at its moorings, while the envoys burbled anxiously about an over-tired child.

"Over-tired!" snarled Henry to his son as they rode back to Westminster, picking their way through the piles of offal and refuse lining the narrow streets. "Over-indulged is more like it. I know what I'd do with her if she were my daughter, and I trust that Madame Isabeau does the same."

Prince Henry was indifferent. He had things on his mind other than the tantrums of an insignificant French Princess. But when he had had his say, his father was found to be equally indifferent to the Prince's demands for more assistance in his Welsh campaign.

"Do you mean to say," the King barked fiercely, "that you and Hotspur can't deal with a pack of Welsh barbarians, even if they *are* led by Glendower?"

"Hotspur says that he will resign his command," the Prince

answered, "as he is unable to pay his troops, having received no money."

"Money! Money! That's all I hear," was the acid retort. "Thomas is in financial difficulties in Ireland—I've just had a letter from the Bishop of Dublin—and I can't give *you* money as well. You won't fare any better, either, if you appeal to the Commons. When I wanted every seaport to provide a ship for defence, Parliament said no! It would cost too much."

So Prince Henry had to return to Wales without having convinced his father that the trouble in Wales was anything more than a petty rebellion, and without having any money in his pocket with which to ameliorate the situation. It was obvious that methods other than the direct ones would have to be employed.

"No!" exclaimed Hotspur disgustedly. "I won't do it! I will not demean my knighthood by luring Glendower here to take the oath of allegiance and then murdering him."

There was an uncomfortable silence in the Prince of Wales's Council Chamber at Chester. Trust a blunt and unrefined Northerner, thought Hugh le Despenser, to state baldly what had only been hinted at in the most circumspect manner possible.

Prince Henry bit his lip. He respected Hotspur and was fond of him in so far as it was in his nature to be fond of anyone. The scorn in Henry Percy's voice took the Prince to task for his own lack of chivalry in countenancing the plan, and Henry was a boy who believed implicitly in his own sense of honour. To have it belied, even obliquely, was more than he could tolerate.

"What else do you suggest then, my lord, since we seem unable to bring Glendower to open battle?"

"We shall never bring him to battle," snorted Hotspur. And, returning to his perennial theme, added: "Especially with no money to pay our troops."

"My father has given everything he can," the Prince retorted defiantly. "There is war everywhere in Ireland and

47

money is needed by my brother, Thomas, as well as by ourselves."

"Wales is nearer than Ireland," Percy snapped, blowing on his rough, red hands, for the November chill seeped in through every crack and cranny of the ill-heated room. He rose to his feet and bowed stiffly. "I warned Your Highness that I should resign if my arrears in pay were not forthcoming. I ask leave to retire to my estates."

The other members of the Council exchanged glances. Hugh le Despenser smiled to himself : he knew that he would be given Hotspur's position as the Prince's chief adviser. Despenser felt that it was no more than his due, for he was a man with a sense of what was owing to his name. His father had led the famous crossing of the Blanche-Taque ford before Crecy and his grandfather had been hanged six feet high at Bristol for being the lover of Edward the second, sent to the gallows at the instigation of Edward's Queen and her paramour, Roger Mortimer. Now, Mortimer's descendant was, since the death of Richard of Bordeaux, rightful King of England and Hotspur was married to the boy's aunt. A consideration, reflected Hugh le Despenser, like Henry Beaufort before him, that the Prince and his father would do well to keep in mind.

It was a point to be borne even more forcibly in mind the following January. Glendower, who had raised his standard at Caernarvon shortly after the Council meeting at Chester, captured Edmund Mortimer the elder, brother to Elizabeth Percy and uncle to the rightful King. This in itself was nothing, but in March came the news, startling both the courts at Westminster and Chester, that Mortimer senior had married Catherine Glendower. Little Edmund Mortimer had acquired yet another aunt-by-marriage; this time no less a personage than the daughter of the man who was the self-styled Prince of Wales and the House of Lancaster's most dangerous enemy.

This apart, King Henry had other problems, mainly financial. In spite of borrowing a thousand pounds apiece from Richard Whittington and the City of London, the King was still desperate for money; and to add to the general air of gloom, the court was plunged into mourning for Edmund of Langley, who died suddenly during the spring.

Albemarle now succeeded to his father's title, Duke of York, and with the weightier appellation, seemed to settle more firmly into his allegiance to Lancaster. Not even the rumours that Richard of Bordeaux was alive and in Scotland had the power to move him.

"A rumour put about by the Scots to make trouble," he remarked to his brother, Cambridge.

"Perhaps!" The younger man adjusted his beautiful crimson doublet. "Henry is taking no chances, in any event. I understand that death is to be the portion of anyone foolish enough to believe the story. Openly believe the story, that is."

"Do you believe it?" The new Duke of York's tone was suddenly sharp.

Cambridge laughed. "Certainly not! I value my skin." He smiled cynically into his brother's troubled face. "My dear Edward, of course I don't believe it. Wasn't Thomas Swynford in charge at Pontefract Castle during Richard's last days? As you say, the Scots are out to make trouble. It's time our cousin taught them a lesson."

The Scots were taught a lesson, but not, unfortunately, by Henry of Bolingbroke. It was the Percys, father and son, who, in July, routed the "children of the Devil" at the battle of Homildon Hill and took the Earl of Douglas prisoner. But for Hotspur and Northumberland it was a piece of good fortune which was to have the most disastrous consequences.

"Read that!" shouted Hotspur.

The Earl of Northumberland, who had been surprised out of his post-prandial nap by the tempestuous arrival of his son, blinked sleepily in the late afternoon sun. Here, in his northern fortress of Alnwick, it was a pleasure to see a brighter day and to take a little comfort from the warmth, particularly when it had been such a terrible summer. He was anything but happy to be confronted by the rampaging Hotspur, obviously about to disturb his peace.

49

Hotspur waved a piece of paper under his father's mottled nose. "The King—" and the younger Percy spat out the word with distaste—"demands that the Earl of Douglas be handed over to *him*. Such an important prisoner, he says, is the property of the crown."

Sleep went flying and Northumberland sat up with a jerk. This was not to be tolerated! Douglas had been taken by the Percys: his ransom was theirs. Henry of Lancaster, the ungrateful cur to whom they had given a crown, wanted to cheat them of it. Northumberland's face grew a dark, apoplectic red.

"By God's wounds," he said slowly, "I've taken as much as I can stand from Bolingbroke."

Hotspur sneered. "Three times he's led expeditions against Glendower and three times he's failed to come to grips with the man. Each time he's ravaged Wales and each time he's said that the Welsh were finished. And each time they've bobbed back again like so many corks. Henry is jealous of our success and ashamed that he can't do likewise. So he intends to punish us for his failure."

Northumberland nodded, getting to his feet and pacing up and down the rushes, the crushed flowers giving off a sweet, delicate perfume. "You're right," he said. "What do we do?"

Hotspur flung himself into his father's vacated chair. "As I see it," he answered, "we owe no loyalty to Henry of Bolingbroke. Didn't he swear to us, when he landed at Ravenspur, that he only came to claim his Lancaster inheritance; his duchy and nothing more?"

"True! True!" The last rays of the sun lay in bars of dusty yellow across the dun-coloured floor and the shadows crept ever closer to the two men by the fire, shrouding the perimeter of the room in a pall of grey and black. Northumberland instinctively lowered his voice to a conspiratorial whisper. "But . . . but we did help to make him King."

"And we can unmake him," Hotspur pointed out.

His father digested this. "We should need assistance. We couldn't do it alone."

"Of course we should need assistance," Hotspur concurred.

He stood up, gripping his father's arm. "And who more natural than Glendower? His daughter is now my wife's sister-in-law. And they are both aunts—Elizabeth by blood, Catherine by marriage—to little Edmund Mortimer."

Northumberland's eyes gleamed. "The rightful King! Do you think that Glendower will join with us?"

"Why not? Doesn't he want the overthrow of Henry of Bolingbroke as much as we do? He wants to be recognised as Prince of Wales. When Edmund Mortimer is King, he shall be."

The Earl nipped his son's hairy wrist on a sudden thought. "What about Cambridge? Shall we approach him? He's married to little Edmund's sister, after all."

Hotspur curled his lip. "That fop!" he exclaimed scathingly. "Besides, I wouldn't trust a brother of Albemarle's —I beg his pardon! Of His Grace the Duke of York's—as far as I could see him. No; leave Cambridge. He'll join us if—when we win. More to the point, will Uncle Thomas join us?"

Northumberland's brother, Thomas Percy, had recently been made Earl of Worcester, Lieutenant of South Wales and tutor to Prince Henry. A powerful man and a good fighter, he could only be an asset to any cause he embraced.

Northumberland considered, then nodded briskly. "I think he will," he said. "He's a man with more than his fair share of family pride. He won't stand for this insult." And the Earl tapped the paper with a grimy fingernail. "I'll write to him today."

"Then choose your messenger carefully," Hotspur advised. "You can be sure that Bolingbroke has his spies at Chester as well as everywhere else. There's not much love lost between him and his heir."

Northumberland raised his eyebrows in interested enquiry, but Hotspur shrugged.

"I don't know why, except that young Henry is a difficult boy to know. He's cold, austere; unlovable perhaps. He commands respect but not affection. I certainly found him so, at any rate. They say that he was very upset when Hugh le

Despenser died this year: maybe that proves that young Henry has some heart. I don't know. Anyway, enough of him. I shall leave for Wales as soon and as secretly as possible. Meanwhile, work on Uncle Thomas."

Thomas Percy was still mulling over his elder brother's proposition when, in February of 1403, King Henry the fourth married again. His second wife was Joanna, daughter of Charles of Navarre and widow of Duke John of Brittany. And although the new Queen left the children of her first marriage behind her in their dead father's domains, she nevertheless brought with her a sufficiently large entourage of Bretons and Navarrese to inflame almost the entire English population.

To the English, the advent of any foreigner was an immediate cause for suspicion, but the Bretons they hated with an intensity that equalled, and even surpassed, their hatred for the French. The term Breton and pirate were synonymous, and in the Cornish peninsula and in the westcountry, where the men of Bristol and Fowey looked upon it as their God-given right to be the only scavengers of the seas, the Bretons were regarded as rivals. And now their King had actually opened England's front door to these men, affording them legal entry into the country.

"You would think," King Henry remarked to his step-mother, Katherine Swynford, "that the whole Breton nation had been allowed to settle in England, so much fuss is being made."

Katherine felt too ill to do more than smile in weak agreement with her step-son, but whatever the climate of opinion amongst those nearest to the throne, popular sentiment continued to be outraged. Why, people demanded, should it be illegal to trade with the Welsh, but not with their old enemies, the Bretons?

And Thomas Percy, always sensitive to feelings of the people, decided that the time had come to throw in his lot with his brother.

6

ON MAY the tenth, Katherine, Dowager Duchess of Lancaster, formerly Lady Swynford, died at the age of fifty-three and was buried beside the High Altar of Lincoln Cathedral.

Henry the fourth and his new Queen were not present, but they were represented by the King's elder sister, Elizabeth, a coarsening, embittered woman in her late thirties, whose unsatisfactory but passionate marriage to John Holland had come to a bloody end three years before at Pleshey, when he had been executed for his part in the Earls' revolt. Lady Swynford had once been governess to Elizabeth and her sister, Phillipa, now Queen of Portugal, and the former had been sufficiently fond of Katherine to squeeze a tear for her from her short-sighted blue eyes.

But if the King were not at the funeral, the Beauforts were there in force. Henry Beaufort, as Bishop of Lincoln, naturally officiated at the ceremony and, on looking round the congregation, was pleased to note the presence of his elder brother, John, Earl of Somerset, together with his wife, Margaret Holland, and their children; his younger brother, Thomas, Earl of Dorset, standing beside their half-brother, Thomas Swynford; and his only sister, Joan, with her husband, Ralph Neville of Raby, Earl of Westmorland. Joan had also brought with her her eldest son, an attractive two-year-old named Richard, on whose behalf she cornered her brother, Henry, during the funeral wake, which was held in several overcrowded rooms of the episcopal palace.

"I want your advice, Henry," she said briskly. "What is the possibility of securing Salisbury's daughter for little Richard?"

Henry Beaufort raised his thin eyebrows. "The granddaughter of a Lollard and a rebel?" he asked, quizzing her.

"That's as maybe," retorted the practical Joan, "but the important thing is that Salisbury's lands and titles were restored to his son. Little Alice Montagu would be no bad match for a Neville. Besides, if Tom Montagu has no son, then the title might, in time, become Richard's." She smiled dotingly upon the small boy who sat at her feet, busily trying to catch the fleas which hopped among the rushes. "Richard Neville, Earl of Salisbury," she purred fondly, patting her son's curly head. The boy returned the embrace with enthusiasm and a grin spread across his square little face, wrinkling the corners of his extraordinarily piercing blue eyes.

"Don't count your chickens, my dear Joan," murmured the Bishop, edging away nervously from this display of maternal affection.

"I don't," Joan assured him, with an abrupt return to her rather masculine manner. "However, it would be a very good match, whatever happens. An alliance with the Montagus might stand Richard in very good stead."

"In what particular way?" the Bishop enquired politely, although his attention was beginning to wander.

"Henry!" said Joan. "Do you know how many children Ralph had by his first wife?"

"Five or six," hazarded the Bishop.

"Seven," snapped his sister. "I intend to have as many, if not more. And it will be *my* children, Henry, who will inherit the Neville patrimony, not Margaret Stafford's brood. That I'm determined upon."

"And Ralph?" asked the Bishop, his interest momentarily recaptured.

"Ralph will do as he is told," Joan answered, brushing the remark aside as an irrelevancy. "But there is a chance that my step-children will make trouble—"

"You surprise me!" exclaimed the Bishop, but his sister continued, unheeding.

"—and I therefore want powerful alliances for my children."

"And what have you in mind for William?" enquired Henry with gentle sarcasm, for his other Neville nephew was barely a year old.

But Joan, the maternal predator, was oblivious to his irony. "I hear," she said, "that Fauconberg's wife has just been delivered of a daughter," and was startled by the Bishop's burst of laughter.

"My dear," he said fondly, "you're the image of our father; old Gaunt to the life when you take the bit between your teeth."

"Talking of father," said Joan, "has the King confirmed our patent of legitimacy?"

"Why? Is the great Ralph Neville afraid that he might be married to a bastard?" Henry Beaufort saw the alarm leap into his sister's eyes and went on reassuringly: "Yes, yes! Henry has confirmed it, don't worry! He has inserted a new clause, however, barring us and our descendants from the throne; although whether he can legally do that might be a debatable point. But as none of us is likely to claim the crown . . ."

He broke off, shrugging, and his sister, satisfied, allowed her attention to be claimed at last by her sister-in-law, Margaret Holland, who had been trying to attract her notice for the past five minutes.

Henry Beaufort drifted away to mingle with his guests and receive their condolences. The death of his mother, however, had not affected the Bishop as profoundly as it might once have done. He was a personage of some importance now, tipped in court circles as the coming man. He had his heart set on the Bishopric of Winchester—the present incumbent was in very poor health—and after that, a Cardinal's hat. So life was very full for Henry Beaufort and left him little time for the luxury of personal relationships. He had remained extremely attached to his mother until the very end of her life, but it was a long time since he had asked for her advice.

He had his problems, too, although one worry, the fear that his half-brother the King would call a Holy Crusade, had been removed. For, a little over a year ago, the apparently unconquerable Turkish Sultan, Byazid, had suffered defeat at last; not at the hands of the Christian armies, thus allowing them to avenge their humiliating defeat at Nicopolis, but by the Mongol hordes under their leader, Tamerlane. And Tamerlane's pretensions to power lying in the east and not the west, the Turkish threat to Europe had, for the time being, been abolished.

But Henry Beaufort had other anxieties. He had a long nose and could scent out danger faster than most people, particularly when it threatened his own interests. Well before his spies had come to him with their tit-bits of information, he had felt uneasy about the Percys. And the news that Hotspur was known to be consorting with Glendower could have only one meaning for anyone capable of putting two and two together.

Henry Beaufort was not the only person with an aptitude for mental arithmetic and the King and his eldest son had long ago drawn their own conclusions about the disaffection of the Percys.

It came as no surprise to either of them, therefore, when, a month after Katherine Swynford's funeral, Hotspur and Northumberland issued their formal challenge to "Henry of Bolingbroke, Duke of Lancaster" and called upon all right-thinking men to rally to the support of King Edmund. Leaving his father to guard the north, Hotspur then advanced with his army, making for the borders of Wales and a rendez-vous with his ally, Glendower.

The King was at Lichfield, already on his way north, when messengers brought him the news that Prince Henry was moving south towards Shrewsbury and was converging fast with the rebel forces as they swung westwards into Wales. The King wasted no time. The Prince was now fifteen years of age, but he had never fought in a major battle. Moreover, he was about to confront one of the greatest soldiers of the day, Hotspur; while Glendower might be presumed to be marching to attack the English army from the west. And, as the King knew only too well, the atrocities committed by the Welsh were every bit as horrible as those committed by the English, the behaviour of the Welsh women towards their prisoners horrifying even their own war-hardened men.

A green boy like Prince Henry must not under any circumstances be allowed to face such an enemy in open combat, alone. Leaving Lichfield at dawn on July the twentieth, the royal forces covered the intervening ground to Shrewsbury by nightfall, and were only just in time. Hardly had the gates shut behind them and the royal standard been raised above the battlements, than the look-outs reported movement on the horizon. And before the opalescent blue dusk faded finally to grey, the whole of the rebel army was encamped about Shrewsbury town.

The meeting between father and son was hardly felicitous : the Prince could not forbear to say : "I told you so !" It was not that he had any wish to upset the King, although he knew quite well that his remark would do so. It was simply that young Henry could never resist holding up his own rectitude as a pattern for others to follow. Sir John Oldcastle, reconnoitring at first light on the morning of the twenty-first, reflected that his Prince was not the youth to be deflected from the path of duty as he saw it, by any consideration whatsoever. He would stigmatise as weakness any deviation from the narrow code of his own beliefs.

Sir John was presently able to report that Hotspur had retired two miles north of Shrewsbury and taken up an advantageous position at Haytely field, a low hill in front of which lay several ponds, affording the rebels a measure of protection. Henry Percy himself had taken charge of the centre, with his uncle, Thomas, Earl of Worcester, in command of the right and his prisoner, the Earl of Douglas, in command of the left. In between each phalanx was a wedge-shaped formation of Welsh and Cheshire archers.

"And Glendower?" queried the King anxiously.

"Sire, there is no sign of his approach at the moment."

Henry of Bolingbroke bit his lip and glanced at his cousin, York, but the Duke had no advice to offer.

The King's dilemma was plain. Would it be better to try

57

to force battle immediately and hope for a victory before Glendower's forces arrived? Or would it be too great a risk to fight with the threat that the Welsh might fall upon his left flank at any moment? It was the sort of decision that no man there, especially York, cared to make. Even Prince Henry made no comment.

After an agonising pause, the King decided on a course of action. "We will send heralds to the rebels for a parley," he said. "Meanwhile, I wants scouts sent north, west and south, as far as they can go by noon, unless they sight Glendower first. Then they must return. If all come back safely, and if no one has seen the Welshman, we will fight."

Young Henry looked on his father with a new respect. His tone, Oldcastle noted, became more deferential. That, at least, was one of the Prince's virtues: he gave credit where credit was due.

By two o'clock, all the scouts had returned. There was no sign of Glendower. Either he had decided to abandon his allies to their fate, or, more likely, he had been delayed somewhere along whatever road he and his men were travelling.

The King prepared to give battle.

Prince Henry sweltered inside his armour. He was thankful that the present hair-style, a thick, close-cropped cap of hair on the crown of the head, cushioned his skull against the weight of his battle-helmet.

There were only two divisions in the battle-formation of the English army, one commanded by the King, the other by the Prince of Wales. Some demur had been raised by the royalist captains about this arrangement. Why only two phalanxes of foot-soldiers instead of the usual three?

"Because," had snapped the King, exasperated by their obtuseness, "when those ponds are reached, we shall have to go around them. The army will therefore divide; one half left, one half right, meeting again on the other side. Hotspur will be unable to charge through our centre because the ponds will impede his advance as much as they will impede ours."

After that, no one had liked to query the choice of Prince

58

Henry to command the left wing, especially with the boy himself glowering at them, anticipating their criticisms. His own people, who had come with him from Chester, seemed to think the King's decision perfectly reasonable. A born soldier, one of his men had called him; but the London men had yet to be convinced of that.

Sir John Oldcastle had been surprised at the King's demonstration of confidence in his eldest son and heir, but to Prince Henry it was so natural that he accorded it no thought at all. Standing now at the head of his troops, he was quivering with excitement, watchful and alert for the King's signal.

Throughout the royalist army, there were a number of gentlemen dressed to resemble their master in order to confuse the enemy. The Prince of Wales knew this to be a common enough practice, but he could not suppress a feeling of contempt. There was to him something that smacked of cowardice about the arrangement: no soldier, be he commoner or King, should be afraid to face death in battle. He muttered as much to Oldcastle.

"Perhaps His Grace regards himself more as statesman than as soldier," Sir John pointed out gently.

"And perhaps," Henry retorted, "these men behind us regard themselves as farmers, sutlers, carters, grooms. . . . I shall be as great a target for the enemy as my father, but I shall never ask another man to play the decoy for me."

The Prince shut his vizor with a click. His arrogance, thought Oldcastle, was appalling, and yet there was a kind of justice in it. Henry of Monmouth would never stoop to ask even the humblest of men to do anything which he was not prepared to do himself.

The King dropped his outstretched arm and the royal host began to move forward. At once, the rebel archers released a storm of arrows from their vantage point on Haytely hillside. Prince Henry, raising his vizor to shout an order to the soldiers on his left, was hit in the face and almost blinded by blood. Immediately, his squires closed around him, while Oldcastle, dashing to the Prince's assistance, vainly tried to staunch the flow.

"I will send some men to help Your Highness to the rear," he said, only to encounter a look of furious disgust from those brilliant blue eyes.

Cutting a strip of linen from his surcoat, the Prince wedged it between his helmet and the wound, thus effectively stopping the bleeding.

"Improvisation, Oldcastle, is the mark of every good soldier," he remarked sententiously and pressed on into the fight. Oldcastle was left not knowing whether he wanted to applaud his Prince or kick him.

Dividing at the ponds as instructed, the royal army encircled the muddy, evil-smelling sheets of water, joining forces again on the opposite side. The rebel army was somewhat demoralised by this unexpected manoeuvre and wavered for a moment or two. But Hotspur, seemingly everywhere at once, rallied them as much by his personal bravery as by his shouted words of encouragement. Indeed, the noise of battle was by now so deafening that his voice was almost inaudible.

The two sides were evenly matched in numbers and equally so in fighting skill and courage. Throughout the long, hot afternoon the battle continued to rage. Twice the cry went up from the rebel lines that Henry of Bolingbroke had been killed and twice the report had to be denied when it was found that the arms of England concealed men other than the King.

By six o'clock, both sides were beginning to tire, but their leaders grimly held on; Hotspur because he hoped to hear at any minute the trumpets of Glendower's advancing army; King Henry because he knew that he must bring this battle to a successful conclusion before that contingency arose.

As the shadows lengthened and the horizon darkened from blue to amethyst and then to grey, Hotspur became desperate. It was obvious that Glendower could not now arrive in time to be of any use. In a blind fury, he flung himself into that part of the fray where the fighting was thickest, about the royal standard. This time it *must* be Bolingbroke! If he could reach and kill him, then the day could still go in favour of the rebel forces. So intent was he upon this purpose that he did not even see the sword that struck him down.

Five minutes later, the cry went up: "Hotspur is dead!" and the rebels broke and ran. The Earl of Douglas and Thomas Percy were both captured as they vainly tried to stem the tide of terrified humanity. Douglas, as a prisoner of war, Henry could not touch, even had he wished to do so: Thomas Percy was summarily tried and executed a few days later.

As darkness finally closed over Haytely field, Henry of Monmouth, resting on his sword amidst the carnage of that reeking hil, tasted the sweets of victory for the very first time.

7

THE victory at Shrewsbury finally convinced young Henry—if, indeed, he were in need of conviction—that his father was the true and rightful King of England. God would not otherwise have given him the victory.

"Now he speaks for God!" Oldcastle remarked with asperity to his friends, while putting his own words into the mouth of the Deity, guided by the writings of Wycliffe and Hus.

Prince Henry's belief in the intervention of the Almighty on behalf of the House of Lancaster was further strengthened by the rapid overthrow of Northumberland. The Earl, broken by the news of his son's and brother's deaths, hastened to make his peace with Henry; then retired to his northern fastness of Warkworth, taking Hotspur's young son with him. His office of Constable of England was given to the King's third son, Prince John, along with some of Hotspur's confiscated estates.

One thing which God seemed curiously reluctant to do, however, was to endorse the superiority of the English over the Welsh. Glendower, whose failure to appear at Shrewsbury had been due to a mistaken belief in Hotspur's military transcendence over Prince Henry and because he had not realised that the King would be in time to join his son for the battle, continued to elude his pursuers. An expedition led by Bolingbroke in the September of 1403 into the heart of Wales, ended as always in ignominious retreat. Although, on this occasion, the English forces managed to occupy Carmarthen, they had to withdraw for the usual financial reasons.

Money, or the lack of it, was fast becoming the bane of Henry of Bolingbroke's life. In November, the court at Westminster was enlivened by the return of Prince Thomas from

Ireland, raging about lack of funds; whilst Prince Henry wrote continuously from Chester complaining of the same trouble. When Harlech and Aberystwyth fell to Glendower at the beginning of the following year, the King pocketed his Plantagenet pride and went cap-in-hand to Parliament, but was curtly refused the money that he so desperately needed.

The Commons, egged on by two of their most active members, Thomas Chaucer and John Tiptoft, spent their energies instead in roundly condemning the number of foreigners employed in the King's and Queen's households. One day, many years later, Tiptoft's son would be known as the Butcher of England, and although the father had none of the indifference to humanity which was to characterise John Tiptoft the younger, he nevertheless had all the xenophobia of the true Englishman. He and Thomas Chaucer led the attack with relish.

The King, returning to Westminster Palace, fell into a Plantagenet rage, almost foaming at the mouth, and Henry Beaufort, to whom the New Year had brought the coveted office of Bishop of Winchester, feared for his half-brother's reason. He begged the King to remember his precious health, but had nothing but cold comfort to offer in return for Henry's self-control. For while the King had been with the Commons, the Bishop had been closeted with two of his spies from France.

"Glendower," Henry Beaufort now told the King bluntly— for there were times when he felt that prevarication did more harm than good—"is in touch with the French. A treaty has been proposed; full recognition for Owen as Prince of Wales and French help for him to obtain your overthrow."

"And what does Owen provide in return?" sneered the King, biting his lower lip to stop it trembling with anger.

"A puppet King in the person of Edmund Mortimer, subservient to France. Northumberland would seem to be a party to this plot, as well."

"I never expected otherwise." The King stared morosely into the fire, his anger, to Henry Beaufort's relief, now spent.

Archbishop Arundel was ushered in by an obsequious page,

who bowed and withdrew. The King raised bloodshot eyes and smiled.

"Come in, Thomas," he said. "We need your advice."

Henry Beaufort bridled. No other man's counsel was needed when he was present. Did the King think that idiot Arundel more capable of sage advice than a Beaufort?

But the King was oblivious to his half-brother's look of sullen reproach. He went on: "Have you heard the news from France?"

"There are rumours," replied the Archbishop, sending a sly smile of triumph in his inferior's direction. He had his own spies, who spied on other people's spies; a simpler and less costly method of garnering information. "A treaty between Glendower and France." He smiled again, enjoying Henry Beaufort's angry interjection of: "Listening at keyholes again, Archbishop?"

The King waved his half-brother peremptorily to silence. "And Your Grace's suggestion?"

Arundel considered his fingertips with their long, beautifully kept nails. "Perhaps a diplomatic marriage might be arranged for Prince Henry in France."

"If it's Isabella you're thinking of," snapped Henry Beaufort, "she has just been married to the Duke of Orleans."

"Charles de Valois has other daughters," the Archbishop pointed out. "The Princess Katherine, for example. Diplomatic feelers might be—ah—tentatively extended."

The King was enthusiastic; but for the time being, the French remained loyal to their new ally, the Welsh. In July, a treaty was signed between the two countries at the home of the French Chancellor, Armand de Corbie; while both France and Brittany continued the traditional policy of harrying English shipping and raiding the south-coast towns. Plymouth and Dartmouth both suffered particularly badly that summer, and, in August, a French expeditionary force commanded by the mercenary, Jean d'Espagne, landed at Milford Haven.

A confident Glendower now surrounded himself with the full panoply of royalty: he had his own Seal, his own court dignitaries and his own ambassadors who were sent to every foreign country that would acknowledge him rightful Prince of Wales.

Others, however, besides the French, were working in the interests of Owen Glendower. As the year 1405 came in with flurries of sleet and snow, and as bitter winds emptied the streets of people, the Duke of York's Windsor apartments were honoured by a call from Lady Despense, one of his sisters.

York, who had just had a tooth pulled by his barber, was in no mood for polite conversation, but, as it transpired, this was not the object of Lady Despenser's visit. She seated herself on a stool opposite her brother and warmed her hands at the fire. Her tone was low but brisk.

"Can we be overheard?"

York was immediately on his guard. "No, we can't," he answered, "but I don't want to be told any secrets. I'm not at all well." He put up his hand defensively to pat his swollen cheek. "I've just had a tooth out," he added in reply to his sister's look of enquiry.

"Hm," snorted Lady Despenser disparagingly. "If you weren't so fat, I suppose I should be able to see that for myself." York made a protesting noise, but this was impatiently waved aside. "It's no good, Edward," Lady Despenser went on, "you're the head of the family now and I have every right—indeed, obligation!—to confide in you. You are not taking refuge behind a plea of ill-health."

"I don't want to know your schemes," York said with as much vehemence as a man of his girth could muster. "Just because your husband was executed after the Earls' revolt—"

"And he might not have been," his sister retorted viciously, "if you hadn't run to father, who revealed the whole plot to —to Bolingbroke. I won't call him the King!"

The Duke of York groaned audibly. He had guessed aright: treason was in the air. This visit of his sister's was her way of taking revenge. She was going to implicate him in a plot of which he would rather know nothing, and when the treason was discovered, it would be remembered that she had paid a call on that brother who, as Albemarle, had dabbled his

65

fingers in so many other pies. York rose hurriedly to his feet.

Lady Despenser, although not inclined to corpulence like her brother, was nevertheless a powerful woman and she pushed the Duke back into his seat as though he had been a baby.

"I am going to Wales," she said quietly, "to Glendower. And I am taking with me our sister-in-law, Anne Mortimer, and her brother, Edmund."

"Cambridge!" spluttered York. "I should have known that he was in this, too."

"Richard is on his estates and knows nothing about it— officially, that is!"

"But Anne is his wife!"

"The girl is too young to be anything but his wife in name for a year or so yet. And there's the point." Lady Despenser sank down again in her chair, happy now that she had her brother's full, if reluctant, attention. "The Mortimers are in constant danger, and as they grow older, nearer the age of puberty, they will be even more so. Edmund is twelve; thirteen this year. If Henry of Bolingbroke is going to lay the ghost of the Mortimer succession, he must do it before either Edmund or Anne can beget more heirs. I intend, therefore, to take them to safety."

"Why Wales?" York bleated feebly, nursing his cheek. The nerve in the cavity was thumping furiously.

"Because their uncle, Glendower's son-in-law, is there."

"I don't believe the King has any intention of harming either child," York protested. "I don't think that it has entered his head."

"Rubbish!" exclaimed Lady Despenser, who persistently refused to hear any good of her husband's executioner. "Now, I must be going. I have other calls to make."

"Other calls?"

"On our worthy Archbishop of Canterbury and also on Tom Mowbray, our Earl Marshal."

"You'll be arrested before you leave Windsor," gasped York, not without a certain measure of relief.

"Oh, I shan't tell the Archbishop anything," his sister smiled. "But when I reach Wales, my visits will be remem-

66

bered." She turned in the doorway, her fur-lined cloak swirling before her. "Will you go to the King, Edward? Just as you did before? Or don't you fancy seeing your sister follow her husband to the block?"

The door shut behind her and York sank back into his seat with an even louder groan than before. And it was not only the pain from his tooth which caused it. He had no father now to whom he could turn for advice, and all his chivalrous instincts forbade his betrayal of a woman.

There were other sources of information at Henry's court, however, apart from the Duke of York; sources perhaps not quite as efficient as they should have been, for Lady Despenser and her two charges had reached Cheltenham before they were apprehended and brought back to London. In one respect, however, the lady was successful: her brother was sent to prison for misprision of treason and Thomas Mowbray, although eventually pardoned, had to stand his trial and was found guilty of complicity in the crime. But the Archbishop was exonerated, Lady Despenser's concern for her immortal soul preventing her at the last minute from implicating an innocent Churchman. A few months later, Henry of Bolingbroke's concern for his immortal soul was not to prove so keen.

The first rumblings of a new rebellion began with reports of the Tripartite Indenture between Glendower, the Earl of Northumberland and Sir Edmund Mortimer, who signed on behalf of his little nephew, the "King". Wales was, of course, to be Owen Glendower's; England was to be divided between the Percys and the Mortimers.

When the King's spies reported the agreement to him, Henry laughed with relief. Anything so absurd could not possibly be taken seriously. Northumberland, if not Mortimer and Glendower, must know that the thing was the sheerest fantasy: the English people would never tolerate it, and whoever reckoned without the noisy, self-opinionated commoners of England, would never manage to seize power. That much even the arrogant Lancasters appreciated.

But rumours were still rife that King Richard was alive and

a guest of King Robert the third at Stirling Castle. A year previously, Richard's Chamberlain, one Richard Serle, had been executed for saying that his master was living in Scotland; but Serle's death, intended as a warning, had not prevented others from saying the same thing. That the French had no faith in the story was obvious. King Charles had despatched Creton to the Scottish court and, on the minstrel's return, had had no hesitation in marrying Richard's widow to her cousin, Charles of Orleans.

Others, however, were more gullible. "Or," as Henry Beaufort remarked to his brother, Thomas, "they pretend to be, in order to overthrow Lancaster. For those who cannot stomach an alliance with Mortimer and Glendower, a belief in King Richard's continued existence is essential."

As was so often the case, the Bishop was correct. Now in his thirtieth year, he had an unendearing habit, which his young half-nephew, Humphrey, found particularly obnoxious, of being nearly always right. "Old Know-all," the Prince called him, and with all the impudence of his fourteen years, did not scruple to say it in the Bishop's presence. Already, there was very little love lost between the two.

In this particular instance, Henry Beaufort had guessed aright that certain peers of the realm, discontented with the man whom they had created King, were making a push to dispossess him. But men like Thomas Mowbray, the Earl Marshal, and Richard le Scrope, Archbishop of York, found nothing to inspire them in the leadership of the Mortimers, and they continued to hope that King Richard was alive. Necessity, however, dictated that they join forces with Northumberland, so they planned and plotted and patiently waited.

The early summer of 1405 seemed as propitious a moment as any for their attempted coup. The King had had to pawn his jewels to pay his troops; in Ireland Prince Thomas's finances were in a worse state than ever; and the people were becoming restless with the inevitable increases in taxation. Trade had slumped, too, following the decree of the Diet of Lubeck which laid a ban on the importation of

English cloth and the exportation of Baltic merchandise to England.

In Yorkshire, the rebel lords began to gather, but they had reckoned without the loyalty of Ralph Neville of Raby to his half-brother-in-law. Sending urgent messages to the King at Westminster, the Earl made preparations to intercept the rebel forces and was fortunate enough to do so before they had got further than Shipton Moor, near York.

Ralph Neville, mindful of the instructions given to him by his Joan, was determined to end the insurrection at any cost.

"Remember," Joan had admonished him, "that we are irrevocably bound to my half-brother. Our future and, more important, the future of our children, depends upon Henry's retention of the throne. 'King Edmund Mortimer' can do us no good at all. Forget your honour if you have to and bring this revolt to an end by fair means or foul before Henry gets here. He will be eternally grateful."

Joan Beaufort was no more unscrupulous than the rest of womankind until her children were involved; then, indeed, she was living proof of the axiom that the female is deadlier than the male. The transformation from cooing dove to raging tigress never failed to astonish poor Ralph Neville; but he had a deep-rooted respect for his wife's common sense and the businesslike acumen which had steadily directed his fortunes.

So when he requested a parley with the rebel leaders and then promptly clapped them in chains, he salved his conscience with the balm of Joan's certain approval. He had sacrificed his honour, it was true, but, as his wife would undoubtedly point out, it was but a small thing to surrender in the interests of his children, Richard, William and, now, little Edward.

When the King arrived at York, therefore, he was met with the happy intelligence that Archbishop Scrope, his nephew, Sir William Plumpton, and Thomas Mowbray were all awaiting trial. The wily Northumberland had not been lured to the parley and, on hearing of the fate of his friends, had escaped to Warkworth, taking his grandson with him. The abandoned rebel forces, finding themselves leaderless, had melted away like frost in the mid-day sun.

Henry of Bolingbroke was in a vindictive mood. Both Archbishop Scrope and Thomas Mowbray had given him their support at the time of the usurpation and he could not understand their reversal of loyalties. Had he not been a good King to them? Had he not heaped them with honours and, recently, pardoned Mowbray for his part in the Despenser plot? If they had been his enemies from the start, he could more easily have forgiven them; but the betrayal by friends went deep. He was out for blood, everyone's blood, including the Archbishop's.

His chief advisers, his Councillors, his well-wishers, were all horrified. To take the life of a consecrated man was unheard of unless he was first excommunicated by the Church, but Henry was determined. He sent for his Chief Justice, Sir William Gascoigne, who adamantly refused to pass sentence.

"Are you afraid for your soul?" enquired Henry bitterly.

"I am afraid for the laws of England," retorted Gascoigne. "They are my Bible, and it is illegal for a secular court to sentence a cleric to death, however justified the sentence may be."

"Then I shall find someone more obliging," shouted the King.

Others, beside the Chief Justice, tried to dissuade him from his course; not from the same motive as Gascoigne, but because Scrope was adored in York. His death would make him a martyr and increase the King's unpopularity with the citizens. The example of Thomas à Becket loomed large in many minds.

But King Henry was not the man to be thwarted once he had reached a decision. There were more complaisant judges than Sir William Gascoigne, and Archbishop Scrope was duly sentenced and executed in a field outside York, along with Mowbray and Plumpton. The day was cold and overcast; the men of York sullen and grim-faced.

Within a month of his death, miracles were reported at the grave of Archbishop Scrope, while the pilgrims flocked in their hundreds to his tomb in York Minster.

8

THE country, the whole of Europe, waited with bated breath for God to strike down the man who had dared to encompass the death of an Archbishop.

Many things happened, but all to King Henry's advantage. He captured Warkworth Castle, and Northumberland and his grandson were forced to escape into Scotland. Then, in the late summer of 1405, Owen's son, Grufydd Glendower, was taken prisoner, and at the beginning of the following year an even more important pawn fell into the hands of the English King. James Stewart, son and heir of King Robert the third of Scotland, was captured, while on his way to France, by Norfolk pirates, who hastened to ingratiate themselves with their monarch by sending him so valuable a prize. A month later, King Robert died, heartbroken at the news, and with the accession of the young prisoner to the throne of Scotland as James the first, his value increased twenty-fold.

There was, however, one piece of sad news which caused men to nod significantly at one another: King Henry's daughter, Princess Blanche of Bavaria, died. But as this was followed by the death in battle of another of Glendower's sons, and as Henry's remaining daughter, Phillipa, was triumphantly married to Eric of Sweden, it could only be felt that the Almighty was biding his time.

It appeared, too, that men were quite prepared to leave retribution in the hands of the Deity. In France, Henry Beaufort was welcomed at the court of Charles the sixth to discuss a possible marriage between the Princess Katherine and the Prince of Wales; whilst King Henry's representatives

71

in Rome, Sir John Cheyne and Dr Henry Chicele, sent to discuss the evergreen topic of the Papal schism, were accorded all honours. At home, Henry's staunch friend and ally, Richard Whittington, was elected Mayor for a second full term of office; Parliament, under the guidance of its Speaker, John Tiptoft, approved the appointment of the King's half-brother, John Beaufort, as Admiral of England; and in Wales, the French withdrew their help from Glendower in spite of his offer to acknowledge the Avignon Pope, Benedict the thirteenth, as head of the Church, rather than Innocent the seventh in Rome.

No; it certainly did not seem as though Henry the fourth was to suffer any immediate punishment for the execution of an Archbishop. But the watchful noticed that, from the very month of Scrope's death, Henry's health began to deteriorate and by the end of 1406 it was necessary for the Prince of Wales to divide his time equally between Chester and London, where, on his father's behalf, he attended Council meetings at Westminster.

Henry of Monmouth was now a man of twenty. His face, beneath its cap of dark hair, was tanned by wind and sun to the colour of mahogany; his body fined down to skin and bone by long campaigning in the Welsh mountains. His had been no spectacular triumph against Glendower; but a dogged persistence allied to his undoubted military genius and a deep-rooted respect for his opponent, was slowly but surely giving him the victory. His reserve resulted at times in conversation which was almost monosyllabic and led to Richard Beauchamp, Earl of Warwick, remarking to Sir John Oldcastle that "still waters ran deep".

Oldcastle merely laughed. He had long ago reached the conclusion that the Prince of Wales's character was no more complex than that of his brother, Prince John. In his own way, Henry was just as simple and straightforward : he was silent because he had nothing to say; cold because he was by nature hard and unemotional. His ruling passion was justice; laudable, but, as Oldcastle reflected with a sigh, unlovely if it did not walk hand-in-hand with its mitigating companion,

72

mercy. That Henry would inspire men, Oldcastle had no doubt; his soldiers because he was at one with them so completely that he could understand even the smallest workings of their minds; his future subjects because he identified himself first, last and always as an Englishman.

Prince Henry's ancestors might have been Norman and Angevin, Spaniard and Fleming, but he regarded himself as English to the backbone. Less than a hundred years ago, French had been the official language of the English court: Henry's great-grandfather, Edward the third, had been the first King since the Conquest to know some English words, but they had been few. King Richard had understood the native tongue, but did not himself use it. It had been left to King Henry the fourth, the usurper, to make English the official language of Parliament. Nowadays, men talked more of *The Canterbury Tales* than the *Roman de la Rose*. After three and a half centuries, the guttural accents and strong earthy humour of the Angle and the Saxon were taking over from the sonorous sophistication of the Gaul. And Society, for so long divided into two strata—Anglo-Saxon peasant and Norman overlord—was fusing together into a single, national identity. Henry of Monmouth, prophesied Oldcastle, would probably do more to foster the growth of this embryonic nationalism than any other King before him.

Some, of course, hated the Prince of Wales: the villains and the rogues found him a hard task-master, as did those who sought to make life easier by a little natural chicanery. Oldcastle was experienced enough to recognise the crusading gleam whenever it shone in Henry's eyes, and remarked to the Earl of Warwick as they went together into the Council Chamber at Chester: "We are in for some new reform, mark my words!"

It was an early spring day. The room was full of a pale, cold sunlight, no chillier than the Prince's voice when he addressed his Council.

"You all know that it has long been the practice, here in the Welsh Marches, for felons to escape the consequences of their crimes by joining the household of a new overlord. An

73

annual payment of fourpence is all that is necessary to secure them their new master's protection. This must stop."

Sir John Greindor, speaking for his fellow Councillors, expostulated: "This practice has always been overlooked. In the Marches, we need every able-bodied man we can muster. How, otherwise, are we to keep back the Welsh? If these men are hanged or imprisoned, we shall lose their services as soldiers in times of trouble."

"That's as maybe," shrugged the Prince. "It is wrong that men should escape their rightful punishment; wrong that the victims should not see justice done. In future, the practice will not be allowed."

Oldcastle gave Warwick a discreet nudge and hissed: "I told you so!" into the Earl's left ear. Richard Beauchamp wobbled his eyebrows in acknowledgment.

Later, the two men were invited to the Prince's solar. Several of the town's prostitutes were present and Oldcastle noted that the Prince was drinking heavily. Even so, his face did not lose its normal, morose expression. Henry was indeed the Prince for the English, thought Sir John with amusement, for the English liked to take their pleasures with a touch of austerity.

The Prince of Wales's increasing predilection for the more dubious forms of pleasure, whoring and drinking, was becoming extremely marked, especially when he was in London. Then he would frequent the taverns of Cheapside with a set of companions who seemed expressly chosen for their lack of morals. As individuals, Henry hated each and every one of them, but they were necessary to his welfare.

Henry of Monmouth was a man of his time and therefore did not indulge in the self-analysis of later centuries. But had he probed even slightly below the surface of his mind, he might have become aware of a streak of cruelty in his nature, normally held in check, but which emerged from time to time, demanding an outlet. Fighting could not provide it, for war had a code of ethics, brutal though it was, to which the Prince rigidly adhered. What Henry needed, and what he found amongst the thieves' dens and bawdy-houses of London, was a savage abandonment that satisfied some deep, animal craving of his nature. He could not enjoy the excesses; he despised not only others, but himself as he indulged grimly in the carnal pleasures of life, his natural asceticism in direct conflict with the other, equally pressing need to inflict pain. He would turn distastefully from his fellow roisterers at the end of such an evening's entertainment, returning to Coldharbour House to bathe and change. But a few weeks later, he would be back with his dubious friends yet again.

Henry's elders, particularly his father, were horrified at his behaviour, the more so as he was the future King. One or two, like the Prince's old tutor and half-uncle, Henry Beaufort, were able to guess at his motives and to realise that the more his father deplored his eldest son's doings, and regretted openly that Prince Thomas was not his heir, the more would Henry indulge in his riotous living. For the mental anguish caused to his father was part of the Prince's pleasure.

The antipathy between father and son was mutual. When and how it had grown was hard to say: it had not always been present in their relationship. On the older man's part, there was jealousy; jealousy of youth and strength and of success against Glendower. On the Prince's side was the natural resentment of a young man waiting to come into his inheritance, plus an unacknowledged fear that his father had unlawfully usurped the crown, thus putting himself and his heirs in peril of their immortal souls.

For Henry of Monmouth was as orthodox in religion as in war, which was why, as Henry Beaufort had realised many years before, it was essential that he believe in the story that Edmund Crouchback had been the true heir of Henry the third—otherwise, his father had deposed and probably murdered an anointed King. Henry of Bolingbroke, a more devious and complicated character than his son, had never believed the story. He had used it merely to salve the consciences of his more guilt-ridden supporters and to win over a conservative and law-abiding people who liked even their chaos to be orderly. A chance remark to this effect, once made by the King in the presence of his youngest son, Humphrey, and passed on by that young man to his eldest brother in garbled form, had left the Prince of Wales with an inchoate suspicion, hastily suppressed, that the throne which he would one day inherit might not be rightfully his. From then on, his dislike of his father, though never openly admitted, even to himself, had grown apace.

It led him to oppose, deliberately, the King's French policy.

"Burgundy!" said the Prince in the Council Chamber.

"Orleans!" roared the King from his sick-bed.

France was now a house divided against itself. Charles the sixth, suffering from ever-increasing fits of madness, was only infrequently an effective King, and, in the interim periods, the government of the country was left to the mercy of rival baronial factions. In the earlier years of Charles's reign, the two chief contenders for power had been his uncle, Duke Philip the Bold of Burgundy, and his brother, Louis, Duke of Orleans, who was also the lover of Charles's wife, Queen Isabeau. In 1404, the Duke of Burgundy had died and his son, John the Fearless, had succeeded to the title. Nothing had changed, however, for John had merely continued his father's policy of opposing Orleans and his paramour, the French Queen, whenever possible.

In the summer of 1407, this rivalry reached its logical conclusion.

"Have you heard?" demanded Prince Humphrey, entering his brother John's apartments in his usual unceremonious manner. He stopped short when he realised that Henry was also present, lying on a day-bed and nursing an obviously thick head. But to Humphrey's relief, the Prince of Wales uttered no words of reproof, simply fixing his youngest brother with a jaundiced and bloodshot eye.

"Heard what?" asked John indulgently, for Humphrey was a never-failing source of amusement to him.

"They're saying that the Duke of Orleans has been murdered! Near the Porte Barbette, in Paris!"

"War to the knife," said Henry.

"It must be Burgundy that we support," urged the Prince, coldly and clearly.

"Why?" asked the King, his eyes beginning to smoulder. He was feeling extremely unwell, troubled by the skin complaint that made his days and nights a misery. Since midsummer, he had been constantly on the move, his doctors deeming it beneficial for him, but November in Gloucester did nothing to raise his low spirits. The town was dank and noisome and the mists swirled up from the marshes making each day a bleaker parody of the preceding one. He had summoned Parliament to him in the ancient city, but Thomas Chaucer, the Speaker, was being a nuisance; and now here was his son being tiresome as well.

"Why Burgundy?" repeated the King, scratching the flaking skin on his arm and leaving a faint streak of blood.

"Because Burgundy lies close to Calais," the Prince answered promptly.

"The trade with Flanders is essential," Henry Beaufort put in. More and more, the Beauforts were attaching themselves to the Prince's party. The Bishop went on: "We need the Flemish weavers."

"And we need the wine trade with Bordeaux," snapped the King, while Archbishop Arundel nodded sagely. "Do you know how much wine this country imports in a year? You ought to," he added with a cackle of mirthless laughter, looking contemptuously in his son's direction.

The Prince's mouth shut in a tight, thin line, like the closing of a trap.

"There is the matter of Your Highness's proposed marriage, too," said Arundel. "Queen Isabeau alone can influence King Charles on that head. The new Duke of Orleans is both her son-in-law and her nephew. She will naturally favour those who favour Charles of Orleans."

"How delicately you put it, my dear Archbishop," sneered Henry Beaufort. "Why not say that Orleans is the son of her dead lover. A more cogent reason for Queen Isabeau's support, surely?"

Prince Henry brought his hand down on the table, his

rings chiming against the wood and making everyone look in his direction.

"Burgundy," he repeated, "is close to Calais. Burgundian support could ensure the town as an effective bridgehead if ever we should wish to further the pretensions of my great-grandfather to the throne of France."

Everyone stared at him. Then the King lay back in his chair, gasping with laughter.

"Further the—! My god, boy—" and he could have used no more insulting word to one who now considered himself a fully grown man—"where do you think that we should find the money to mount an invasion of France?"

"It could be found," the Prince replied sullenly, the red glint of anger sparkling in his eyes. "The people would find it for that."

"This year," said the King, slowly and impressively, "this year alone, I have borrowed four thousand pounds from Richard Whittington; three thousand pounds from John Hende. And now, Thomas Chaucer, on behalf of that . . . that assembly down there, has forced me to recognise formally that Parliament alone has the right to initiate the granting of loans to the crown. Do you realise what that means? I can no longer force them to give me money unless they are willing. And you sit there and talk about invading France. And *why* invade France? Tell me that!"

"The throne of France is rightfully ours through your great-grandmother, Isabelle of France," the Prince replied doggedly, and Henry Beaufort looked at his half-nephew with sudden interest.

"Invade France, indeed!" the King was snorting. "A fantastic dream!"

But was it such a fantastic dream? wondered the Bishop. The King's chief objection to it seemed to lie in the conviction that Parliament would not vote, nor the merchants lend, money for such a purpose. Henry Beaufort thought otherwise. The English hated the French with a deep, unreasoning hatred which appeared to be endemic rather than acquired. An invasion of France, provided that it was successful, would certainly have their support and might be the very thing needed to relieve the House of Lancaster of the constant plague of rebellion.

The beginning of the year 1408 saw Lancaster eased of two of it most persistent opponents. On the nineteenth of February, Northumberland was killed in battle at Brabham Moor whilst making his last abortive attempt to unseat the man whom he had helped to make King nine years earlier. Hotspur's son succeeded to his grandfather's title and, being still young, had no inclination to continue the feud.

Later in the same year, the siege of Harlech Castle resulted in the death of Sir Edmund Mortimer. Glendower himself escaped, but his power was broken. He would not give up easily but he was no longer a serious threat to the English crown. He had missed the greatest chance of his life when he had failed to support Hotspur at Shrewsbury Field.

But Henry of Bolingbroke was too ill to care. In the early spring, he suffered a severe epileptic fit at Mortlake, and in December, he was so bad that his ministers judged it wise to send for Prince Thomas from Ireland.

Henry of Monmouth watched and waited, displaying neither grief nor, to the disappointment of the onlookers, elation. He was young and healthy; his father was middle-aged and ill. He had only to bide his time and the crown would be his for the taking.

9

THE King recovered, but relations between him and his heir became more strained than ever. There were plenty of people to hint at Prince Henry's absence of grief during his father's illness. They did not do so openly : Henry of Monmouth was still their future King. But by concentrating on the extravagance of Prince Thomas's sorrow, they managed, subtly, to convey Prince Henry's lack.

The King said nothing, but thought the more. He drew closer to Thomas and to his unfailing supporter, Archbishop Arundel. The Beauforts, also being young, gave their loyalty to the rising star, and the court gradually, imperceptibly, split into two factions.

Henry of Bolingbroke turned to religious matters. His last illness had frightened him, bringing him, although only forty-one, to the brink of the grave. He knew his health to be precarious and, contrasting his decaying body with his splendid physique before the usurpation, saw, terrified, the judgement of God. He had never had the hubris of his eldest son; never seen the Deity as his personal friend and ally; never, except for the benefit of the world at large, believed that his actions had been divinely inspired. What he had done, he had done defiantly, knowing full well that he might one day have to pay the price. And now, he felt, was the time to begin propitiating his God.

That disgrace to the Christian world, the papal schism, was the most obvious area for his placatory efforts. And when, early in 1408, the Sacred College of Cardinals at Pisa had decided to call a Council with a view to resolving the breach, King Henry had hastened to send his representatives to the conference. Shortly before his second illness, he had received, at Westminster, Cardinal Francis Ugguccione, Archbishop of Bordeaux, and had discussed the matter with him far into the cold winter nights. Afterwards, he had sent Sir John Colville and the Papal Auditor, Nicholas Rushton, to reinforce the English delegation at Pisa.

At home, egged on by the fanatical Archbishop Arundel, Henry instigated a serious attempt to suppress the rapid spread of the Lollard heresy. Like many another before and after him, the King saw the universities, particularly Oxford, as centres of dissidence, and this caused trouble. The undergraduates resented the probes into their personal beliefs and student riots became more frequent.

"The students," Henry Beaufort told his half-nephew delightedly, "say that their religious views are their own and not the property of the King. They argue that how they worship God can have nothing to do with their studies."

Henry of Monmouth found himself in a dilemma. He knew that the Bishop was not so much a progressive thinker as the dedicated enemy of Thomas Arundel, and, as such, bound to support anyone who opposed the Archbishop. Consequently, Prince Henry, in his turn needing the support of the Beauforts in a court where the hierarchy was becoming ever more hostile towards him, discovered that he, the most orthodox of men, was committed to the side of free thought. It was an anomalous position and one which caused him great embarrassment; for when Hus was excommunicated, Henry was in full agreement with the Church's decree, but could not say so openly for fear of offending the Oxford undergraduates and their champion, Henry Beaufort. One student named Peter Payne had actually gone to Czechoslovakia and obtained a post in the revolutionary government.

Prince Henry's indecision of mind resulted in the fiasco of Badby's execution. John Badby was a tailor from Evesham who had been sentenced to be burned for his Lollard beliefs.

"If the doctrine of transubstantiation is true," he had told the Bishop of Worcester's court defiantly, "then at each Mass, when the consecrated Host is swallowed, there must be twenty

81

thousand Gods in England, for every man then holds the Blood and Body of Christ within himself." He glared at his judges. "Transubstantiation must therefore be the greatest blasphemy thought up by mankind."

Badby was sent to London for execution. On his father's orders, Prince Henry attended the burning, but in a state of mind bordering on the schizophrenic. He believed implicitly in the justice of Badby's fate, but felt himself impelled to act the role of Lollard champion, if for no better reason than to antagonise his father.

Therefore, as Badby began to scream and writhe in agony, Henry ordered the fire to be doused and had the half-burned victim dragged before him. He had intended to pardon the man in order to show that he, Henry of Monmouth, was above the edicts of State and Church. But, faced at last with the moment of decision, he found that he was unable to declare for heterodoxy. Instead, he offered Badby a pension for life if he would recant. Badby refused.

"Let the execution proceed," Henry said, grim-faced.

When Henry Beaufort heard of the incident, he was guilty of some extremely unclerical language. Like his half-nephew, he had no particular sympathy with Lollard beliefs, but he needed the Lollards' support if he were to unseat Archbishop Arundel. In addition, as he pointed out in round terms to the culprit himself, the incident had done the Prince's popularity untold harm. The Londoners were perfectly happy to see a man burned to death for heresy : they enjoyed their public executions, whatever form they took. But they would not tolerate seeing a man suffer twice over : it offended their notions of fair play.

"Before you become King, you must learn to understand your subjects better," the Bishop upbraided his half-nephew.

The Prince eyed him coldly. It occurred to him that although he was fond of his half-uncles, Thomas and John Beaufort, he and Henry Beaufort were uneasy allies.

"When I am King," he answered tartly, "I shall give my subjects something other than theological disputes to occupy their minds. I shall encourage them to think about France."

To France, the year 1409 brought no relief from its political unrest. Isabella, widow of Richard the second and wife of Charles of Orleans, died. Shortly afterwards, the Duke married Bonne, the daughter of the Count of Armagnac, and these two great factions were now united against Burgundy. Caught at the centre of the maelstrom were King Charles, mad for more than half his time, and Queen Isabeau, pitting her sharp German wits against the entire unruly baronage.

"And succeeeding," Henry Beaufort pointed out.

The Earl of Warwick, to whom this remark was addressed in Prince Henry's house of Coldharbour in East Cheap, languidly applauded a minstrel as he finished playing.

"Well, they do say," he answered, "that a virgin will save the throne of France. Perhaps it's Isabeau," and the assembled company joined in his ribald cackle of laughter.

Queen Isabeau's morals were a household joke, even here in England. It was common knowledge that the murdered Duke of Orleans had been his sister-in-law's lover and there were rumours that the Dauphin, Louis, was his child. At the French court, the poor boy was openly referred to as "his uncle's son".

Prince Henry looked up from his seat by the window and said: "I've heard that story, but the virgin, I believe, will come out of Lorraine, not Bavaria." He was smiling and Henry Beaufort grimaced at the Earl of Warwick.

"My half-nephew has a sense of humour, then," he whispered, and Warwick raised his eyebrows.

"A pity," he retorted, "that he doesn't let it see the light of day more often. Jocularity doesn't last long with Henry."

It was of short duration now: the Prince was already claiming Henry Beaufort's attention with some question about the newly elected Pope, Alexander the fifth. Would the two deposed pontiffs accept Peter Philargi in his new role?

"It's extremely doubtful," the Bishop replied, sending a look full of meaning in Warwick's direction. "We are probably about to find ourselves in the position of having three Popes instead of two," and he laughed.

Henry shrugged disgustedly. He had recently returned

from Wales where the surrender of Harlech Castle had resulted in almost all Glendower's remaining family being taken prisoner. But once again, the principal actor had eluded his pursuers, apparently dissolving into the Welsh mists which lay for ever cloaking the mountains.

The Bishop, regarding the Prince closely, thought he detected shadows under the young man's eyes, a certain weariness in his posture, and was alarmed. Henry had always seemed such a golden youth, a Hector, untouched by the fatigues of ordinary mortals, and it was unusual to see him display any strain. And it did not suit Henry Beaufort that the Prince should show signs of lethargy just now, for the Bishop felt that the moment had almost come for dislodging Archbishop Arundel from his post as Chancellor. Henry Beaufort needed the Prince's unflagging support.

The King was in his usual financial straits. The Council in Ireland had written deeming it desirable that Prince Thomas should receive two thousand marks from the Irish revenues and a thousand marks per annum from the King. Henry of Bolingbroke had been forced to refuse, for Parliament, in the ebullient form of its Speaker, Thomas Chaucer, had made it plain that it would not vote the money. Antagonism towards the King and his chief ministers was growing : anti-clericalism was rife everywhere amongst the common people. Undoubtedly, the moment was approaching for unseating Thomas Arundel and the Bishop scrutinised his half-nephew closely as Henry rose from his seat. Then he sighed with relief. The shadows beneath the eyes had been nothing more than a trick of the light; the weariness merely a too-relaxed pose.

In November, the overthrow of Archbishop Arundel as Chancellor of England was accomplished with very little fuss. The King had no option but to comply with the combined wishes of his Parliament, his heir and his most powerful subjects. Henry of Bolingbroke knew at last something of the humiliation suffered years before, at his own hands, by his deposed and dead cousin, Richard the second.

There was great surprise, however, when the name of the

new Chancellor was made public; not Henry, but Thomas Beaufort. Why the phlegmatic Dorset had been selected instead of his more erudite brother, was a matter for much speculation and gossip. Had Thomas been Prince Henry's choice? And, if so, was there a rift within the Prince's party?

What was not generally recognised, or believed, if it was guessed at, was that Thomas was the Bishop's own choice. The Prince had assumed as naturally as did everyone else that Henry Beaufort would wish to accept the office, but his old tutor was far too shrewd.

"My dear Henry," he had said, "yours must be the popular party. We have brought about Arundel's dismissal because of the people's support. And they support us because they are feeling anti-clerical. To replace one Churchman by another would be to court their displeasure. No, no! Thomas will do very nicely: he will do just as I . . . just as *we* tell him."

And so, Thomas Beaufort became Chancellor. The King, outwardly acquiescent, awaited his turn.

The Duke of York was ushered into his brother's house and stood, blinking, in the dim light of the great hall. Cambridge, resplendent in satin, moved towards him like a flickering ray of light; a stray rainbow glimmering amongst the sable shadows.

"Edward! How good of you to come! And such terrible weather, too. But a sight of your first nephew is something that I know you wouldn't want to miss."

"How is Anne?" York asked gruffly as he followed Cambridge up the twisting stair at the end of the room and into his sister-in-law's solar.

"Tired," admitted the Earl, "but no more so than most women after giving birth to a child."

York, however, when he saw his sister-in-law, was of the opinion that Anne Mortimer was more fatigued than the average woman in similar circumstances and suspected that she would not make old bones.

The baby was lying in its cradle, a surprisingly lusty little creature with a square red face and a precociously aware expression for one only a few days old. Why the baby's physical strength should so amaze him, the Duke had no idea. Anne Mortimer might be delicate, but no one realised better than York that his brother's effete appearance was an illusion; an impression created by Richard's foppish clothes and his languid air. People always referred to Cambridge in a slightly contemptuous fashion, as a harmless idiot concerned with nothing but the cut of his doublet and the colour of his hose. But the Duke knew that Richard's foolish smile and fluttering, inane gestures concealed an intelligent mind. Moreover, Cambridge gloried in his deception; laughed up his elegant sleeve at this trick which he perpetrated upon society.

Why did his brother do it? York wondered. It was as though, all his adult life, Richard had been hiding behind this innocuous façade, waiting his opportunity—for what? Perhaps Cambridge, too, had been asking himself that question, but now, in his son, the puzzle had resolved itself.

The Earl bent, smiling, over the cradle. "An heir for Mortimer," he said. His long lashes fluttered against his pale cheek. "And an heir for York." He turned and faced his elder brother, his blue eyes now wide open and as alert as York had often seen them in childhood, when Richard had been intent upon some secret purpose. Cambridge continued: "An heir, in fact, to two uncles, neither of whom has children of his own. One," and he inclined his dark head in his brother's direction, "is the great Duke of York, holder of vast titles and estates. The other—" the eyes kindled, taking on an oddly hazel glow in their lapis-lazuli depths—"is the rightful King of England. And, as I said, my son, my little Richard, is heir to both."

York swore fluently under his breath. What a family he was burdened with! First his sister, and now his brother embroiled in dangerous treason. Why could they not accept Lancaster as he did? More important, why had King Henry not taken steps to ensure his own—and others'—safety, by getting rid of Richard the second's heirs? York was not generally an advocate of murder. He was fond of his sister-in-law in a negative way and felt no particular animosity towards her brother, but he valued his own peace of mind more. And without Anne, there would not now be this baby, this possible heir to both Mortimer and York, to constitute a threat to his serenity.

"You should never speak of Edmund Mortimer as King," he protested uneasily and his brother laughed.

"It's the truth."

"Perhaps so! The truth, however, is not always palatable."

"Ah! But I should say nothing to anyone but you—for the present, at least."

York stirred, shifting his position on the hard joint-stool.

"You should not say it to anyone at all. You have never interested yourself in your brother-in-law before."

"I have never had a son before." And Cambridge smiled, stooping to warm his hands at the small fire burning on the hearth. "You can rest assured that I shall do nothing foolish. I shall bide my time—if that time ever comes." Once more, the Earl gave his urbane, almost moronic grin. "But there is little doubt that Henry of Bolingbroke is not the popular young Prince he was ten years ago when our father assisted him to a throne."

The King's popularity was indeed at its lowest ebb. Thomas Hoccleve, attending the great banquet given by Sir Henry Somer, Chancellor of the Exchequer, was aware of unrest and disunity all about him, and all of it centred upon the Crown.

Hoccleve himself was a little happier than usual. The Prince of Wales had asked him to translate Aegidius Romanus's *De Regimine Principum*, and in Henry of Monmouth's patronage, the Clerk of the Privy Seal saw some cause for optimism. He could write his own prologue to the work, underlining the duty of Princes to be liberal and generous to their underpaid servants, particularly those in government employ. He would hint—not too openly, but none the less clearly—at his own impecunious circumstances, and felt sure that the Prince of Wales would accept the nudge and reward the translator as he deserved. Certainly the future seemed a little rosier, thanks to the King's eldest son who, for the present, had all Hoccleve's devotion.

Young Henry had the devotion of others, as Hoccleve and everyone else well knew; but it was unfortunate that one of the Prince's most ardent supporters, John Beaufort, Earl of Somerset, should recently have died. This eldest child of John of Gaunt's and Katherine Swynford's illegitimate progeny had been only thirty-eight years of age and might have been counted upon by the Prince's party for at least another decade.

But even John Beaufort's death had worked in one respect to Prince Henry's advantage. It was common gossip in London that Prince Thomas, home from Ireland and irrevocably identified with his father's cause, was already casting greedy eyes upon his half-uncle's relict; although not so much upon the widow herself, reflected Hoccleve, as upon the vast Beaufort and Holland estates which she would bring as dowry to her second husband. This scandal was doing the King's faction no good and Henry Beaufort had gone so far as to sound out certain of the more influential magnates concerning the possibility of deposing the ailing Bolingbroke in favour of his son. King Richard, thought Hoccleve, must be laughing in his grave.

He continued eating, busy with his own thoughts amid the clatter and steam of the Grocers' Hall, and listening with only half an ear to his neighbour, the ex-Mayor Richard Whittington, who insisted on telling him, in his depressing Gloucestershire monotone, of his latest good works; the endowment of Whittington's parish church of St Michael Pater Noster; the handing over of Leadenhall to the Corporation; the opening of Bakewell Hall for the sale of broadcloths. Hoccleve glanced at the thin, clean-shaven face and grunted. Prosy, pious old fool, he thought briefly; then became immersed once more in his own reflections.

A member of the Watch entered and pushed his way to the high table. Shortly afterwards, the Sheriff and the Mayor departed in a hurry, amid a buzz of speculation.

"They say," Whittington remarked presently, looking disapprovingly down his long nose, "that there has been a riot in East Cheap and that Prince Thomas and Prince John are involved. Disgraceful!"

Hoccleve smiled into his fish tart. If true, this incident would scarcely redound to the court party's credit, either. A wild lot, these Plantagenets, but it would never do to underrate any one of them, especially Henry of Bolingbroke.

10

HOCCLEVE was perfectly right; it was never wise to under-estimate the King's recuperative powers. Henry had no intention of letting the reins of government slip from his hands into those of his son, so long as he retained his faculties. His body was sick, but his mind was as strong as ever. Prince Henry and the Beauforts might, for the moment, be riding high, with Dorset as Chancellor and the Prince of Wales as Captain of Calais, but the political see-saw could swing just as suddenly in the opposite direction—and who should know that better than Henry of Bolingbroke, who, in six months, had brought his cousin crashing from the throne into the grave? But sometimes, the King felt that his time was short and then a terrible urgency would possess him.

On a cold February day in the year 1411, when the grey London skies pressed in on all sides and the river, or what showed of it beneath its skin of refuse, was a dull leaden colour, Henry sent for his Queen.

"You are a rich woman," he said, motioning her to sit beside his couch. "I've endowed you well." He took her hand and patted it. "You will be well provided for when I'm gone."

Joanna's grip on his arm immediately tightened. She did not like allusions to his death : she could not foresee life here in this miserable island without Henry. She did not love him. She had never loved any man, apart from her sons; and in rare moments of complete honesty she knew herself incapable of deep physical enjoyment. She had never been able to give herself with abandon to anyone : love, for her, was a restricted emotion, centred, with the exception of her children, almost entirely upon herself.

But she was capable of great affection and was very fond of this husband of hers who had treated her kindly and generously. So, when he said now : "I want you to do something for me," she replied at once : "Oh course! Anything!"

He gave her a grateful smile and, in spite of the reassuringly martial look in his eyes, she was alarmed by its feebleness. She thought of her eldest step-son who would be King in her husband's place, and shivered. She was afraid of Prince Henry, which was odd because his nature was very much akin to her own. And perhaps that was why she feared him : she knew that when love sang its song only in the minor key, the major chords were apt to be harsh and discordant and cruel.

"What do you wish me to do?" she enquired.

"I want you to give your manor of Woodstock to Thomas Chaucer."

"A little bribe?" she asked quickly and Henry laughed.

"As you say, my dear, a little bribe. If I were to give the Speaker of the Commons such a gift, it would look . . . suspicious. But coming from you there can be no objection." He raised his hand and patted her cheek. "I want Archbishop Arundel back as Chancellor before the year is out."

The Queen nodded. She would like to keep Woodstock, but she would like to see Prince Henry and his friends disgraced even more.

"I shall see that the gift is made," she answered, "and at once. I cannot imagine that Master Chaucer will refuse."

The Speaker did not refuse, taking his gift with both hands and thanking his stars for such an open-handed patroness.

But the douceur seemed, for a while at least, to have been given in vain. The Prince's party continued in the ascendant, with Prince Henry's Burgundian policy being vigorously pursued. The King's plans for a marriage between his eldest son and Katherine de Valois were cast aside in favour of the Prince of Wales's proposed union with Anne, a daughter of Duke John the Fearless of Burgundy.

"Which should refute those slanders," Prince Henry remarked with a sneer to his brother, John, "that I think more

91

of my own enjoyment that I do of my duty. If people think that it will be a pleasure to marry her"—and, contemptuously, he cast a miniature in front of his companion—"they have a strange notion of felicity."

John studied the picture carefully, smoothing the quiet young face with his finger.

"She looks a gentle girl," he said at last.

"Pious! Or so I've heard."

"That should suit you, Henry." John looked up at his elder brother, but the blue eyes were unshadowed, guileless.

John's hero-worship of Henry was quite genuine. He was neither jealous of him, like Thomas, nor fondly discerning, like Humphrey. John's devotion was unclouded by either envy or criticism and Henry, to his credit, had the perception to recognise its true worth; to know it for the purest emotion that he would ever be offered by another human being.

"Perhaps!" he answered briefly, taking up the miniature again and putting it aside with other state papers. "If it furthers the alliance with Burgundy, I shall be satisfied. I must be."

John accepted this, but asked: "Will the alliance become a fact? Our father was too ill to meet Duke John, as he promised."

"He said he was too ill," grunted Henry. He glanced out of the open window, across the bustle of East Cheap, to Sir John Oldcastle's house which stood opposite. "I intend to send an expedition to aid Burgundy against the Armagnacs. Oldcastle will lead it."

Prince John never failed to be surprised by Henry's continuing friendship with a known Lollard. Since Archbishop Arundel's persecutions and the excommunication of Hus by the Pope, the Lollards had been less vociferous, but Sir John was the exception. He and his new wife, Lady Cobham, spoke openly of their beliefs, even before the conformist Prince. But of course, reflected John, it was part of his brother's present policy to support the Lollards. How long, however, would Henry continue to do so when there was no further necessity? Meantime, Oldcastle was useful to him.

92

The expedition to France turned out to be successful even beyond Prince Henry's wildest dreams. Under the direction of Sir John Oldcastle and the Earl of Arundel, it sailed from Dover at the beginning of September, and by the middle of the month had reached Paris. Then came the news that, in a clash with the Armagnacs near St Cloud, this small English force of just over a thousand men had driven the enemy beyond the Loire.

Prince Henry was thoughtful. If such a small contingent of English troops could achieve so much, what could a full-sized army not accomplish? Now, surely, his father must admit that an invasion of France had its possibilities; must see that the Prince of Wales's policies were superior to his own.

The King neither admitted nor saw anything of the kind : he wanted the way of marriage, not of war. He was too ill to lead an expeditionary force himself, and he wisely foresaw trouble if his already popular son and heir became more of a hero to the English people than he was now.

So, in November, the King made his move. Six of Prince Henry's household, including his Steward, were arrested; the Prince himself was dismissed from the Council; and by the end of December, Thomas Beaufort had been relieved of the office of Chancellor and Archbishop Arundel reinstated in his place.

Outwardly, the breach between father and son was formal and precise. Before the Council was relieved of his presence, the Prince was thanked for his services. But beneath the surface, rage and frustration ran. The Prince of Wales left London, ostensibly on a progress through the Midlands, but word soon reached the capital that he was arming his tenants on the borders of Wales. Henry and Thomas Beaufort hastened to join him at Chester.

"Don't be a fool, boy," the Earl of Dorset said bluntly, stooping to warm his hands at the fire, for the March day was cold. "Rebellion can gain you nothing."

Henry Beaufort sent his brother a warning look as he saw the anger flash into his half-nephew's eyes. Nevertheless,

Thomas was right. The Lancastrian throne was shaky enough without proclaiming to the world that the House was divided against itself. Whatever else the King had done, he had taken pains to avoid an outright quarrel.

"Appearances are everything," the Bishop told the Prince. "There are those in Europe waiting eagerly to see Lancaster bring itself to ruin. And there are many in this country who would be glad to see Edmund Mortimer on the throne. So before you march against your father, sleep on it!"

Henry did so, and the result of his lucubrations was that he took—albeit reluctantly—his half-uncles' advice. But news from London that an Armagnac delegation had arrived, offering the restoration of Aquitaine, Anjou and Angoulême to King Henry in return for English help against the Burgundians, prevented the Prince from actually disarming his retainers.

This was a grave mistake, for rumour was soon rife in the capital that civil war between father and son was about to break out, and the city was in a ferment. Trade came virtually to a standstill. In Wales, Glendower stirred once more— for the last time, it was true, but no one could know that at the time—while the Scots resurrected the old story that King Richard was still alive, a guest in Stirling Castle.

The Prince of Wales was no fool and he realised that if he plunged England now into civil strife, he might well have no throne to inherit. For a while he was nonplussed. He could not deny that he had levied troops in the Marches and the Midlands: too many people knew it to be the truth. But the news that a force was being raised under the command of Prince Thomas to aid the Armagnacs in Normandy gave him a chance to save his face.

Declaring that he had armed his men only to assist this expedition of his brother's, he went to London and vigorously denied what he called "these slanders against my character", and even demanded that the King punish the rumour-mongers.

In the privacy of Coldharbour House, however, he gave vent to his feelings and told his Beaufort half-uncles his precise opinion of the proposed expedition. The Bishop was fascinated by his half-nephew's command of the Anglo-Saxon tongue in all its cruder forms; but Thomas Beaufort regretted the passionless manner in which the diatribe was delivered. He had all the soldier's admiration for the man who could swear fluently, but the Prince's oration lacked fire : the deliberate, calculated utterances endowed the words with an obscenity which, for Thomas Beaufort, they had hitherto lacked. For the fisrt time in his life, they embarrassed him.

The Bishop was soothing. "The King will soon find out that he has made a grave mistake," he said. "The Armagnacs are not to be trusted and your brother will be made to look a fool."

Henry Beaufort spoke more in hope than in certainty. Prince Thomas had recently married John Beaufort's widow and a legal wrangle had ensued between him and the two remaining male Beauforts concerning their sister-in-law's possessions. The Prince of Wales, disgusted by what he considered to be an incestuous match—Margaret Holland was Prince Thomas's half-aunt, if only by marriage—had supported the Beauforts, while the King had naturally thrown in his weight on the side of his favourite son. It had done nothing to ease the already strained family relationships and made Prince Henry's party all the more anxious to see disaster in Normandy.

At first, it seemed as though these pious aspirations were to remain unrealised. Prince Thomas achieved a certain measure of success in the Cotentin and, in consequence, was created by his father Duke of Clarence and Lieutenant of Aquitaine. But before the victories could be followed up, the Armagnacs made peace with the Burgundians and begged their now embarrassing allies to go away. All Europe laughed; the Londoners, who, from time to time, displayed the peculiar English faculty of being able to enjoy a joke at their own expense, also laughed; and the Prince of Wales laughed loudest of all.

It was his second mistake within a few months. Henry of Bolingbroke, ailing and beset by qualms of conscience, was in no mood for his heir's unaccustomed mirth. Scarcely had the Prince recovered from his bout of levity than he found himself facing charges of misappropriating the Calais funds, which, in his capacity as Captain, it was his duty to administer.

Never before had the Prince been so icily angry. The inference that he could stoop to petty peculation goaded him as no slur upon his courage, or even his chivalry, could have done. The imputation that he would appropriate official monies for his own pleasures amongst the bawds and doxies of Cheapside left him speechless by its sheer vindictiveness. He had never dreamed that his father could stoop so low. The fact that he could—and did—easily refute the charge brought against him, did nothing to alleviate his feelings. His honour had been impugned and by the very man who should have been at the greatest pains to protect it. Only a dramatic gesture could do justice to the enormity of the situation.

Consequently, on September the twenty-fifth, the court at Westminster was startled by the appearance of Prince Henry clad in a bright blue satin doublet, sewn all over with eyelet holes, the needle with which each hole had been embroidered hanging by a silken thread : a garment which symbolised by the eyelet holes the wearer's ability to see through his enemies' actions, and, by the needles, his own diligence in doing his duty.

Prince Thomas sneered in open contempt of the display and informed his brother that the King would not see him. Henry shoved Thomas aside; the new Duke of Clarence retaliated in kind; and the courtiers crowded round in anticipation of a royal brawl. Fortunately, the King's Chamberlain informed him of what was towards and orders were given to allow the Prince of Wales entry.

The Prince stalked into his father's presence-chamber and stood glowering : but he was shaken. He had not seen the King at close quarters for some while and realised suddenly that he was facing a dying man. The bloated, flaking flesh was putty-coloured, the hair almost non-existent and over all the room hung a smell of decay and corruption. Henry of

Bolingbroke was forty-six years of age and he was a man haunted by the consequences of his deeds.

The King was not an evil man, but one who, thirteen years before, had been caught in a mesh of circumstances and desires, opportunity and ability, which had swept him inexorably along the road to power. His own and his cousin's characters had combined to inevitable effect, and once the fact of the usurpation had been established, the murder had been a necessary corollary. The King had done nothing, however, with his eyes shut and had always known that he would pay the price with his conscience. This and the bitter realisation that he was as vulnerable to treachery amongst his so-called friends as Richard had been, had slowly undermined his health. Now he knew that his death was not far off; that the day of reckoning had almost arrived. Had it been within his power, he would have restored the throne to Edmund Mortimer, but, as he had remarked sadly to a friend: "My sons will never allow my regality to pass out of their line."

But what sort of a King was he leaving England? He had never been able to fathom this eldest son of his. Did Henry have any deep feelings for anyone? He looked at the Prince's set face and thought: "He is a hard man, but perhaps a hard man is what England needs. His conscience is clear at all events, provided that he remains convinced that he, and not Edmund Mortimer, is the rightful King."

But the King knew that he had been vindictive and spiteful; that he had acted from pettiness because his son was young and popular and he was middle-aged and disliked. He had had such wonderful visions of what he would achieve for England; instead, he had been forced to dissipate his energies fighting to keep what he had won. The dream and the promise now belonged to his son: he could not go to meet his God with the added guilt of the quarrel between them left unresolved.

So he rose to his feet, saying nothing, but feebly holding out his arms. To his surprise, and perhaps to Henry's, the response to this gesture was overwhelming. The Prince threw himself into his father's embrace, tears running down his face, cling-

D

ing about the King's neck as he had not done since he was a child. The years fled away for both of them; Henry of Bolingbroke was again the handsome, magnificent soldier; Henry of Monmouth the adoring young son.

Such a moment could not last; the pitch of intensity was too strong; the emotional atmosphere too rare to last more than a few fleeting seconds. But they had touched the peaks and throughout the remaining months of the King's life, they were able to offer each other a greater understanding and a larger measure of tolerance than if those moments had never been.

During Christmas, the King lapsed into unconsciousness, but rallied again. On March the twentieth, he went to pray at the tomb of Edward the Confessor and there collapsed. He was carried to the Abbot's lodging in Westminster Abbey and laid in the Jerusalem Chamber, but by the time his four sons arrived, he was incapable of speech and had been shrived. As the winter's day drew to its close, his spirit passed also, borne away on a great gust of wind that seemed to shake the Abbey from one end to the other. And the heralds went out into the murky dawn to proclaim King Henry the fifth.

PART TWO

THE GOLDEN YEARS, 1413–1420

11

HAD anyone told Henry the fifth, on the morning of his coronation, that he would outlive his father by a bare nine and a half years, the new King would have laughed in his informant's face. He had never felt healthier nor happier in his life.

Henry was taking his burden of regality very seriously. He had spent the night of his father's death praying in the cell of a Westminster recluse and was determined to show by his actions his support for the orthodox Church. On the morning of April the eighth, therefore, the morning before the coronation, his brother John's attention was diverted from his many preparations by a red glow in the sky and a pall of smoke rising in the vicinity of St Paul's. The Prince at once sent one of his servants to discover the cause.

The previous week, in the presence of their brothers, the King and the Duke of Clarence, John had been made Duke of Bedford and Humphrey Duke of Gloucester. And it was the latter, in all the glory of his new title, who was ushered now into John's Westminster apartments.

"Something is happening at St Paul's," he announced. "In fact, there's a burning. A heretic, do you think?" and Humphrey grinned in that callous way of his which never failed to revolt his more sensitive elder brother. At the same time, John found himself forced to return the smile because Humphrey, like so many other Plantagenets both before and after him, combined insensitivity and charm in equal measure. What in other men would have appeared downright hard-heartedness, the Duke palliated with a deprecating twinkle of the eye.

"I've sent to discover the cause," John answered, motioning his brother to a chair and pouring him some wine.

As Humphrey accepted the mazer from his brother's hand, grimacing ruefully to himself over the paucity of its contents, John's servant returned, grimy and scorched.

"Some heretic?" enquired Humphrey cheerfully, before his brother could speak. He took in the man's appearance and laughed. "Don't tell me that they tried to push you into the bonfire as well!"

John frowned Humphrey down, but his irrepressible brother only grinned into his cup.

"It's not an execution, Your Grace," the man explained earnestly. "It's books that they're burning."

"Books?"

"Sir John Oldcastle's books, my lord, by order of the Convocation of Canterbury."

"Oh, Lord!" exclaimed Humphrey. "I'd forgotten that that set of old gudgeons was gracing St Paul's." He saw Bedford's look of outraged reproof and giggled, turning once more to the servant. "Lollard books, are they? Yes? I thought so! I guessed that our brother would repudiate his old friend, but I didn't expect him to do it quite so speedily or so drastically."

"Will you be quiet?" John demanded, nodding a hurried dismissal to his servant. When the man had gone, he said angrily to Gloucester: "Do you think that he's a block of stone? A thing without ears? You are not immune from charges of treason and heresy, you know, just because you are the King's brother."

"Oh, I realise that," Humphrey said, lazily rising to his feet and stretching. "I should be a fool if I didn't. Henry will never let anything stand in the way of his duty, not even ties of friendship or blood. That Archbishop Arundel has been dismissed from the office of Chancellor and our beloved half-uncle, Henry Beaufort"—Humphrey spat viciously at the name—"installed in his place, I can understand. The Archbishop was never a friend of brother Henry's. That Chief Justice Gascoigne has been retired in favour of Sir William

102

Hankeford, I can also understand. Gascoigne, after all, is sixty-three. But Oldcastle! Now there's a different story. Because I think that, in his own peculiar way, Henry is quite fond of Sir John. Certainly, he's made enough use of him, Lollard beliefs and all, in the past few years. But now, my dear John," and Humphrey smiled knowingly into Bedford's perturbed face, "now, the support of the Lollards is no longer necessary to our brother. He is the King, and a very unschismatical King as you and I have always known he would be. It may grieve Henry to hurt his friend, but he would never use his influence to prevent the Convocation from doing anything it thought right and proper."

With a shimmer of velvet and a flash of jewels, Humphrey went on his sumptuous way, leaving John, Duke of Bedford, to some new and disturbing thoughts concerning his adored eldest brother.

The interior of Westminster Abbey was stifling, packed with a vast concourse of people all moving and swaying together like ripples of a multi-coloured ocean. The resplendence of the Confessor's tomb paled into insignificance beside that glittering throng, and even the richest of tapestries adorning the ancient grey walls was nothing but a dim glow in the background; a muted setting for the diamonds and rubies, the ermine and sable, the cloth-of-gold and glimmering velvets that today adorned the bodies of the greatest in the land.

Outside, on this coronation morning of April the ninth, it was snowing heavily, but the crowds which thronged the busy streets were undeterred by so small a consideration. The people might grumble to each other about the inclemency of the weather, but they warmed their chilled extremities by getting drunk on the free wine in the conduits, and cheered vociferously every figure, whether recognised or not, who made his or her way into the welcoming warmth of the Abbey. They even raised a shout for the Dowager Queen Joanna, but although she smiled graciously in response, her thoughts were busy elsewhere.

One of Henry's first acts after his accession had been to order the immediate completion of the church of St Mary's-in-Newarke at Leicester, where his mother was buried. He had also commissioned Mary de Bohun's effigy from one of London's leading coppersmiths, and although these could be considered as nothing more than acts of filial piety, Joanna saw a more sinister purpose behind them. She regarded these gestures as a direct warning to herself that the King had never accepted her in place of his mother; that he had in fact never looked upon her with anything but resentment. Her friends suggested in vain that she was allowing her dislike of Henry to distort and discolour her judgement; pointed out without success that he had never treated her with anything but the most punctilious courtesy. Joanna trusted more to her own intuition than to the opinions of less interested parties.

But if the Queen Dowager were feeling uneasy, Henry Beaufort, Bishop of Winchester and Chancellor, was regarding the future with considerable optimism. King Henry was winning golden opinions, not only amongst his contemporaries, but also from his former enemies, his father's old friends. The Lords Spiritual, who, for years, had been afraid that on Henry the fourth's death they would find themselves with a heretically inclined monarch, now discovered that they had a more rigid precisian than his father had ever been.

Of the Lords Temporal, those who had supported Henry the fourth loyally throughout his troubled reign were glad to see upon the throne a younger, stronger man, to whom the stigma of usurper or murderer could not be attached; those who hankered after the old régime or felt their consciences stirred by the thought of Richard and his heirs, were placated by Edmund Mortimer's release from years of house-arrest and his apparently happy acceptance of the Lancastrian dynasty. Of the younger sprigs of the nobility, there seemed no one, not even Richard de Vere, Earl of Oxford, whose father had been King Richard's closest and most dearly beloved friend, who did not regard Henry the fifth with complaisance, if not outright enthusiasm. The new generation of Hollands and Montagus and Scropes seemed as much Henry's men as their fathers had been Richard's.

Nevertheless, thought Henry Beaufourt, as he walked in his place in the coronation procession, it behoved his half-nephew to be as much upon his guard as his father had been. The King would do well to remember that his cousin Cambridge had, until her recent death, been married to the sister of Edmund Mortimer and that Cambridge's three-year-old son was his Uncle Edmund's heir; that Thomas, Lord Camoys, was married to Hotspur's widow, Mortimer's sister; and that Henry le Scrope of Masham was a nephew of the murdered Archbishop. There was, reflected the Bishop, the nucleus of a treasonable plot in the friendship of these four men and he considered it wise to keep them under surveillance. Henry Beaufort particularly distrusted Cambridge. An air of cunning and treachery hung about the Earl like a cloak; a kind of mocking self-awareness that robbed his actions of sincerity and made a travesty of genuine belief. Whatever cause Cambridge embraced, he would do so from the most cynical of motives; not from any passionate conviction, but from a perverted desire to make mischief.

Glancing to his left, the Bishop saw Joanna Beaufort, daughter of his dead brother, John. Joanna had inherited the looks of her beautiful grandmother, Lady Swynford, and Henry Beaufort had been quick to notice the young King of Scots' interest in his lovely niece. As the great triumphal anthem rose from a thousand throats, the Bishop of Winchester's thoughts were not upon God but upon dynasties. A Beaufort might yet sit upon the throne of Scotland and be the progenitor of her future Kings. He, Henry Beaufort, must see if he could prevail upon his half-nephew to release James the first of Scotland from his seven-year-long captivity.

"No!" said the King.

Together, he and his half-uncle were strolling in the grounds of Lambeth Palace, guests of an Archbishop Arundel who, although he could never totally overcome his former dislike of his old friend's son, had the grace to admit that

Henry the fifth was proving a competent and highly conventional King. The June sunshine lay pale and delicate about them and the lemon-sharp smell of newly scythed grass told them more plainly than the thrusting spears of betony or the clear, sweet trilling of the birds, that summer had arrived at last. Both men were tired : they had returned only that morning from Canterbury and the elaborate funeral of King Henry the fourth.

Now, at the King's short answer, Henry Beaufort raised his eyebrows in delicate enquiry. "Might I," he ventured "ask why not?"

He knew that he must tread warily with Henry, who disliked his fiats being questioned. But it seemed to the Bishop that the restoration of her rightful King to Scotland's throne —with, of course, a Beaufort wife—could do nothing but good to Anglo-Scottish relationships.

"No!" Henry repeated; then relented, feeling perhaps that some explanation was due to this uncle who had been his boyhood's tutor and who shared with him memories of those uncertain weeks in Ireland which had loomed so large in the life of a terrified child. "I may need him—as a hostage!"

Henry Beaufort was now thoroughly confused and was annoyed because of it. His half-nephew's processes of thought were surely not so devious that he, one of the subtlest minds in the country, could not follow them.

"Hostage?" he murmured.

"If I invade France," Henry said patiently, "the Scots will almost certainly support their old ally, Charles the sixth. But if I still have James to bargain with, I can possibly restrain their active intervention."

"Oh course! How very stupid of me," apologised the Bishop, and was astonished, as he was constantly being astonished, at his half-nephew's ability to foresee all the ramifications of a military situation. He added tentatively : "You intend to make war then?"

"If negotiations fail, yes." Henry's thick lips compressed, emphasising the heavy lantern jaw. He continued his silent pacing along the pleached alleyway. After a moment or two, he added: "I am sending Henry Chicele and the Earl of Warwick to King Charles next month; possibly Zouche and Scrope, as well."

The King's face softened as he uttered the last name and his uncle wondered, not for the first time, why, when Henry had at last allowed his heart to be touched by the tender emotion of friendship, he should have bestowed his affection upon young Scrope. It was true that it had already produced some good, in so far as the King had granted a licence for offerings to be made at the tomb of Archbishop Scrope in York Minster. This had not only placated those Yorkshiremen who regarded the murdered prelate as a saint, but had also successfully frustrated the would-be agitators who, for years, had made political capital from the execution. Nevertheless, young Henry le Scrope of Masham was on cordial terms with the Earl of Cambridge, and although this might mean nothing at all, Henry Beaufort could not overcome his conviction that York's younger brother was playing some deep and dangerous game of his own. The Bishop prayed that his half-nephew's new-found capacity for friendship would not be crippled by any treachery on the part of that friend.

"A formidable deputation," Henry Beaufort smiled, lengthening his stride to match the King's. "What do they ask of the French?"

"All those territories—Ponthieu, Aquitaine, Normandy—granted to Edward the third by the Treaty of Bretigny and never handed over by them."

The Bishop nodded, but felt constrained to remind his sovereign: "By the same treaty, Edward the third also renounced his claim to the French throne."

Henry shrugged. "If France still fails to honour her part of the agreement, why should this country honour hers?"

The Bishop's eyes dilated in appreciation. Oh, yes! A master strategist, Henry! He said: "And you expect, of course, that your demands will be refused?"

"I should think it likely, wouldn't you?"

"Very likely," the older man concurred with a smile.

Arundel came flapping along the path behind them, his

107

face, already puffy with ill-health, strained and tense from more immediate causes.

"That woman," he moaned. "That woman!"

"What woman?" enquired the King and the Bishop almost simultaneously.

"Margery Kempe," sighed Arundel, looking with longing at a rustic bench which stood at the end of the pleached alleyway.

The sudden burst of sunlight, unfiltered now by overhanging leaves, made him blink and rub his eyes. He was getting old, thought the King, and made a rapid mental survey of the possible candidates for the Primacy of All England. Would his half-uncle expect the post? If so, then Henry Beaufort would be a disappointed man, for Henry of Monmouth, reaching one of his lightning decisions, had already settled upon Henry Chicele, Bishop of St David's, as the future Archbishop of Canterbury.

"Margery Kempe?" repeated Henry Beaufort, his brow furrowed in a concentrated effort of memory. "I've heard that name before. Isn't she the woman from Norfolk who has visions?"

"She says she has visions," snapped the Archbishop. "Hears voices, too! And, like Cassandra, she prophesies doom."

"She also," murmured Henry Beaufort, "or so I've heard, cries."

The Archbishop flung up his hands and nodded his head in an agony of agreement. "All the time," he shuddered. "Today, she has had ten crying fits and tells me that she has been known to have as many as fourteen in one morning."

"Is that the noise which has been coming from the servants' hall?" Henry Beaufort asked in some amusement, but the King snorted in disgust.

"What is she doing here? Why do you permit her in your palace, Archbishop?"

"She has been sent by the Bishop of Worcester, Your Highness, for examination; to decide whether her visions be of God or the Devil."

"Is she a Lollard?"

"No, no! The Bishop of Worcester thinks her a sincere daughter of the Church. So does the Archbishop of York, even though he was forced to pay her to leave his diocese."

"Now I remember!" Henry Beaufort turned towards the King, who had at last indicated that the exhausted Arundel might be seated. "She told His Grace of York that he was an evil man and would never get to heaven unless he mended his ways."

"The woman needs a whipping," Henry answered angrily, "but so long as it's proved that she is not a heretic, I suppose it would be safer to speed her on her way."

"She goes tonight, thank God," muttered Arundel. "She is going on a pilgrimage to Jerusalem. Let us hope that she doesn't return." He rose to his feet and laid a hand on his sovereign's arm. "However, mad or not, she offers some advice which Your Highness would do well to heed." Arundel's hand tightened its grip and his eyes shone with an unlovely fanaticism. "She advises Your Grace to beware of your enemies. It could be that she warns you against the Lollards."

12

THE Archbishop need not have worried. The King was always on his guard against heresy in the Church.

In May, at the end of his first Parliament, before the magnates and the Bishops had dispersed, Henry had summoned Sir John Oldcastle to Kennington, where certain of the knight's books and papers, specifically saved from the April bonfire, were read aloud to the assembled company. These included the writings of William of Ockham and of the excommunicated Hus.

"Do you not think that such works as these should be utterly destroyed?" Henry had demanded of Oldcastle in minatory accents.

And Sir John, sensing that his old companion-in-arms was, most surprisingly, offering him a chance to avoid imprisonment, agreed that the books were indeed heretical and denied having read more than a phrase or two in each of them.

Later, however, Oldcastle had realised that he was not to escape so easily, being sent for again by the King, who had promptly engaged him in theological argument in an attempt to make him see the error of his ways. Unfortunately, the knight's counter-arguments had proved to be both more lucid and more logical, leaving the King floundering in a morass of indecisive words and bad temper. In the end, Henry had been forced to resort to the final refuge of the verbally defeated, threats.

"If you persist in these opinions, Sir John," he had said coldly, "I shall have no choice but to hand you over to the ecclesiastical courts for examination."

Oldcastle, feeling that he should be grateful for the amount of latitude already shown him, forbore to argue further. A week or so later, he had sent a party of his wrestlers to entertain the King at Windsor and had been gratified to hear of their generous reception. After which, Sir John had retired to his castle of Cooling in Kent, while the King had proceeded to Canterbury for his father's belated funeral.

From then on, however, the relationship between the two men deteriorated rapidly and in September, the King, pressed by his clergy, issued a royal writ for Oldcastle's arrest. In view of his persistent reassertions of his beliefs, Sir John himself had to admit that there was nothing else Henry could do and submitted without resistance to the officers who came to take him to the Tower.

From there, on September the twenty-third, he was conducted before the Archbishop and Convocation of Canterbury in the Chapter House of St Paul's. It was a beautiful morning, as warm and as transparent as a bubble of spun glass, and the excellent weather seemed to have affected Authority's mood. Either that, reflected Oldcastle with a derisive little smile, or they were acting on instructions from the King. Indeed, judging by Arundel's acidulated countenance, this was probably the case.

The hearing began.

"Do you believe in transubstantiation?" the Archbishop demanded, leaning forward painfully in his chair.

"You have my deposition."

"Do you believe in it?" the Archbishop persisted.

"No."

A slight noise, like the sighing of wind in the summer trees, went whispering around the court.

Henry Beaufort asked sharply : "Do you believe that confession to a priest is a necessary part of Christian penance?"

"Again, you have my deposition. But again, if you wish to hear it from my own lips, no !"

"Take him away !" shouted the Archbishop.

To Oldcastle, it was quite plain that he was to be given every chance to recant and was horrified to discover that this

111

knowledge in no way endeared the King to him. It seemed, rather, to increase his resentment; a resentment which had slowly and silently grown inside him over the years, reaching fruition with the burning of his books. Henry had used the Lollards in his fight with his father, just as his grandfather, John of Gaunt, had once used Wycliffe. Now, the King wanted to placate his conscience by allowing Oldcastle his freedom. He should not have that satisfaction: if Oldcastle had to suffer the bodily torture of death at the stake, Henry should suffer the mental anguish of watching him burn.

Two days later, Sir John was once more taken before the court. Yet again, he was asked to recant.

"No," he answered firmly, looking into that row of sweating faces. "If the Church persists in its teaching that the bread and wine turn into the Blood and Body of Christ after consecration, then the Church corrupts the teachings of Christ Himself." There was a gasp, but he continued inexorably: "And the only necessity for salvation is true repentance. Confession of sin to a priest is irrelevant and stupid." He smiled serenely at their apparent horror. "As for your crucifixes, you turn them into heathen idols with your genuflections and your bowings. They are man-made objects of wood and metal and as such are fit for nothing but to be kept clean, like ornaments."

"And the Pope?" queried the Bishop of Rochester in trembling accents.

Oldcastle's voice rose. "The Anti-Christ," he answered simply.

After that, there was nothing else to be said. Arundel formally excommunicated him and handed him over to the secular courts for judgement and execution. There was nothing more that the King could do.

There was, however, plenty that others could do. As one disgusted monk recorded: "Almost the whole of the mother-land is involved in the Lollard heresy."

Notices appeared, nailed to church doors, condemning Henry as the priests' King. Others proclaimed that a hundred thousand men would rise as one should Oldcastle be executed; and throughout the entire country, anti-clericalism burned like a fever in the blood. Money, too, was available from the rich cities of Bristol, Norwich and York; money with the power to open doors—even the doors of the Tower.

On the afternoon of October the nineteenth, Sir John lay quietly on his bed in his cell, listening to the muffled sounds of the city and the river, and, closer still, the muted noises of the fortress itself. An early autumnal fog blanketed the grey stones and the leaf-strewn gardens outside, finding its way through the damp, moss-lined walls of the prison quarters and making even the warmly clad guards shake and shiver with the cold.

"A visitor to see you. A priest," one of these worthies informed Sir John through chattering teeth, and the knight groaned in despair, turning his face to the wall.

During the first twenty-four of the forty days which must elapse between condemnation and execution, Oldcastle had been subjected to a never-ending procession of clergy, all urging him to abandon his heretical beliefs and return to the bosom of the Church. Sir John had laughed in their faces, informing them brusquely that he was no apostate and, in the beginning, rather enjoying the verbal battles. Now, however, he was weary of the whole business and wanted to be left alone to compose himself for death.

"Go away, Father! I have nothing to say to you," he grunted as a friar glided silently into the cell.

The man, undeterred, bent nearer and tapped Oldcastle on the shoulder.

"Tonight," a voice whispered in Sir John's ear, "you will find the door of your room unlocked. Follow the guard whom you will find outside. He will not be your usual gaoler. God go with you. Life to the Lollards and death to the priests."

Before the startled knight could reply or put any questions, his visitor had gone as noiselessly as he had come, only the door clanging ominously behind him. For a while, Oldcastle found it hard to credit that the whole experience had not been a dream; but when, near midnight, he tentatively pushed at the door of his cell, it opened and a man came forward out of the shadows.

Half-an-hour later, Oldcastle was safely hidden in the Cheapside home of a Lollard friend and his eager ears were being regaled with the first brief outlines of a Lollard conspiracy which would overthrow the government and bring down the King.

The Chancellor, Henry Beaufort, was seriously perturbed. Sir John Oldcastle's escape from one of the most impregnable fortresses in England had indicated, as nothing else could have done, the King's increasing unpopularity throughout the country. Even the re-interment, in early December, of the body of King Richard in Westminster Abbey—in the tomb which he had designed for himself alongside his beloved first wife, Anne of Bohemia—failed to revive public opinion in favour of Henry.

"We are becoming a nation of heretics," the Bishop snorted savagely to his younger brother, Thomas Beaufort.

The Earl of Dorset, a man not much given to soul-searching, either his own or other people's, could not help wondering on this occasion if his half-nephew and his brother had not brought the present crisis upon themselves. They had tacitly condoned heresy during the previous reign in order to attach the Lollards to their cause. King and Bishop could hardly be surprised, therefore, if their abrupt reversal of policy antagonised the heretics more than their consistent hostility would have done. Thomas, however, said nothing. He had learned while still very young that to argue with his clever older brother was pointless: he could not hope to prevail against that subtle and brilliant mind. Instead, he obeyed Henry's behest to keep his ear to the ground.

And there was plenty to hear. The Lollards, like every other community, had fools and traitors within their ranks; those who were afraid for their lives and those who simply could not resist talking. By the time that the King arrived at Eltham to celebrate Christmas, his spies were able to put him

114

in full possession of the facts concerning the projected Lollard rebellion.

Henry was appalled to discover how widespread was the disaffection. In the memories of the older men, the peasants' revolt of thirty-four years earlier loomed large. With pallid faces and trembling tongues they recalled how England had tottered on the brink of anarchy; how close the government and the nobility had come to being entirely wiped out. Life as they still knew it had hung in the balance: only luck and the courage of the young King Richard had prevented the scales from tipping in Wat Tyler's direction.

"And we are not dealing with an ignorant peasant now," Archbishop Arundel said querulously. "Oldcastle and his henchman, Roger Acton, are literate men, able to organise and stir the multitudes as John Ball and Wat Tyler could never do."

"Nonsense!" put in Henry Beaufort sharply. "Ball was a priest. And in my opinion, a man does not need to be able to read and write in order to make other men follow him. He needs a . . . a personal spark . . . a flame! You talk of organisation." The Bishop laughed, glancing mockingly round the table at his fellow Councillors. In the distance could be heard the sweet, clear notes of the chapel-children and the deeper accompaniment of the palace waits as they sang their Christmas carols. "Have you never realised, Archbishop, that unless one is in a position of supreme authority, it is almost impossible to organise the English into action of any kind? Our countrymen's predilection for individuality of thought breaks up every faction into innumerable smaller ones—as the Lollards themselves will discover if ever they become strong enough to repudiate the authority of Rome."

Humphrey of Gloucester grinned insolently across the table at his half-uncle. "Is that something you anticipate?" he queried. "Because if so—"

"I do not anticipate it," Henry Beaufort snarled angrily. "I am merely pointing out—"

The King brought his hand crashing down on the table, making Archbishop Arundel jump like a startled fawn.

"Silence!" he roared, losing for a moment his usual icy calm. "We want no hypotheses, no jibes, no quarrels." Anger glowed redly at the back of his eyes and, with a final withering glance at the protagonists, he returned to the matter in hand.

"We know," he said, "that the Lollards intend to meet in St Giles's Fields on the night of January the ninth. Whatever some of you may think, the Archbishop was right to remind us of the peasants' rebellion. The gravity of that situation arose because the rebels were allowed to take London. That must not happen this time!"

There was a general murmur of assent and, in consequence, as soon as the Christmas festivities had come to an end, the King, his three brothers and all the court removed to London, taking up their residences in the Priory at Clerkenwell. There, the Mayor and the magistrates were summoned to receive their orders.

"Every gate in the city is to be guarded night and day and the men for this job must be most carefully chosen. If a man is so much as suspected of Lollard sympathies, he must not be allowed near the gates." The King glanced around the assembled company. "Alderman Whittington, you shall be held responsible for the New Gate"—Whittington, still in mourning for his wife who had died the preceding November, bowed—"and Thomas Chaucer, you will be held responsible for the Lud Gate."

"And what do we do?" the Duke of Clarence hissed in his brother John's ear.

The Duke of Bedford smiled and squeezed Thomas's arm. "Don't fret! We haven't been overlooked. You, Humphrey and I are to lead the patrols stationed about Temple Bar." He saw his brother's face brighten, and grimaced. "I don't believe that we shall see much action," he cautioned. "Something in my bones tells me that for the Lollards this will be a sorry affair."

It was a sorry affair.

The Lollards had reckoned on the element of surprise and,

116

therefore, without the King's genius for military organisation. Their plans were defective; although it was not altogether the plans, but, as Henry Beaufort had prophesied, the waywardness of the insurgents themselves.

Instructions had been specific : the Lollard forces were to meet in St Giles's Fields on Wednesday, January the ninth. Messengers had been sent into Derbyshire and Leicestershire, two countries where heresy was particularly rife, with information concerning date and time. In spite of this, the Lollards of the Midlands had started their own riots on the fourth of January; riots which had been speedily suppressed.

For the most part, however, the conspirators kept to their instructions, and, from all over the country, little bands of men, mainly artisans, together with a few scriveners and renegade priests, made their way along the roads in the bitter January weather. Essex sent a considerable contingent, the instigators, John and Thomas Cook, having offered sixpence a day to everyone who would support Sir John Oldcastle; Bristol, then, as always, a hotbed of nonconformity, despatched forty craftsmen and half a dozen chaplains; Sir Thomas Talbot of Davington led the men of Kent; and Thomas Maureward, ex-Sheriff, the men of Warwickshire.

The prime movers in the rebellion had failed, however, to see further than success. They had told their followers that the Lollards of the capital would open the city's gates and let them in—going so far as to arrange sleeping accommodation for the leaders among families of the faithful—but had provided no instructions on what to do should the gates remain shut. They had not anticipated treachery and had not foreseen, therefore, the presence of the King with an array of armed men. Neither had they allowed for the fact that their followers would be less inclined to violence than the peasant rabble of 1381.

As a result, the various groups of men from town and country were nonplussed by London's inhospitably closed portals and by the inimical young King who confronted them at the head of his troops. They surrendered without a fight, each man allowing himself to be led off to prison, "like lambs to the slaughter", as Archbishop Arundel remarked with his death's-head grin to Henry Beaufort.

But, in the event, only sixty of the Lollards were hanged, a number which could have been less had any of the condemned recanted. And those who were left could rejoice in the knowledge that Sir John Oldcastle had again escaped, gone to earth no one knew where.

Only Archbishop Arundel was disgruntled at the outcome, and as he died in February, his dissatisfaction was short-lived. Henry Beaufort and all those about the King could feel that the whole affair had redounded to Henry's credit: his prompt and decisive action had prevented possible bloodshed in the streets, winning for him the gratitude of the Londoners; and he had shown clemency, earning for himself the grudging admiration of the younger and more heterodox elements throughout the country, especially at the Universities.

Nevertheless, thought Henry Beaufort, it was time that the energies and prejudices of the restless English were channelled in other directions. Perhaps an invasion of France had merits which he had not hitherto perceived.

13

HENRY flung the book from him in disgust.

Beyond the walls of the Greyfriars' House where he was lodging, the Leicestershire countryside was awakening to the glories of April. Along the banks of the Soare the marsh-marigolds offered up cups of pure gold and the fragile, lilac tracery of the cuckoo-flower was reflected, cobweb-like in the grey-green torrent of the waters. The more modest butterbur sheltered, squat and pink, beneath the spread of foliage and, in the woods, bluebells lay in dark, shadowed patches of undisciplined beauty.

The King was in Leicester for the sitting of his second Parliament and it was Henry's intention to instruct his Speaker, Thomas Chaucer, to proceed with negotiations for a Burgundian alliance. He did not particularly desire the marriage except as an act of self-immolation upon the altar of duty. As a woman, Anne seemed to him neither attractive nor exciting; but as a political necessity, binding England and Burgundy closer together in the ties of their mutual hatred of France, she was all that he found most desirable in a wife.

But his marriage was far from being uppermost in his mind at the present moment.

Humphrey of Gloucester stooped to pick up the folio which his eldest brother had discarded with such vehemence.

"*The Lantern of Light,*" he read aloud, and Thomas of Clarence looked up curiously from his resting-place on a day-bed by the door.

"What's that?" he enquired, and the King snorted angrily.

"A Lollard tract," Henry answered. "A book of sermons and lectures at present being circulated throughout the country." His heavy jaw tightened ominously as he signed for the minstrel to cease his singing. Then, turning to John, who was sitting quietly near the fire, trying to make the fleas and lice hop into the flames, he said : "If I am to invade France, I cannot afford this kind of disunity and unrest at home. This Parliament must be empowered to take the sternest measures against heresy. Heresy breeds treason," and he twitched the Lollard book from under Humphrey's interested gaze.

The Duke of Gloucester made a moue of resentment at his elder brother's back and then grimaced conspiratorially at the grinning Duke of Clarence. "The universities won't like it," he warned, but Henry merely shrugged.

"I daresay they won't, but I've tried leniency and the students haven't responded to that. Arundel—God rest his soul!—warned me on his death-bed that I had made a grave mistake in showing clemency."

"His reasons, though, were entirely religious," Thomas gibed, raising himself on one elbow and playing with the end of the fringed coverlet.

Henry ignored him, addressing himself once more to the deferential John.

"For the same reason, the Channel must be cleared of pirates. The men of Devon and Cornwall are constantly at war with the Bretons, and acts of piracy on either side do nothing but evoke reprisals on the other."

"The men of Devon and Cornwall rely on freebooting for their livelihood," John of Bedford suggested tentatively.

"And the merchants of London and Bristol rely on peaceful trading for *their* livelihood," the King retorted coldly. "Until the Channel is free from these marauders every ship that sails it is subject to attack. We have lost more shipping in the past year than Richard Whittington and others care to think about." And Henry stooped to warm his chilled hands before the leaping fire.

"Will the people back you in this?" John asked, his pleasant, honest face more than a little troubled.

"Do you know what Froissart wrote about the English?" that well-read young man, Humphrey of Gloucester, demanded. "He wrote that the English take their greatest delight in battle and killing; that they are always richer and happier in times of war than in any other; and that any king who does not love war will never win their hearts."

"They'll back me," the King replied, answering John's question more directly than Humphrey had done. "The English have always hated the French. Nothing will please them more than another Crecy or Poitiers."

Thomas of Clarence sneered. "It might be difficult to emulate such resounding successes," he pointed out, but Henry remained undisturbed by his brother's disparagement. And, as always, Henry's arrogant confidence in his own ability touched Thomas on the raw. "How will you pay for this war?" he continued, swinging his feet to the ground and sauntering towards the fire.

"In the usual way," Henry replied impatiently, "with taxes." He looked thoughtful for a moment or two, then added: "I also intend to confiscate all property owned by French, Norman or Breton religious houses. The Commons petitioned for such an action as long ago as our great-grandfather's time. With a little prompting, they will be only too happy to do so again and I shall be only too happy to oblige them."

"But most of that land has been held by Frenchmen since the Conquest," expostulated John.

"Precisely! And it is high time that such an iniquitous state of affairs was ended. The English Church gives me its whole-hearted support in the matter."

Humphrey looked up with his sly grin. "Quite right!" he exclaimed, nodding. "England for the English, but France . . . ah! France for the English, too!"

The French seemed bent upon proving themselves Henry's staunchest ally in his determination to invade their country.

There were a few Frenchmen, of whom, in his rare moments of sanity, Charles the sixth was one, who realised that the salvation of France lay in uniting her warring baronial factions and presenting a united front to her enemies. Unfortunately, Charles's periods of lucidity and understanding were becoming shorter and less frequent. His mind clouded very quickly and then he would have to be chained in the dark like an animal, screaming and howling in his own filth, until such times as the clouds lifted and his reason returned.

Meanwhile, the internecine feud between the Burgundians, led by their Duke, John the Fearless, and the Armagnacs, headed by Charles, Duke of Orleans, continued its blood-stained course, laying waste France's beautiful land and dissipating the lives of her most hopeful young men. Queen Isabeau, whose political acumen and shrewd judgement were too often blunted by her insatiable bodily needs, exercised some controlling influence, but her ambitions and her achievements were too personal to be of much service to the general good. France remained a country vulnerable to attack, while the English, closing their ranks after the schisms and ruptures of the previous reign, presented an ever-growing threat.

Spending the Christmas of 1414 at Kenilworth as the guest of King Henry, the Duke of York remarked with satisfaction to his younger brother that there would be war with France before the coming year was out.

Cambridge, huddled in his miniver-lined cloak and deprecating Edward's partiality for walking in all kinds of weather, made earnest representations that they should make their way back to the comparative warmth and comfort of the castle.

"As for all this talk of war," he murmured, "I thought that the peace negotiations were still under way."

"Of course they are," answered York, surprised. "The last Parliament—the one that sat at Westminster in November—advised that all forms of bargaining be exhausted first."

Cambridge laughed, his breath hanging in little frozen clouds in the quiet air. "Our worthy Archbishop Chicele was satisfying his conscience, no doubt."

York ignored this. "And next month," he continued

blandly, "Thomas Beaufort will head a further deputation to demand the crown of France." Cambridge choked, but his brother went proudly on : "And if that claim is rejected by the French, as it undoubtedly will be—"

"Oh! Undoubtedly!"

"—the embassy will demand Normandy, Tourraine, Anjou, Maine; in short, all the lands which should have been ours under the Treaty of Bretigny when our grandfather renounced his claim to the French throne. Plus the ransom of two million crowns which was never paid for John of Bohemia after his capture at Poitiers. So, you see—"

"I see only too well!" Cambridge curled his lip in disdain. "If our extortionate second and third demands cannot be met, then our first, to the French crown, is held to be valid."

York concurred with a placid, almost fatuous, smile. The prospect obviously pleased him and the two men retraced their steps along the snow-powdered path in silence. The sky was as flat and unbroken as a pewter plate, not a wisp of cloud or a snippet of blue anywhere to be seen. The ground was stone-hard and put hunting out of the question; a fact greatly deplored by York, for whom the sport was the grand passion of his life. His childless marriage had been uneventful and all the energies and enthusiasm of which his large body and sluggish mind were capable had been expended on the pleasures of the chase. He was, at present, busy making his own translation of Gaston de Foix's *Master of Game*.

"Hunters," York had written only that morning, "live far more happily than other men. When a hunter gets up he sees a beautiful morning, brilliant weather and hears the singing of the birds, full of melody and love. And when the sun comes up, he sees fresh dew and twigs and grasses and the sun making everything shine. There is great joy in the hunter's heart. . . . I say again that hunters live in this world more joyously than other men and go to Heaven when they die. . . ."

His brother's voice cut stridently across his pleasant reverie.

"By what right," demanded Cambridge, "does Henry claim the throne of France?"

York blinked like a man awakened from a dream and forced his wandering attention to concentrate upon his brother's words.

"By the same right as our grandfather claimed it," he replied.

"And that was?"

"You know very well what that was," York answered with asperity. "His mother was the rightful heir of her father, King Philip the fourth, after her three brothers had all died without heirs."

"But France obeys the Salic Law. No one may inherit through a woman."

"The Salic Law," York explained with massive patience, "is a French law and therefore not applicable to Englishmen."

"And, of course, the English Church endorses this view?" Cambridge mocked.

"Yes. . . . No. . . . What do you mean, the *English* Church?"

"The English Churchmen, if that suits you better."

York rounded on Cambridge with unusual irascibility. "You denigrate everything," he snapped.

Cambridge stopped in his tracks, the laughter suddenly wiped from his face, and caught his brother's arm in a cruel grip. Gone was the fop, the degenerate, the lazy cynic. In his place was the man whom York had always known to exist beneath that illusive exterior; hard, strong and passionately ambitious.

"Then think on this, my dear brother," hissed the younger man, bringing his face to within an inch or two of the Duke's. "You talk glibly about our cousin's claim to the throne of France, but has it occurred to you—" and the clasp tightened until York gave a protesting yelp of pain—"that the claim is not Henry's to make? The claim, if it exists at all, belongs to my quondam brother-in-law; my son's uncle, Edmund Mortimer."

Cambridge's words were to cause the Duke of York innumerable anxious moments and sleepless nights, and it was

124

as well for his peace of mind that he was not a witness to his brother's future actions.

It was as well, also, that the King was to remain in ignorance, if only temporarily, of the treachery of his chosen friend, Henry le Scrope of Masham.

For while Cambridge retired to his castle of Conisborough in the company of Sir Thomas Grey, Hotspur's cousin, to begin the task of suborning the northern lords to Mortimer's cause, the King was busy with his preparations for invasion and could ill afford the distractions of a broken personal relationship. It did occur to him from time to time that Scrope was more than usually taciturn; less than his customary pleasant self. But Henry had too many other things to claim his attention to give the circumstance more than a passing thought.

As the Hampshire countryside blossomed under the touch of yet another spring, as yellow flags and water avens appeared along the banks of the Itchen, and as common vetch and speedwell pin-pointed the fields about Winchester with clusters of red and blue stars, a great army and all its accoutrements began to assemble along the southern coast. Henry, dividing his time between Henry Beaufort's episcopal manor at Waltham and his headquarters at Portchester Castle, with frequent visits to the fortified town of Southampton, had his time fully occupied. Along the rutted roads rumbled the siege machines; the ballista, the trebuchet and the marngonel. More spectacularly came the lords and their retainers, forgathering from every part of the country; the knights with their armour and their horses; the archers in their leather jackets and hats of boiled tarpaulin; the master-gunners in charge of the siege artillery; the surgeons, the grooms, the smiths; the yeomen, the cooks, the carpenters and the scullions.

The Solent flowered with the painted sails of ships which had been especially built in places as far distant as Bristol and Newcastle, or hired from Holland and Burgundy. The air was filled with the plangent twanging of bowstrings and the acrid smell of "Greek Fire". Each inhabitant of every village was, willingly or unwillingly, host to one or more of Henry's soldiers; while those troops unable to commandeer a comfortable billet slept under hedges, in barns and cowsheds, or simply on the open ground.

And at the head of this unwieldy mass of men and equipment, the King drove himself on night and day, deciding on rates of pay, ensuring that his army was adequately fed, settling disputes and arranging transportation. Apart from that, he had his realm to set in order before setting forth to conquer that of Charles of France. As Regent he appointed his brother, Bedford; good, reliable John who would rule wisely and firmly, accepting the appointment without any of the sulks or hysterics which would have accompanied a decision to leave behind Gloucester or Clarence.

Henry felt reasonably confident that he was entrusting a peaceful kingdom to John of Bedford's care. Glendower had not been heard of for some years now, and the Lollards appeared to be suitably cowed since the fiasco in St Giles's Fields twelve months earlier. The news that Jan Hus had been lured to Constance by the promise of the Emperor Sigismund's safe-conduct and there seized and burnt at the stake, arrived whilst Henry was in the midst of his preparations and made him doubly confident that the Protestant heresy was in a fair way to being crushed once and for all.

His brothers and friends, his magnates and captains might insist that the King should take more ease, but Henry's self-assurance, both in the righteousness of his cause and his ability to work out his destiny, gave him resources of strength which he might otherwise have lacked. He felt that nothing now could go awry, and not even the news that the Earl of Cambridge had made a bid to capture Murdoch, the son of the Scottish Regent, Albany, disturbed him unduly. He did exhort the Duke of York to keep his younger brother under control, but as the King had never regarded his cousin Cambridge as anything but an effete dandy, the admonition was accompanied by Henry's rather mirthless laugh and was obviously not intended to be taken too seriously. He was standing at the time with his back to Lord Scrope and so

126

failed to see the swift, tell-tale flicker of emotion that passed over his friend's countenance as he heard the news of Cambridge's failure.

For it had been the Earl's hope to secure the person of Murdoch, on his way to the Border in exchange for the young Earl of Northumberland, as his own bargaining counter; not for Henry Percy, but for the man who still lived on in Stirling Castle and called himself Richard the second. Before proceeding with his plan to proclaim Edmund Mortimer King, Cambridge wished to lay this particular ghost once and for all by proving that the body in the tomb in Westminster Abbey was indeed that of Richard of Bordeaux, and that the creature of Stirling was an impostor. But his design had been frustrated by the efficiency of the royal captains escorting Murdoch Stewart through the wilds of the Border country, and so Cambridge and Sir Thomas Grey had now left Conisborough and were moving slowly south to join the invasion forces at Southampton.

Scrope shifted his position so that he could see across the solar of Waltham Manor and so bring into focus the fair head and pallid features of the latest acquisition to that princely gathering; Edmund Mortimer, Earl of March, twenty-two years old and rightful King of England.

14

THE Earl of March walked slowly across the inner ward of Portchester Castle.

The King had gone on a pilgrimage to the shrine of St Winifred in Flintshire, but activity had not ceased with his absence. Tents for the most important of his captains had been erected in the outer ward of the castle and the constant braying of trumpets, the continuous advent and departure of messengers, the rattle and rumble of the battlewagons as they poured through the main gate and the arrival of the great siege-guns from Bristol and London all contributed towards making the site of the ancient fortress of Portus Adurni as busy as it had been in the heyday of Rome.

Edmund Mortimer was a troubled young man. Not only was he at the centre of a treasonable plot to kill the King and his brothers—Henry, Thomas and Humphrey here in Portchester; John to be assassinated by the Lollards in London—but, in addition, the Earl had fears for his own life. Of all the people close to Cambridge, Edmund, with the exception of the Duke of York, was the only one to realise how dangerous a man his former brother-in-law could be; the only one who constantly remembered that Cambridge's maternal grandfather had been Pedro the Cruel of Castile. Long years of imprisonment, of living with the nightly possibility of being murdered in his bed, had rendered Edmund Mortimer unusually sensitive to the hidden motives, the unspoken words of his fellow men.

As he wandered aimlessly in the direction of the church, all that remained of the Augustinian priory which had once stood on the site, and as he dodged the smiths and armourers going purposefully about their business, the Earl of March asked himself why Cambridge should risk his life in order to put his erstwhile brother-in-law upon the throne. They were, of course, cousins, but bore no closer relationship to one another than King Henry did to either. And Edmund could not believe that Cambridge cared so much about the law of primogeniture that he was willing to stake his life upon restoring the Mortimers to their rightful inheritance.

No; the truth of the matter must surely be that Cambridge's son, the five-year-old Richard Plantagenet, was his uncle's heir. Restore the Mortimers and Cambridge would immediately become the father of the heir-presumptive. But there, in that last word, lay the rub. For Edmund Mortimer was a young and virile man : he could be expected to marry and produce heirs of his own, thus leaving Cambridge of no more importance than he was at present. But if Edmund Mortimer were also to die during the uprising, the Earl of Cambridge would at once become the father of the new child-King.

In spite of the warmth of the day, Edmund Mortimer shivered. Knowing Cambridge as he did, seeing so clearly the streak of Iberian cunning beneath the apparent stupidity of the Angle, he could not doubt that such an intention existed in Cambridge's mind. What was he to do? He could not let himself tamely be led to the slaughter, but what was his alternative? To throw himself upon Henry's mercy? To reveal the plot and send not only Cambridge, but Scrope and Grey also to their deaths? The two latter intended him no harm and trusted him implicitly. They would never dream that he of all men, the one in whose interests they thought themselves to be working, would betray them to the King.

Mortimer stopped at the church door, suddenly awakened from his reverie. He became aware of the clatter and noise of the encampment; conscious also that he was being jostled by impatient soldiers as they forced their way past him, into Confession and out again, anxious to resume their labours. The Earl of March turned, blinking cat-like in the strong sunshine, and saw Cambridge and Scrope wending their leisurely way between the stationary baggage-wagons; two brilliant peacocks who had somehow strayed into a nest of starlings.

"Ah! My dear Edmund! We have been looking for you." Cambridge laid a hand, with its incredibly well-shaped and well-cared-for nails, on Mortimer's sleeve. His blue eyes smiled sleepily into the younger man's. A snake with a rabbit, Edmund thought in panic.

As Cambridge propelled him gently into the shadow of the church porch, and while the Earl's voice droned on softly and sibilantly in his ear, Edmund Mortimer's thoughts raced down little by-ways of their own, considering the most convincing arguments with which to persuade the King of his innocence in this conspiracy; of his intention to betray it from the start.

In London, Henry took formal leave of his step-mother. The Queen Dowager had paid handsomely towards this war which might well result in the death of one or more of her sons, depending upon what part Brittany decided to play in the forthcoming struggle. Her reward was that Henry, for the time being at least, left her in peace, with no more than a highly covetous glance at the enormous income which she enjoyed under the terms of the late King's will. But Joanna was not really deceived: she knew that the day might come when her immense wealth would prove too great a temptation for her eldest step-son. And she wondered how Henry would then reconcile the violation of his father's wishes with that depressing monster, his conscience.

For there was little doubt that Henry was becoming more and more obsessed with the idea of himself as God's Elect; the Chosen One who would punish the French for their iniquities against mankind in general and the English in particular. It was the theme of his farewell address to the Mayor and Aldermen of London, and while it aroused nothing but fervour in the breasts of such patriots as Richard Whittington, it caused more sceptical souls like Thomas

Chaucer to wonder how long it would be before the King had cause to rue his words; how long before he was driven ignominiously from French soil.

The French, however, were paying Henry the compliment of taking him seriously. When he reached Winchester, yet another French embassy, headed by the Archbishop of Bourges, the Count of Vendôme and the Bishop of Lisieux, waited to greet him in a last-minute attempt to avert an invasion which, whatever its outcome, would ravage still further their already war-torn country.

They offered Henry the Princess Katherine in marriage. The King, amidst the round of jousts and banquets, Masses and official diplomatic meetings, considered the proposition. But, at the back of his mind, there always hovered the picture of Katherine's elder sister, the now dead Isabella, spitting venom and hatred at his father and himself all those years ago. There might be too much of Queen Isabeau in all her daughters to make any one of them a comfortable wife.

Nevertheless, because he had deluded himself into a genuine belief in his desire for peace, Henry was forced to show some interest in the lady. It was Henry Beaufort, strolling with his half-nephew in the cloisters of Winchester Cathedral, who intimated how he might appease both his conscience and desires.

"Eight hundred thousand crowns seems a paltry dowry with which to ensure England's King for a Princess of France," the Bishop murmured.

The King eagerly agreed, and so : "A dowry of two million crowns and I will marry the Princess Katherine," he informed the horrified French ambassadors.

Negotiations faltered and died, even though Henry was induced by the more moderate members of his Council to reduce his extortionate demand to a million crowns. The final official wines were drunk, the remaining diplomatic presents exchanged, and the sad and weary Frenchmen made their dispirited way back to Dover. The English rode triumphantly on to Portchester, cheered extravagantly in every village and encampment through which they passed, the

131

royal cavalcade enlarged each day by the hundreds of men still flocking to join the army about Southampton.

But the King's complacency, his growing confidence in his universal popularity, was about to be rudely shattered.

The night of July the thirty-first was stormy, a wild summer squall blowing in from the Solent, tossing the trees in a demented dance and bellying the ships' sails into fat pincushions of purple and green, red and brilliant azure. Henry was with his captains in Portchester Castle's great hall, its beautiful oriel window letting in the last streaks of a watery dusk. The King's dark head was bent over the lists on the table before him, his brothers and captains clustered respectfully around to receive his instructions for the loading of the horses and provisions.

Henry cursed with annoyance as a page bowed low by his chair; but the boy, undeterred, whispered: "My master, the Earl of March, begs an audience of Your Highness. Privately! He apologises for bothering Your Grace, but says that the matter is extremely pressing."

"In God's name—!" Henry was beginning, but something in the boy's face, some urgent gleam in the eye, made him abandon the curt refusal which was trembling on his lips. Instead, he rose, scraping his chair angrily against the rush-strewn floor.

"Very well!" He glanced at his interested captains. "You will all oblige me by going about your business for a while. The Earl of March, it seems, has something of importance to tell me." He resumed his seat and nodded curtly to the page. "Bring your master in. But no more than five minutes, inform him."

The Duke of York saw his brother for the last time in Southampton prison.

The interview was less difficult than it might have been, for Cambridge, having at last accepted death as inevitable, was perfectly calm and composed. That was not to say that he had not fought for his life with every weapon at his disposal. Sir Thomas Grey had already been executed, but

Cambridge and Scrope had demanded trial by their peers, refusing to be condemned by the jury of twelve solid Hampshire citizens who had been empanelled for the purpose. Unfortunately for the two conspirators, there were so many magnates assembled ready for embarkation that the delay thus gained had been infinitesimal. The two men had been re-condemned to a traitor's death before Grey had lain a week in his grave.

Cambridge, his pride in his pocket and his tongue in his cheek, had then written a letter to Henry begging for clemency. As he remarked to the disgusted Scrope, pride would avail them nothing once they were dead. Not that he really expected the King's pardon: he had planned to show no mercy to Henry. He thought it worth the attempt, however, and suspected, correctly, that if he grovelled a little the King would at least commute the sentence to death by beheading instead of the agonising hanging, drawing and quartering.

So it was in almost a jaunty mood that he said goodbye to his brother.

"For God's sake, Edward, don't start blubbing now," he begged, and laughed uncertainly. "I deserve to die. I made a grave mistake."

York nodded, the fat of his pendulous jowls quivering dismally. "Treason," he began, but his brother interrupted him contemptuously.

"I'm not speaking of treason! That's a risk but not necessarily a mistake. A fact to which our present beloved King"— he spat—"and his father can testify. I'm talking about the more serious error of underrating a man; of thinking him to be a bigger fool than he really is."

"Edmund Mortimer?" York queried.

"Edmund Mortimer!"

"I don't understand. Why—?"

Cambridge smiled. "It doesn't matter now. There's one thing I want you to promise me, Edward: that you will take care of little Richard. The boy is your heir. When you die, he will be Duke of York. I don't want him to suffer for my

mistakes and there may be some people"— he paused significantly; then continued—"who will try to make you disinherit
him."

"I should never do that." York saw his brother's eyes intent
up him and added : "I promise."

Cambridge was satisfied. "Keep your eye on him, Edward.
It won't be easy for him; the son of an attainted rebel."

"He's a sensible little chap," York said comfortingly.
"Solid! No imagination!"

"Yes, most of the time," Cambridge answered. "That part
of him is like you. But there is a streak of rashness in him,
his inheritance from me. So keep a watch over him, Edward,
in the years ahead. I wouldn't want him to meet the same
fate as his father." He smiled wryly.

The gaoler was by now knocking anxiously at the cell door,
and with a muffled promise that he would indeed keep his
nephew safe, York embraced his brother for the last time—
neither man knowing that within less than three months York
would also be dead.

The following day, August the sixth, 1415, the Earl of
Cambridge and Henry le Scrope of Masham were executed
outside the north gate of Southampton.

Five days later, on Sunday the eleventh of August, the
English flagship, *La Trinite Royale*, spread her silken sails;
sails above which floated the King's banner embroidered with
the figures of Father, Son and Holy Ghost, and with the arms
of St Edward and St George. The sun struck sparks of gold
from the copper-gilt crown adorning the top-castle, and at
the deck-head a golden leopard in a silver coronet gleamed
and shimmered in the afternoon light. And the crew, three
hundred strong, leapt as one man to do the bidding of her
Master, Stephen Thomas.

Throughout the previous day and most of the night, ten
thousand men had been embarking in the fifteen hundred
ships that crowded the roadsteads. Since dawn, they had been
manoeuvring into departure positions, and matters were not
helped by a fire which started mysteriously in the hold of one

of the ships, destroying it and two others and spreading alarm and despondency throughout the fleet.

"An ill-omen," said everyone, and the Duke of Gloucester hurriedly put off from the *Katherine de la Toure* to know whether or not his brother meant to proceed. He was hoisted aboard the flagship a little ahead of the Duke of Clarence, who arrived from the *Rude Coq de la Toure* on the same mission.

Henry received them on the poop-deck in the company of his Admiral, their half-uncle, Thomas Beaufort, Earl of Dorset. The King's face was blackened with smoke from helping to fight the fire and the skin about his eyes was puffy from lack of sleep. His nose, always his most prominent feature, stood out sharply from a face grown suddenly old.

But it was not lack of sleep or cares of office which had caused his haggard appearance. The discovery of his friend's and his cousin's treachery had bitten deep into his soul, but even that had had less effect than the realisation that there were people who still looked upon Edmund Mortimer as the rightful King of England. Henry had been very tempted to dispose of the Earl of March, in spite of his betrayal of the plot, and for several days Edmund Mortimer's fate had wavered in the balance. In the end, one factor had militated against the King's decision in favour of March's execution; the consideration that the Earl's death would leave Cambridge's son the holder of the Mortimer claim. And never again, Henry felt, would he trust anyone belonging to Cambridge.

Even the Duke of York he looked upon with distrust, recalling that York, as Albemarle, had once been in a plot to assassinate his father and himself. And if common sense whispered that that was all a long time ago, and that there was no more loyal man alive today than Edward Plantagenet, Henry still could not bring himself to cast a friendly look or a civil word in the direction of Cambridge's brother.

For Cambridge's treason was as nothing compared with his heinous crime of having suborned the King's best friend. It was not in Henry's nature to admit that his judgement had been at fault; that the man on whom he had lavished an

135

affection of which he had hitherto believed himself incapable, had been an enemy from the start; in short, that he had made a fool of himself. And so the hatred which should have been Scrope's and the contempt which should have been his own, Henry directed against his dead cousin. Even the clemency which he had shown over the death sentence had stemmed from family pride : it would have offended his dignity as a Plantagenet to permit another of the same name to suffer a traitor's execution.

The King felt tired and drained of emotions as he stood now on the poop-deck, listening to his brothers' demands that the sailing should be postponed and to their clamorous insistence that the fire had been a portent of bad luck. The trouble was that he half-believed it himself, and yet he could not credit the fact that God had shown Himself antagonistic towards Henry Plantagenet.

Thomas Beaufort stepped forward, urgently gripping the King's arm and nodding in the direction of the main-mast. High above Henry's fluttering banner, their wings stretched like a cloud in the brilliant sunshine, flew a flock of swans, and the Swan was one of Henry's emblems. A storm of cheering arose from the assembled ships.

"You have your answer," Henry said, and imperceptibly his spirits began to rise. The thought of Scrope gradually receded, pushed into some remote corner of his mind; a memory to be buried beneath an accretion of apparently more important things.

At three o'clock in the afternoon, the war-drums beating from every deck, the great fleet set sail for France.

15

THE English army lay encamped about Harfleur and, on this morning of August the nineteenth, word had just been brought to Henry in his headquarters at the Priory of Graville that his brother, the Duke of Clarence, had at last suceeded in encircling the town. It was unfortunate that before this feat had been accomplished, the commander of the Harfleur garrison, the Seigneur d'Estoutville, had been reinforced by several hundred men under the gallant leadership of the Seigneur de Gaucourt.

The King's uncle, Thomas Beaufort, had not been the only man to wonder aloud why Henry had chosen the strongly fortified Harfleur, at the mouth of the Seine, for his point of entry into France, instead of one of the two French towns still remaining in English hands: Calais or Bordeaux.

"Two reasons," the King had informed his captains brusquely. "First, Harfleur is less than a hundred miles from Paris. Second it is in my own duchy of Normandy."

The irreverent Duke of Gloucester had muttered to the Duke of Clarence that to listen to Henry no one would imagine that Normandy had been lost to the English since the reign of King John. "Let us hope," he had added piously, "that the Normans feel the same way about Henry as he does about them." And Humphrey's high-pitched laugh had rung out.

The majority of Normans, however, were at one with the Seigneur d'Estoutville, who, on seeing the English ships in the Seine estuary, had had no hesitation in closing the town's three gates and sending immediately to the Dauphin at Rouen for reinforcements.

The nineteen-year-old Louis, sickly and soon to die, was disinclined to help. He considered that Harfleur's formidable fortifications—its three gates were each protected by moat, drawbridge and portcullis; its walls and twenty-six crenellated towers were all of twelve feet thick—sufficient protection against the Goddams, who would no doubt dissipate their energies in their customary fashion; drinking themselves into a stupor and raping every woman in sight.

Henry, however, who was as well aware as the Dauphin of his countrymen's shortcomings when let loose in a foreign land, had issued stringent orders to prevent these particular crimes. He made rape as well as murder punishable by death and added, to the disgusted amazement of his troops, that if any man forced himself into the presence of a pregnant woman, thereby causing her death from miscarriage brought on by shock, the offender would also be hanged unless pardoned by the King himself. It was a capital offence, too, to desecrate a church in any way whatsoever and, to add insult to injury, every English soldier had to wear on back and chest the red cross of St George so that he might be easily identifiable.

"As well dress us all alike," grumbled John Hanham, Clerk of the Poultry, to William Sharpeton, Clerk of the Scullery, as they hurried between the lords' tents on Graville hill towards the priory at the summit.

"I thought," Sharpeton said, wiping his nose on the back of his hand, "that this siege wouldn't take more than a day or two." He coughed and spat against the Duke of York's tent. "That's what they said when we arrived. An' it's a week gone now."

"A few days!" exclaimed a third man who had been trudging up the hill in their wake.

William Balne, Clerk of the Kitchen, with his two underclerks, Robert Allerton and Richard Reston, respectfully in tow, delivered himself of a raucous laugh. "A few days! It'll be more like bleedin' weeks before this lot surrender."

Being at that moment taken short, he relieved both his body and feelings in the direction of Harfleur. "Bloody

French!" he continued rancorously. "We can't even cut off their water supply. Some damn river runs right through the centre of the town."

"The Lizard," supplied John Hanham, mispronouncing the word Lézarde with all the Englishman's relish for mangling a foreign tongue. "We'd better hurry," he added. "The King'll be wanting his dinner."

"He doesn't care what he eats," Balne said, but quickened his pace nevertheless.

"It's all right for this lot," the aggrieved Sharpeton panted, nodding his head towards the Priory. "Sat up here in comfort! But what about the poor soddin' bastards down in the marshes, eh? Tell me that!"

"What I want to know," grunted Balne, who had been giving a sharp word of encouragement to his two accolytes, both of whom showed a lamentable tendency to dawdle, "is what them bloody gunners is doing. Why haven't they made a breach in the walls by now? Bleedin' inefficient, if you ask me."

And the three men, with the two boys running behind, disappeared into the priory, greatly refreshed by their grumblings.

The gunners, however, had no time even for that luxury. They worked by night as well as by day, feeding into the insatiable iron jaws of 'London', 'The Messenger' and 'The King's Daughter' entire millstones covered in pitch and tar, and set alight before they were rammed into the gaping mouths. At first, that quartet of Master Gunners, Hans Joye, Walter Stotmaker, Gerard Van Willighen and Drovankesell Coykyn, each with his team of two serving gunners, had bombarded the walls of Harfleur only during the hours of daylight. They had found, however, that by dawn the indefatigable Frenchmen had closed the gaps with the fallen debris. In consequence, they had decided that, working in relays, they would continue firing throughout the night. Unfortunately, the guns had a habit of breaking down from time to time. The old-fashioned siege-machines would then come into their own, to the unbounded mortification of Gerard Van Willighen, who was as touchy as a woman on the subject of his beloved artillery and inclined to indulge in a fit of mild hysterics every time anything went wrong.

Meanwhile, the miners were at work, burrowing like moles in the dark, dank bowels of the earth. But as the French sappers worked just as fast and just as competently as the English, the situation underground was stalemate.

Henry himself was everywhere.

"You are burning yourself out," Thomas Morestead, one of his two Chief Surgeons, warned him.

But the King could not rest until Harfleur surrendered. His pride had received a severe blow : he had been arrogantly confident that he could take the town with the minimum of trouble.

August went out in a blaze of tropical heat and September came in with nothing except an increase in the humidity of the atmosphere and a resurgence of French defiance. At the beginning of the previous month, the garrison had shown signs of weakening and Henry had written to the Governor of Bordeaux that at last the end was in sight; the town would be his within a week. But by the time that the Governor's congratulations were received, the French had made a totally unexpected sally from the town, burned two gun emplacements and killed a substantial number of English soldiers who had been sheltering in the trenches.

These, however, were by no means the only casualties among the English troops, whose losses had been heavy. For in the last few weeks, a more fearsome enemy than the French had begun to decimate Henry's army. Dysentry was rife in the English camp, striking down lord and commoner alike. The responsibility for this lay not merely with the weather and the fetid, fly-infested marshes that surrounded the town of Harfleur. The real causes were ones against which Henry had warned so many times, but his words had been constantly ignored. English stomachs, used to beer and ale, revolted against the rough, cheap Norman wine which was poured into them in an almost continual flow. In addition, they were stuffed with shell-fish, small, sour apples and unripe grapes. It was little wonder, therefore, that by the time Harfleur sought to surrender, Henry had lost over a third of his men, and half of these dead not from blazing arrows, boiling oil or red-hot pitch, but from dysentery.

The Bishop of Norwich was dead as was Michael de la Pole, second Earl of Suffolk. The Earls of Arundel and March, along with hundreds of others, had been shipped back to England, too ill even to walk. And by mid-September, when the citizens of Harfleur made their first attempt to parley, it was obvious that the Duke of Clarence had also succumbed to the disease.

Henry looked at his brother's pallid, sweating face and laid a hand on Thomas's damp forehead.

"You must return home as soon as it is safe for you to do so," he remarked dispassionately.

The King felt no pang of regret at losing his brother. He valued Thomas as a soldier and as his heir, but other than that the old dislike, which had its roots in their father's reign and before, had not diminished.

"Will the town fall?" Thomas asked, tossing on his bed and cursing his page for not bringing him more water.

"They have three days in which the Dauphin can send them aid. The Sieur de Hacquville has gone to Rouen. If they have received no assistance at the end of that period, d'Estoutville and de Gaucourt have agreed to surrender."

The tent was stifling under the glare of the relentless September sun. The smell of sickness made Henry retch, but he kept a firm hold upon himself: he hated to show weakness of any kind.

Thomas groaned and rolled on to his side, heaving into a basin. When the spasm was over, he gasped: "And will Louis send aid, do you think?"

Henry's lips curled disdainfully. "Oh, I think not! Not even with Constable D'Albret to stiffen his sinews. And I hear from my spies that Marshal Boucicaut is having trouble raising recruits at Honfleur. The French are more concerned with the taxes being levied on them by their own government than with fighting the English."

The tent flap was lifted to reveal a sliver of incandescent whiteness and Humphrey of Gloucester entered, his robust health almost an insult to the emaciated Thomas.

A spark of affection kindled in Henry's eyes. There was something about the irrepressibly ebullient Humphrey that commanded the King's goodwill, in spite of a natural tendency to despise him.

"Chester Herald has returned from Paris," Humphrey announced, wrinkling his fastidious nose against the smell and hurriedly following his eldest brother again into the open air.

Chester Herald brought a letter from King Charles, who was enjoying a period of sanity; a fact which his letter made abundantly clear.

"None of your forbears had any right to the throne of France," he wrote, "and you have even less."

The implication was obvious and brought the hot blood pounding into Henry's head, rushing in a red tide up to the close-cropped hair, then receding again to leave the King's face white and taut with fury.

The letter continued: "You have no right to cause this country trouble and with the help of the Lord, in whom we have profound trust, we shall resist you to France's honour and England's shame."

That Charles, that gibbering idiot, should claim the assistance of God was so intolerable that for a moment or two Henry was almost unconscious from rage. He was aware of nothing except the tempestuous beating of his heart and the fierce passion consuming him like a flame.

"How dare he!" the King choked. "How dare he!" Had not God shown clearly that He was on Henry's side; that Henry was His Chosen One, His Soldier?

Chester Herald recoiled a step, frightened by the expression on his sovereign's face, but Henry quickly had his emotions under control. Nevertheless, he would not forget this letter, nor forgive it.

"Where is Charles now?" he demanded.

"At Mantes, Your Grace. He has taken the Oriflamme with him."

Henry's mouth shut like a trap; then, after a moment, he sneered: "Much good may his sacred banner do him! Harfleur will soon be mine."

Harfleur formally surrendered on Sunday, the twenty-second of September.

Henry, with Sir Gilbert Umfraville on one side and the Earl of Huntingdon upon the other, and attended by all those of his court who were neither sick nor dead, sat in a silken tent, on a golden throne and waited for the keys of the city to be brought to him.

The twenty-four French hostages were led by Thomas Beaufort towards the splendid pavilion; and the English soldiers who spat and jeered at them as they passed, noted with satisfaction that even de Gaucourt and d'Estoutville had been forced to wear the shirt of penance and tie a felon's halter about their necks. Henry of Monmouth would teach these foreigners that it was unwise to trifle for too long with the victors of Crecy and Poitiers.

Henry, still smarting under the lash of King Charles's letter, kept the hostages on their knees for twenty minutes, neither looking at them nor speaking; only ending their ordeal by signing to Thomas Beaufort to accept the keys on his behalf, which Dorset was glad to do.

The King, however, also knew when to display humility and entered the city barefoot, going at once to the church of St Martin to offer up thanks for his victory. The Harfleur churchmen were deeply impressed, and if they did not openly applaud his intention to turn their city into an English colony, they did not oppose him either.

All able-bodied adults were allowed to remain within the walls so long as they swore allegiance to the English crown. But the indigent and the old were evicted, a ragged, straggling column, each person clutching a pathetic little bundle of possessions; turned out of homes and parted from loved ones in the name of that God who had preached Peace on Earth and Goodwill towards Men.

The command of the new garrison was given to the Earl

of Dorset, who, in common with the remainder of Henry's captains, assumed that the King and the bulk of his army would now withdraw by sea to England, in readiness for the winter months. Henry, however, had other ideas.

At a Council meeting in the Priory of Graville, held on October the fifth, he announced his plans. "I intend to march to Calais for embarkation."

There was a stupefied silence. Gloucester, York, Huntingdon, Dorset, all of them stared at Henry as though he had taken leave of his senses.

The dying days of September had brought the first chill blast of autumn sweeping in from the sea; the burning heat had given place to more temperate weather; and a faint crusting of frost in the early dawn intimated that winter was close at hand.

"Harfleur to Calais," protested York, the first to recover the powers of speech, "is all of a hundred and fifty miles. Perhaps more!"

"And the main French army lies at Rouen," Dorset added.

Henry shrugged. "By the time that the Dauphin has grasped our intention," he said, "it will be too late. They may follow us, but they will be unable to overtake us. We shall march parallel with the coast to the ford at Blanche-Taque and, once across the Somme, again follow the coast road to Calais."

The men around the worn refectory table stirred uneasily. It sounded so simple : too simple, thought York.

"Your Highness realises," he asked, leaning forward, "that if—if, I say—by some means the French should manage to overhaul our forces"—he paused for dramatic effect—"they would outnumber us by four or five to one."

A fleeting expression on that fat, earnest face reminded Henry of the dead Cambridge.

"And would you be afraid of that, cousin?" he jeered, anger snapping in the depths of his almond-shaped eyes.

Sir Thomas Erpingham, sensing trouble, hurriedly intervened.

"What His Grace of York says is true, Your Highness," he

144

argued. "The losses we have suffered have decimated our army. The Earl of Arundel's troop alone has lost its commander and a hundred of its archers."

Henry was fond of Erpingham and respected both his courage and his judgement. Nevertheless, his mind was made up. He had intended to march on Paris, but the prolonged defence of Harfleur had ruined all his plans. The French army lay between him and his goal and he dare not risk a winter campaign. This raid along the coast to Calais would be better than returning to England with nothing more to show for his subjects' money than the surrender of a solitary French town.

"Then we must ensure, my lords," he answered calmly, "that the French do not overtake us. And I cannot believe that they will."

16

HENRY was far less confident in private than he was in
Council and had spent many a sleepless night before reaching
his decision to march on Calais.

He missed the sage counsel of his half-uncle, Henry Beaufort; but when his own wisdom failed, he would ask himself
what the Bishop of Winchester would be likely to do in similar
circumstances and thereby found a solution.

The King was fully aware of the foolhardy nature of this
reconnaissance raid through a hundred and fifty miles of
hostile territory with an army already shattered by combat
and disease. But he knew his countrymen; sympathised with
their longing for another Crecy or Poitiers; recalled guiltily
the promises with which they had been induced to part with
their money. Henry might not have said in so many words
that he would be in Paris by Christmas, but it had been
tacitly understood.

When he had set sail from Southampton three months
earlier, hopes had run high. He had been equipped with the
best ships and the best guns that money could buy and
thousands of willing men. All he had to show for it was
Harfleur. If he went home now, disappointment would soon
bubble over into discontent. The Lollards were still active
and it would need only a hint of public dissatisfaction with
the King, for Oldcastle and his men to seize upon it and turn
it to their advantage. And who knew what support Edmund
Mortimer still commanded? The House of Lancaster was as
yet too new, too raw to hold men's lasting affection. What it
needed was a hero; someone with whom the English could

identify in their growing sense of national pride and their quest for martial glory.

Yet another consideration obsessed Henry's mind as he paced restlessly to and fro in the narrow cell which served him as a room. If he returned to England, he would leave at Rouen a sizable French army whose first task would undoubtedly be to re-take Harfleur. Although he could victual the garrison by sea, it was always possible that, in the end, the sheer weight of French numbers would force the town to surrender. But if Henry set out for Calais, he would draw the French troops after him, thus giving Thomas Beaufort and his men time in which to rebuild the city's battered defences.

"Moreover," he pointed out to his recalcitrant captains, "we shall have to cover only the first hundred miles unescorted. As soon as we cross the Blanche-Taque ford, we shall be met by a force from Calais. I have already sent word by one of our ship's masters to the Earl of Warwick to rendezvous with us at the mouth of the Somme in just over a week's time."

The English army left Harfleur on the morning of October the seventh.

It was a morning of heavy frost and needle-sharp sunlight; all white and gold. In the distance, the hills were nothing more than a vaporous grey shadow, lost behind a shimmering veil of amber. Everywhere was brilliance and light, from the sparkle of rimed branches and rooftops to the glitter of ice-bound road and the sun-spangled glint of the harness.

Henry embraced his half-uncle, Thomas Beaufort, who, for his part, was convinced that he would never see Henry again. He had a sudden vision of the young boy whom he had fetched from Ireland all those years ago and the recollection nearly unmanned him.

The King had left Dorset twelve hundred men to occupy Harfleur. The rest marched in three columns; the van commanded by Sir Gilbert Umfraville and Sir John Cornwall; the middle by Henry and Gloucester; and the rear by the Duke of York. (Henry had known a grim satisfaction in consigning his cousin to this particular position.)

Six days later, the English army, weary but not dispirited, was approaching the mouth of the Somme, and the prospect of meeting with members of the Calais garrison cheered even the most inveterate grumblers.

There had been a little trouble at both Montvilliers and Fécamp—"but nothing as what an Englishman couldn't 'andle," as Nicholas Brampton, Stuffer of Basinets, proudly reminisced with his companions.

At Arques, the citizens had had the temerity to threaten opposition to the English troops. Henry, however, had sent a terse message to the Castellan demanding immediate passage across the River Béthune or else he would not hold himself responsible for the conduct of his soldiers: Arques, he had intimated, might well be razed to the ground.

The Castellan, who, like every Frenchman, had been brought up on stories of the Englishman's hideous rapacity and his depredations in France during the campaigns of the previous century, had made haste to comply with Henry's wishes and not only allowed his army access to the bridge over the Béthune, but re-victualled it as well.

"A pity, that was," remarked Albright Mailmaker, who, as his name implied, was an Armourer, "I could have fancied a bit of arson."

This conceited attitude on the part of the English was not diminished by the fact that they had successfully withstood a French cavalry attack as they had prepared to cross the River Besle near Eu. And although this skirmish had indicated that the French were on their tail and fully cognisant of the English army's whereabouts, the islanders were not unduly troubled. Very soon now, they would meet with their compatriots at the Blanche-Taque ford.

It was in the early dawn of October the thirteenth that the bad news burst about their astounded ears. As the advance column wound its way into the cobwebby depths of the Somme valley, mist swirling knee-high over the saturated ground, two scouts returned with a talkative Gascon prisoner. And what he had to say, sent Sir John Cornwall pelting back along the lines to find the King.

By noon, the army had ground to a halt and every man in it knew the awful truth. The French advance-guard had overtaken them, and the Blanche-Taque ford was securely held by Marshal Boucicaut at the head of six thousand men. The Calais reinforcements had been routed.

The French captains held a Council at Bapaume, but the division of opinion was sharp.

"Let the Goddams go," D'Albret advised, and in this he was supported by Marshal Boucicaut.

"Let them go!" spluttered the Duke of Bourbon. "Not bring them to battle?" There was an outraged murmur from the Dukes of Orleans, Alençon and Bar.

The Constable leaned forward, resting his hands on the table. He was a dark, swarthy man whose looks and colouring would be perpetuated by many of his descendants (notable amongst whom would be King Charles the second of England).

"Yes! Let them go," he repeated. "The English are broken in body and in spirit. You all know that as well as I do."

They did indeed know it. For five days, the massive French army had paced the north bank of the Somme, while along the south bank had stumbled the dispirited and demoralised English, conscious that each passing mile, each passing hour took them farther away from the safety of the coast and deeper into enemy territory. Henry had hoped to use the bridge at Abbeville, but the Duke of Berry had been before him and the structure destroyed. It had needed little imagination on the part of the French to realise that this disappointment would have had the most devastating effect upon their foes.

Marshal Boucicaut now raised his voice. "D'Albret is right," he said. "If we stand contemptuously aside and let this broken remnant of an army straggle through to Calais, no one can accuse us of cowardice : we outnumber them four or five to one. Indeed, we are more likely to be praised for our chivalrous action. At the same time, this pretentious fool, Henry Plantagenet, will be made the laughing-stock of Europe—the man who set out in a lion's skin but was revealed as a bumbling ass."

149

"No!" exclaimed Alencon, rising to his feet in a shimmer of amber and scarlet. "We must crush the English once and for all and we shall never have an opportunity like this again. We simply cannot fail."

D'Albret caught Boucicaut's eye and the Marshal shifted unhappily in his seat. He shared the Constable's unease, for the English, in his experience, were a people with the most uncanny knack for survival. Who would have thought that they could have crossed the Somme at all? Yet they had eventually done so at Voyenne and Bethencourt. Within twenty-four hours, working in the most appalling conditions, up to their armpits in water and mud, the stricken English had built two causeways, one for men and one for the baggage-wagons. And wherever the work had been filthiest or most dangerous, there had been Henry Plantagenet, urging his men to ever greater efforts. Boucicaut, the soldier, could guess how they loved him for that. What a contrast, he thought bitterly, to France's mad King and sickly Dauphin, both of whom had been left for safety at Rouen.

D'Albret tried another tack. "Have you considered, my lords," he asked, "the possibility and all its consequences if the English should be victors in the forthcoming battle?"

For a moment there was a dumbfounded silence. Then Bar broke into a roar of laughter that reverberated amongst the smoke-blackened rafters of the ceiling, swelling in volume as the mirth of Alençon, Bourbon and Orleans was added to its already riotous proportions. Only Boucicaut remained silent.

"If the Goddams should beat us," D'Albret insisted, his voice rising imperatively above the clamour, "it would take this country generations to recover morally from such a defeat. The blow to French prestige would be incalculable."

Bourbon wiped his eyes and nose on a crimson sleeve. "Tell me you were joking," he begged. "You're not serious! We outnumber the English by five to one, as Boucicaut said just now; our men are fit, theirs sick with dysentry and famine."

"They still have the Welsh long-bow," the Marshal reminded them quietly.

"Faugh!" spat the Duke of Alençon.

The Constable compressed his lips until they were nothing but a thin thread of scarlet in the dark-brown skin of his face. How many Crecys, how many Poitiers did his countrymen need before they could be brought to believe in the deadliness of the long-bow of Gwent? In comparison, the cross-bow was archaic and cumbersome, the short-bow a child's plaything. But because the French noble despised men of plebeian birth, he despised the Welsh archer; an error, reflected D'Albret savagely, which could have the gravest results.

He rose and went towards the door. As he opened it, he turned and faced his companions once more.

"Let me advise you, my lords, to renew your acquaintance with the Book of Samuel. The story of David and Goliath makes most interesting reading."

The morning of Friday, October the twenty-fifth, the day of the cobbler saints Crispin and Crispinian, was gloomy and cold. Throughout the night it had poured with rain, adding to the discomfort and misery of the English army. There was hardly a man in that exhausted and starving host who did not believe himself doomed.

It had not needed the wild gestures and incoherent stutters of the scouts for the troops to picture the size of the French army which now lay across their path. Ever since they had managed to cross the Somme—a river whose name would for ever be engraved upon their hearts—the trampled cornfields and churned-up mud had spoken to the Englishmen of the vast host which had recently passed that way. Even Henry had been daunted enough to attempt to come to terms with the French. All prisoners taken during the march had been returned, and Chester Herald had been sent to offer the restitution of Harfleur in exchange for an uninterrupted passage to Calais.

"Accept! Accept!" Boucicaut and D'Albret had pleaded, but the other French captains had remained adamant.

"Why?" had demanded Alençon. "Why, when we can have Harfleur and Henry Plantagenet as well? And when we have finished with this upstart Englishman, we can deal at our leisure with the Burgundians."

The Duke of Burgundy was hunting on his estates, ostentatiously leaving his King and countrymen to their fate. D'Albret had been foolish enough to hope that internal feuds might have been forgotten during this threat from an outside foe.

"I wish to God," he had said, "that Burgundy was with us now."

In the English camp, Sir Walter Hungerford had been rash enough to voice similar sentiments.

"I wish we had ten thousand more archers with us," he had sighed.

The King, already bitterly ashamed of the momentary weakness which had led him to treat with the enemy, had rounded angrily on his friend.

"You speak like a fool, Walter," he had snapped. "By the God in whose Grace I firmly believe, I wouldn't wish for one more archer than we already have. We are God's people. He has given to me the sacred trust of humbling these French, whose pride in their numbers and strength is an offence in His sight."

Camoys and Hungerford had exchanged speaking glances, but the advent of the Duke of York had prevented more being said.

York had been upset because some of the archers had abandoned the heavy stakes which, on the Duke's advice, Henry had bid them cut as far back as Boves. Following instructions, the archers had sharpened these stakes at both ends so that they could be driven into the ground to form, collectively, a wicked-looking *chevaux de frise*.

"If we are forced to fight the French, we shall need them," York had insisted, his flabby jowls quivering earnestly.

Henry, who respected his cousin's judgement and was fast forgetting his resentment of Cambridge's brother in the face of their common danger, had immediately ordered that no man, however sick, however tired, was to leave behind his wooden stake.

And York's vigilance proved to be justified, for the bristling ferocity of the *chevaux de frise* planted firmly into the rain-soaked ground, gave the outnumbered and dispirited English at least a modicum of consolation on this grey and miserable Friday morning.

The English troops were drawn up four lines deep in a field of uncut corn. Henry and Gloucester commanded the centre; York the right and Camoys the left, with the customary wedge of archers between each formation. Behind them lay the village of Maisoncelles; to their right the woods and hamlet of Tramecourt; and to their left the woods about the castle of Agincourt. Inside these two thick belts of trees lay an open stretch of country less than half a mile in width, into the far end of which was packed the bulk of the French army.

And it was at the sight of this dense mass of men, jammed shortsightedly into so narrow a space, that Henry's spirits began to rise. The French might have the numbers, but in their choice of a battleground they had shown that they did not have the tacticians. They were confident that weight alone would crush the enemy.

They seemed, however, in no hurry to put their theory to the test. Four hours after daybreak, they were still sitting in their battle-lines, eating, gaming or sleeping. The effect of this upon the English was demoralising in the extreme.

Henry had expected an attack soon after dawn and his army had been alert and in position since the first ribbons of light had swathed the blackness of the sky. He had addressed his men and, like them, received absolution. He had donned his armour of plated gold and his squires had placed over his battle-helm a circlet of rubies and pearls. His surcoat glowed with the arms of England and France and there was no other man on this battlefield dressed to resemble the King.

"I shall not be taken captive for ransom," he had told his archers. "I shall die with you."

A thin, ragged cheer had risen from the ranks, and men, some of whom had nothing but the bow in their hands and the sheath of arrows on their backs, had felt heartened in spite of their naked bodies trembling in the chill morning air.

Now, however, the long wait spent in contemplation of the French host unnerved even the Welshmen and Henry realised that he dared delay no longer. Raising his arm, he shouted: "Forward! In the name of Jesus, Mary and St George!"

The trumpets sounded. Each man, kneeling, made the sign of the Cross and touched the ground with his lips in recognition of his mortality.

"Dust to dust," muttered Ifor Evans, Archer. "Mary, Mother of God, preserve me."

Then the English and Welsh began to advance towards their lines of pointed stakes.

The Duke of York swung his sword time after time, the sweat pouring down his back inside his armour. The field was one mass of bodies, pressed together in a mêlée of arms, legs and weapons. Never in all his experience had he known anything like it.

The French were trapped, unable to move, hemmed in on either side by the trees, by the immovable wall of English to the front and by their own men behind, who, oblivious to the dangers of suffocation, pushed inexorably forward. The air was alive with the hum of arrows as the Welsh and English archers wrought havoc in the enemy lines.

It was almost impossible now to recognise anyone, so thick was the atmosphere·with flying dust and blood. York did see Gloucester fall, however, and identified his attacker as the Duke of Alençon. Next moment, Henry, his coronet glittering about his helmet, the arms of England blazing even through the mist, was standing over his fallen brother and had thrown the Frenchman to the ground.

What happened then, York could not see. A swaying muddle of bodies closed off Henry from his view, just as a severed hand ricocheted against the Duke's breast-plate.

York felt ill. His heart was thumping in a most unfriendly manner and there were pains across his chest and up his arms. He was finding it difficult to breathe and a red mist hovered in front of his eyes. He thought he saw his brother, Cambridge, smiling and beckoning him on; a mocking ghost wreathing in and out of the mist.

York would have fallen, but there was no room to fall: the

living and the dead propped each other up. Ahead was a great bank of corpses and he was being dragged towards it. He tried to lift his arms, but could not. . . . The pain in his chest was crushing him. . . .

It was finished.

In some places, the piles of French dead were over eight feet in height and the triumphant English, looting their hysterical way across the blood-drenched field, were forced to climb the sides of these gruesome mountains.

But no one cared. Each man was drunk, not only with the wine rifled from French baggage-wagons, but with the headier brew of total and undisputed victory.

There was hardly a Frenchman of repute left alive. Alençon, Bar, D'Albret, the Duke of Burgundy's two brothers, who had defied his edict and come to serve their liege-lord, and men whose illustrious names were to fill nearly a dozen scrolls were all dead. Dead, too, on Henry's orders, burned, stabbed or strangled, were all the French prisoners taken during the battle.

"The Frenchies' own fault," opined William Carpenter, Carpenter of the Hall, casually slitting the throat of a man still breathing and starting to despoil the body. "It wouldn't have happened if they hadn't looked like making another attack. Some of them prisoners—" he slipped a ruby ring on to his finger and regarded it admiringly—"weren't even disarmed. There hadn't been time. Well! I ask you! Stands to reason you can't have hundreds of armed men at the back of you while you're busy fighting up front."

"But there wasn't an attack," snarled his companion, who had been one of the captors thus robbed of a future ransom. "Ten prisoners I had an' I split their bleedin' throats for nothing."

"But it looked like an attack," argued Carpenter, irritated by his friend's paucity of understanding. "The King had to make a decision, quick-like. I think he made the right one."

The other grunted derisively, but it was an opinion which would be endorsed by contemporary French and English chroniclers alike; and although half the army was disgruntled by the order, the other half regarded it as just retribution for the French raid upon the English baggage-wagons, when all the boys and the horses had been slaughtered.

Certainly none of Henry's captains entertained any thought of censure, and Humphrey of Gloucester, nursing a dagger wound in his left arm, embraced his brother fervently with his right.

The King, who had removed his dented battle-helmet to reveal a face grey with fatigue, submitted for once to his youngest brother's enthusiastic welcome. But all he said was: "York is dead. Caught in the press and suffocated in his armour. Suffolk is gone, too." He smiled wryly. "The father at Harfleur; the son here at . . ."

His weary voice tailed away. He had not yet decided what this battle should be called and at present was too weary to decide. For a moment, to the watching Walter Hungerford, he seemed almost human, beset by a man's frailties and emotions.

Walter himself was still overawed; a sense of disbelief in their victory mingling with a dazed elation. Like many another, he had learned that day a valuable military lesson: sheer superiority of numbers was uesless unless there was room to manoeuvre. The French, trapped between the woods of Tramecourt and Agincourt, their advance lines impaled upon the English *chevaux de frise*, had degenerated into a stagnant body of men; the lords crushed inside their armour, the rearguard unable to move forward, the van unable to retreat. To Walter Hungerford, therefore, it was hardly surprising that for every thousand Frenchmen dead only a handful of English had been killed.

But Henry saw things differently. The tired man, worn out by the stress of command and hand-to-hand fighting, suddenly vanished to be replaced by the Soldier of God. The English victory against incredible odds, the enormous French losses, the utter rout of the latter's Chivalry proved to him one thing only. God had shown His hand; had proved conclusively that Henry Plantagenet was to be the scourge of the French even as Attila had been the scourge of Rome.

Successive French Kings and governments had sinned too long in keeping the rightful heirs of King Philip the fourth from the throne of France. The Will of God and the will of Henry Plantagenet had clearly been proved to be one.

As the King turned away to order the quartering of his men and the singing of *Te Deums*, Walter Hungerford saw for the first time the dangerous glow of fanaticism shining in Henry's eyes.

17

THE November day was cold and a chill wind blew the clouds into an ever-changing panorama of shapes—human faces, pewter-coloured lakes amidst iron-grey hills, fleecy lambs asleep in their folds—and the light which filtered through the overhanging roof-tops was murky and unwholesome. A day for the agues and the shivers, but nobody cared. The London streets were as close-packed as they could get with people without impeding altogether the returning, victorious army.

Ever since the news of Agincourt had been read by Henry Beaufort at Paul's Cross, the bells had hardly stopped ringing out their triumphant peals, whilst all over the country men and women had danced in the streets and lit bonfires and shaken each other by the hand in an ecstasy of national pride. Crecy and Poitiers were as nothing compared with this devastation of the French nobility; this humbling of France's pride; this amazing victory snatched from the jaws of almost certain defeat. Henry of Monmouth was their darling, their adored, their god—"and the House of Lancaster is safe so long as he lives," Henry Beaufort thought complacently as he stood with seventeen other Bishops on the steps of St Paul's.

Meanwhile, the royal procession had halted at Blackheath so that Nicholas Walton, the Mayor, could deliver his welcoming speech. As far as the eye could see stretched a vast patchwork of people; scarlet, blue, amber and saffron, every guild or craft was represented. Trumpets blared, clarions rang, horns tooted, until the din, thought Humphrey of Gloucester, was enough to make a man lose his mind. Even the noise of the battle had not been so deafening, but it at least had the merit of drowning the Mayor's oration.

As the cavalcade moved towards the Southwark end of London Bridge, where two mammoth-sized statues stood in crimson splendour amid a flurry of pennants and banners, Humphrey smiled with a secret elation. How his brother Clarence must be cursing, railing against the fate which had sent him home from Harfleur with the humiliating affliction of dysentery. Humphrey knew his Thomas; guessed that he would never recover from the disappointment of having missed one of England's greatest victories; understood his bitter jealousy for the two brothers who had been present. Bedford would never entertain such feelings : kind, self-effacing John would rejoice at his brother's good fortune and take pride in their martial achievements. Humphrey's gnome-like features lit with pleasure as he contemplated the many small jibes with which he would taunt the envious Thomas.

As the procession reached the far side of London Bridge, progress was again hindered by an archway, on top of which was a pavilion of red velvet and the glittering, gem-encrusted statue of St George—that saint so recently adopted by King Edward the third as England's patron, and who had so soon and so dramatically justified his selection. Marshal Boucicaut, from his ignominious position amongst the ranks of prisoners, reflected bitterly that the jewels adorning this one statue alone, would be sufficient to pay his ransom. Would the enormous sums demanded by Henry for himself and the Dukes of Orleans and Bourbon ever be paid? Could such money now be raised in war-torn France? God! If only he might have died there on the battlefield with D'Albret! If only their advice had been heeded before that terrible travesty of a battle had ever been fought! If only . . .!

It was as well for Boucicaut's sanity, and also for that of the Duke of Bourbon, that neither man knew on that November morning in 1415 that he would never see France again. The Duke of Orleans would be luckier, but even he would have to wait for twenty-one years before he returned to his native land.

A crowd of little boys, their faces painted gold, laurel wreaths in their hair, burst through the archway to sing a

159

song specially composed for the occasion. Clear and high rang the voices like the chiming of glass upon glass.

> "Our King went forth to Normandy
> With grace and might of chivalry.
> Our God for him wrought wondrously . . ."

"Our God," thought Henry, his eyes glowing, the only sign of emotion in his still and sombre face. "*My* God." Had he not told the Duke of Orleans to "be of good heart. Know, cousin, that God has given me the victory not because I deserve it, but because He wished to punish your countrymen and your people for the disorders, sensuality and vice which has for generations corrupted and corroded your way of life. It is not to be wondered at if the Almighty has been provoked."

After that, his high-ranking French prisoners had tended to avoid Henry's company; a circumstance which the King found incomprehensible. But there were too many other things on his mind for him to brood over their apparent ill-manners.

As he approached the Tun in Cornhill, there came from another tent of crimson brocade a stream of "venerable prophets" dressed in cloth-of-gold, each man releasing sparrows and doves from cages of silver-gilt. All this rejoicing, Henry thought, all this money spent as though Agincourt were the sum total of everything that England need achieve in her conquest of France, was infuriating. What fools his compatriots were! Agincourt was merely the beginning; the prelude to the years of hard campaigning that lay ahead. And for that Henry would need more money, more men. France would never give in without a struggle: even now the Armagnacs were rallying to King Charles and the Dauphin in Rouen.

Other problems, smaller, yet no less important in their way, nagged at the edges of Henry's mind. His cousin of York's death could not have been more unfortunate, leaving as it did Cambridge's son, the five-year-old Richard Plantagenet, as the new Duke of York; a potentially dangerous little boy in

160

so far as he was also the son of Anne Mortimer. How wise he had been, Henry reflected, not to have had Edmund Mortimer executed in July along with the other conspirators. God grant that the Earl of March live many more years and have sons of his own; for the power of York combined with the claims of Mortimer could well spell trouble in the future for the House of Lancaster.

As he approached the doors of St Paul's, Henry glanced up into the confidently smiling face of his half-uncle, Henry Beaufort. And as he fell to his knees and kissed the ground amidst a shower of golden rose-petals tossed from on high, the King felt an infinite relief at having his most competent adviser once more close at hand.

Henry Beaufort looked in faint surprise at the little Duke of York standing so sturdily before him. How in the world Cambridge had fathered such a prosaic child, the Bishop had no idea. A phlegmatic boy, if he read little Richard aright, and therefore likely to grow into far less dangerous a man than his father had been. Nevertheless, the Bishop was entirely of the King's opinion that an eye must be kept on Richard Plantagenet, and he turned towards Henry, who sat busily writing in the royal apartments in the Tower.

"I suggest, sire, that His Grace of York's wardship should be given to my sister, Joan Neville of Raby. She has, as Your Highness knows, a sizable family of her own"—Joan had fulfilled her vow to have a larger family than her lord's first wife—"and our young cousin here won't lack for companionship. The eldest boys, Richard and William, are perhaps a little old for him, but there are others."

And another child on the way, if he knew his Joan. She would be pleased, too, to have such a lucrative ward as the Duke of York, and who could tell? The boy might one day prove an eligible husband for one of her daughters; Catherine, maybe, or Eleanor or Anne.

The King was pleased to approve. He considered it an excellent solution to the problem, for he knew his half-aunt and her husband to be devotedly loyal, but he did not say

F

so aloud, merely grunting his assent and dismissing the child from his presence.

"I will make the necessary order presently," he said to the Bishop, "meantime, tell me the news from France."

The faint March sunlight touched his cheek, stressing its thinness and showing up a network of wrinkles which looked like shadows under his eyes. Kingship, thought Henry Beaufort, was taking its toll.

The Bishop laid his hands together over a growing paunch. "John the Fearless has withdrawn to his own territories again. He has apparently grown tired of besieging Paris, for the time being."

"A pity," snapped Henry. "He had reached as far as Lagny. Why did he not persist? Many Parisians favour the Burgundian cause, or so I've been led to believe."

"Oh, undoubtedly." The Bishop fluttered his hands expressively before lowering them to lie once more quiescent on his ample stomach. "But perhaps Duke John now feels that he holds the advantage over King Charles and has no need to resort to bloodshed."

Henry snorted. "You refer to the new Dauphin?"

"Precisely!" Again the hands fluttered and lay still.

In December, the Dauphin Louis had died in Paris, leaving his brother Jean, an equally sickly youth, to succeed to his title. Unfortunately for the Armagnac faction, the new Dauphin was married to the Duke of Burgundy's niece, Jacqueline of Hainault, and the young couple were living in Burgundy. John the Fearless now held them virtual prisoners, hostages against King Charles's good behaviour.

Henry rose to his feet, stretching his arms until the bones cracked. Watching him, Henry Beaufort was aware of a widening gulf between his one-time pupil and himself: nothing had been quite the same since Henry's return from France. Every day saw the King growing more isolated from his fellow-men, even his friends; withdrawn behind some intangible barrier of his own making. There was little doubt that he saw himself as a man apart; one of the chosen few who perform some special deed of great renown; an Arthur or a Roland. A dangerous conviction, thought the Bishop, and one which could, if his half-nephew were not careful, lead to disaster—if not for himself then for others. And this pride was a self-consuming emotion, burning the King from within; re-fuelling itself with his strength and exhausting him with its intensity.

"I must return to France this year," the King said, speaking almost to himself. Then, over his shoulder, he asked his half-uncle: "You know that, don't you? You are prepared to persuade the Commons to levy further taxes?"

The Bishop smiled. "I have found a most appropriate text for my opening address to Parliament next week. 'God has opened for you a way.' And, in any case, I believe that there will be no opposition. For the present, our countrymen are in a frenzy of self-pride and would grant you the moon should you ask for it."

Henry laughed derisively, but as it turned out his half-uncle was correct. The Commons even permitted him to make use of certain subsidies which should not, by rights, have come into his possession until the following autumn.

And Henry needed all the money he could get, for not only did he have to finance a new invasion force, but he also had to re-victual the Harfleur garrison. And, at the beginning of March, due to the foolhardiness of its commander, the city was very nearly lost to the French.

Henry was still at Westminster, attending Parliament, entertaining Henry Percy—who had at last been exchanged by the Scots for Albany's son, Murdoch—and coping with the fiery Talbot of Shrewsbury, who had arrived from Ireland to complain about the non-payment of his wages as Lieutenant. Both these gentlemen, as well as the Dukes of Clarence and Gloucester, were with the King when the messengers from Harfleur arrived to tell of yet another English victory. But how nearly a disaster it had been was appreciated perhaps only by the King and his half-uncle, Henry Beaufort.

The Bishop, who had personally conducted the two men into Henry's presence, motioned to the taller of the two to begin his story; a tale which started on the ninth of March when the Earl of Dorset, seconded by Sir John Fastolfe, had taken a thousand men and raided along the French coast as far as Fécamp. (And who, wondered Henry Beaufort, would have expected his dear, staid young brother, Thomas, to be so rash?)

"What then?" demanded the King, his eyes intent on the messenger's face.

The second man took up the story. "At Valmont, sire, near to Fécamp, we were attacked by the French. Their leader was the Count of Armagnac—the Constable since the death of D'Albret."

Henry nodded. The mention of D'Albret immediately filled the room with memories of Agincourt, adding a golden lustre to the greyness of the day.

The man went on: "The Earl of Dorset was severely wounded"—here he half-turned towards Henry Beaufort standing beside him; then hurriedly turned back in the direction of the King—"but he rallied the men, Your Highness, and we retreated as far as Etretat"—this was near the Chef de Caux and, as everyone knew, within spitting distance of Harfleur—"when the French cavalry caught up with us and at once engaged us in battle."

"And?" Henry's voice was sharp with fear.

"The French dismounted, sire, before attacking."

Henry breathed again. What fools these Frenchmen were! How easily they could have ridden down the exhausted and wounded English: instead, they had chivalrously fought on foot. The King signalled for the man to proceed. He had no doubt now as to the outcome.

"We routed them, sire, and took eight hundred prisoners with us into Harfleur."

When Henry welcomed the Holy Roman Emperor, Sigismund, on the first of May, the victory of Valmont was still being spoken of as a further sign of Divine support for the English cause. This in spite of the fact that the Count of Armagnac and his forces, besieging Harfleur, had twice almost succeeded in capturing it. Also, English supremacy in the Channel was

164

being severely challenged by the Genoese, whose knowledge of the sea and all things pertaining to it was to make their city the cradle of the world's greatest explorers. Famine stalked the streets of Harfleur as Henry's ships found it increasingly difficult to get supplies into the beleaguered city.

It was the most unpropitious moment that Sigismund could have chosen for a projected alliance between England and France. The Emperor had know it, secretly, ever since he had been sped on his way from Calais by the Earl of Warwick; polite, but obviously preoccupied with other and more military matters.

Henry was an equally attentive, but equally unresponsive, host. He accepted Sigismund's gifts—the arm, heart and part of the skull of St George—with unfeigned delight; deplored wholeheartedly the effect of the Papal schism upon Christianity; agreed that a crusade against the Turks by the united heads of Europe was eminently desirable; but plainly considered that the only possibility of an alliance between England and France lay in the two countries' unification under one King.

And Sigismund, making his lecherous, wine-bibbing way around Windsor, found himself, most unexpectedly, beginning to agree with Henry. The Emperor had been very disturbed by the situation which had greeted him in France; the country rent by warring Burgundian and Armagnac factions; Charles chained up like a wild beast; the Dauphin a prisoner in the Duke of Burgundy's hands; and by Isabeau's promiscuity which had shocked even his threadbare moral standards.

The Louvre palace had been shabby, with dirt in the corners and mice scurrying across the floors. The French, anxious for Sigismund's friendship, had entertained him lavishly enough, but they could not hide from him the poverty of the de Valois court nor the sad state of the French people in general.

What a difference there was in this country of rain and cloud and ever-changing skies! From the moment of his reception by Archbishop Chicele at Canterbury, and through-

165

out his progress to London, the Emperor had seen nothing but well-fed bodies, fields awash with the pale green of early crops and fruit trees so thick with blossom that they looked like snow in the sunrise; all witnesses to the uninterrupted life of this island which had known no major foreign invasion for well over three hundred years.

Henry had made a pretence, at least, of willingness to form an alliance.

"Let Charles honour the Treaty of Bretigny," he had said. "Let him return Aquitaine, Poitou and Normandy and I will withdraw my claim to the French crown."

Both men knew that this was a gesture, nothing more. The French would never restore these lands to the Plantagenets.

Sigismund looked from his window at the shining opalescent sky above Windsor and for a moment could think of nothing but its beauty. The English sunlight rarely had the dazzling whiteness of Italy or the clear sapphire brilliance of the south of France. It shone, instead, in washes of pale primrose, shimmering behind veils of gauze; mysterious, glowing, imparting to every flower and leaf a radiance of pure gold.

The Emperor turned away with a sigh : he had a decision to reach. Yesterday he had been created a Knight of the Garter and today he must make up his mind whether or not to treat with Henry; whether or not to sign an agreement which would ally the Holy Roman Empire with England and so acknowledge as valid that country's claims to the throne of France.

18

On August the fifteenth in the year 1416, the Emperor Sigismund and King Henry signed and sealed the Treaty of Canterbury.

One final consideration had tipped the scales in England's favour so far as Sigismund was concerned. The Council of Constance, which he had convened and which was to be his lasting monument to the cause of Christian unity, was in danger of becoming dominated by the French delegation. Sigismund's gesture of friendship towards England at once indicated his displeasure at this fact and withdrew from France the protecting arm of the Holy Roman Empire.

Nevertheless, Sigismund was not entirely happy at the thought of disinheriting the ancient House of de Valois, and so, as he strolled a few days later with Archbishop Chicele in the gardens of Canterbury Cathedral, he broached the subject of Henry's marriage.

"He will be twenty-nine this coming October, I believe," Sigismund said. "A great age for a man—especially for a King—to be single. This country needs an heir, my lord Archbishop. This country needs an heir!"

Chicele cautiously agreed: it was a matter to which he had given much thought. However, he resented this old lecher's interference, particularly when Sigismund dug him in the ribs and whispered: "They say he hasn't slept with a woman since he became King. It's not natural. All right for you dessicated priests"—the voice swelled from a confidential whisper to a full-throated roar—"but not for a young man. Especially not for one who was as randy as he was."

Chicele's face wore its most repressive look; a cold slip of a moon beneath his nimbus of greying hair. Sigismund saw it and laughed quietly to himself, but it was not part of his policy to alienate one who stood so high in the esteem of his newly acquired ally. So he took the Archbishop's arm in a friendly hand, his hot, wine-laden breath brushing the other man's cheek, and never guessed how Chicele's fastidious soul mentally recoiled from his effervescent embrace.

"What I am saying, Archbishop," he went on, only edging closer as Chicele's body shrank from his touch, "is that the French offer of the Princess Katherine, made last year, should be seriously considered. In her children by King Henry the two crowns could be satisfactorily united. And I understand that the Burgundian alliance has never really appealed to King Henry." Sigismund's rotten teeth showed in a wide, unattractive grin. "And who shall blame him? A pious girl, Anne, by all accounts; full of good works, ministering to the poor. Faugh!" The Emperor spat, most accurately, into a clump of buttercups. "But the daughter of Madame Isabeau, now there's a different story! I should be surprised if she couldn't teach Henry a thing or two. Eh? Eh?"

And Sigismund's roar of laughter echoed riotously through the cloisters into which they had just turned.

"The Princess Katherine is also her father's daughter," Chicele said meaningfully, able at last to withdraw his arm from Sigismund's clutching fingers. He rubbed it surreptitiously as though to free it from all contact with the gross figure beside him.

The Emperor shrugged the Archbishop's oblique objection aside. "There's a little madness in all families," he said. "We all have our skeletons rattling around in our cupboards. Nothing in that, and no one that I know of considered it an impediment to her sister's marrying King Richard. Besides, the advantages would outweigh the disadvantages and Henry's son would then be acceptable to both England and France."

The Archbishop thought the Emperor over-optimistic, but what he might have answered was lost by the sudden appearance of the King and two of his brothers at the far end of the cloisters, all obviously in the grip of great excitement.

"My lord Archbishop!" Henry's voice sounded triumphantly beneath the stone vaulting and his eyes smouldered fanatically in his lean, hard face.

Chicele hastened forward.

"My lord Archbishop," Henry repeated, "great news! God has again given us the victory." His eyes, hooded for a moment by his heavy lids, blazed open. "My brother Bedford, on the very day that the treaty was signed here in Canterbury, engaged the Genoese fleet at the mouth of the Seine and inflicted such a crushing defeat on the Italians that four of their carracks were sunk and five more captured."

"God be praised!" exclaimed Chicele. "And my lord of Bedford?"

"Wounded, but by no means fatally. I have ordered the bells to be rung and bonfires to be lit in all the principal towns; and free wine, my lord Archbishop, in all the conduits."

Sigismund, who had stood quietly by throughout this exchange, cynically enjoying the Englishmen's conviction that the Almighty was their personal ally, now moved forward, but the clamour of the cathedral bells breaking suddenly above their heads, he was unable to offer more than the briefest of congratulations.

Humphrey of Gloucester did manage to make himself heard, however, as he hissed wickedly in Clarence's ear: "Well, well! John has provided his own Agincourt. That leaves only you, my dear Thomas, to cover yourself in glory."

And as Thomas rounded on him, his eyes burning with rage, his arm threateningly upraised, Humphrey's laugh rang out, slicing through the racket of the bells.

Thomas of Clarence was not the only one to be provoked by the twenty-four-year-old Duke of Gloucester during those autumn days of 1416.

Crossing to Calais in the wake of his brothers and Sigismund, the Duke was present at the farcical negotiations between England and France; the Emperor's final and very half-hearted attempt to bring unity to western Europe. The representatives of King Charles the sixth did not stay long and were speedily replaced by Duke John of Burgundy and his son, Philip, Count of Charolais.

It was this latter young man to whom Humphrey took instant exception. No one, least of all himself, could say why; but the immediate antipathy which he felt for the somewhat priggish Philip almost wrecked his eldest brother's bargaining with John the Fearless.

"For God's sake behave yourself!" Henry stormed at a sullen but unrepentant Humphrey after some outrageous piece of rudeness.

"I can't help it : I loathe him," protested the Duke defiantly.

"Heaven alone knows why you should," the Duke of Clarence cut in. "You and Philip are two of a kind; both after the women."

"But I enjoy it," Humphrey retorted, and Thomas was grudgingly forced to admit that he knew what his brother meant.

Philip of Charolais was a womaniser, but coldly pious with it. There was no joy in him and his opaque, fishy eyes rested calculatingly rather than lovingly upon the damsel of his fancy. They so rested upon his cousin, Jacqueline of Hainault, who, together with her husband the Dauphin Jean, had been brought to Calais by the Duke of Burgundy for safer keeping.

And perhaps, ruminated Clarence, that was at the root of the trouble between Gloucester and Charolais, for there was no doubt that Humphrey was also attracted to the seductive Dauphine. Thomas suggested this to Henry in extenuation of Humphrey's conduct, for, like all the brothers, he had an affection for the benjamin of the family which no amount of misbehaviour on Gloucester's part could totally allay.

Henry, however, was disinterested. He had neither the time nor the inclination to bother himself over Humphrey's concupiscence, but a part of his busy brain did register the fact that the lady, who was palpably bored by her weak and ineffectual husband, was not averse to the handsome Humphrey's attentions. This was a potentially perilous situation and Henry had no compunction, therefore, in insisting that his youngest brother return with him to England, instead of remaining at Calais to speed Sigismund on his way to Constance.

"The Earl of Warwick is capable of managing without your help," the King snapped. "Moreover, your presence will be necessary at the opening of Parliament."

Whether this was true or not, Humphrey was in his appointed place to hear his half-uncle, Henry Beaufort, urging the Commons to consider carefully the need for another invasion of France.

"It is true to say," thundered the Bishop, "that it is sometimes necessary to make war in order to keep the peace."

The Commons, a little more reluctantly than heretofore, agreed; and with the coming of the New Year preparations began in good earnest for the assembly of another invasion fleet along the southern coast.

Returning from Kenilworth, where he had spent Christmas, Henry pawned the crown jewels to the City of London, and the crown itself to Henry Beaufort for twenty-one thousand marks. The Bishop was in a generous mood, his brother Thomas having recently been elevated by the King to the dukedom of Exeter. The Beauforts, those bastard children of John of Gaunt and Katherine Swynford, were rising high, high, high! Nothing could please the Bishop of Winchester more. If only Joan would have the good sense to secure the little Duke of York for one of her daughters, and if only the King would permit the marriage of Joanna to the captive King of Scots, Henry Beaufort felt that the family would be nearing the apogee of its attainments. That, however, would only be reached when he himself obtained a Cardinal's hat.

He broached this subject with something less than his usual diplomacy while entertaining the King at Waltham; but realised at once from Henry's high-nosed stare that over-eagerness had led him to err.

"This is hardly the time, my dear uncle," Henry reproved him, "to be thinking of self-aggrandisement. We are here to mount an invasion."

171

After this rebuff, the Bishop wisely let the matter drop, and although, secretly, it continued to occupy the greater part of his thoughts, he entered into the preparations with such enthusiasm that he was quickly reinstated in Henry's good graces.

Throughout the remainder of that winter and during the following spring and early summer, the scenes of two years before were busily re-enacted. Men and munitions converged upon Southampton and Portchester; every goose in England lost six of its wing-feathers to supply the flights for the bowmen's arrows; and the Solent was again crammed with shipping. Over fifteen hundred vessels, the blossoming of their sails turning the cramped and muddy stretch of water into a many-hued flower garden, bore witness to Henry's conviction that England must be "master of the Narrow Sea". And at the end of June—"as if," Henry Beaufort told him, "you have but to wish for a thing for God to grant it"—his cousin, John Holland, Earl of Huntington, won another resounding sea-victory for England off La Hogue, trouncing a combined French and Genoese fleet.

In France, too, events were moving in Henry's favour. In April, the Dauphin Jean died and the Duke of Burgundy was forced to look for another ally, willing or unwilling, at the French court. And once more fate provided the answer. The quarrel which had been simmering between Queen Isabeau and the Count of Armagnac boiled over into open warfare, and the Constable arrested and banished the Queen, first to Blois and then to Tours.

It was from Tours that the soldiers of Duke John the Fearless made an audacious rescue of the raging Madame Isabeau, sweeping her back to power as Regent for her insane husband. As Burgundy's ally, she now extended her hand in friendship to England, and in the name of both King Charles and herself offered Henry yet again the hand in marriage of the Princess Katherine.

"Undoubtedly God is on our side," chuckled the Bishop of Winchester, rubbing his hands in glee.

But Henry knew that God only helped those who helped

172

themselves: he knew, also, that France would not drop into his arms like a ripe plum. The Armagnacs still fought on in the name of the new Dauphin, the ugly, timid and uninspiring young Charles. And when he finally set sail from Southampton on July the thirtieth, 1417, Henry guessed that no swift and sudden glory awaited him; only the long and weary boredom of besieging one French town after another.

Bonneville had fallen; Caen had fallen; the Earl of March was plundering in the Cotentin. And as December set in with iron-grey skies and a powdering of snow on the ebony hills, Henry and his army settled down to besiege Falaise.

The preceding month, Henry had made peace with his step-brother, Duke John of Brittany, an event which in some measure belatedly reconciled him to his father's marriage to Joanna of Navarre. With his right flank thus secure, the King could afford to take Falaise and its massive castle at his leisure. He dispensed with the discomforts of tents and had his carpenters erect a timber city; the long huts with their turfed roofs coyly sheltering behind a substantial palissade.

"Will de Mauny hold out?" the Duke of Exeter enquired of his half-nephew as the two men walked briskly, viewing their defences. The air was crisp and dry, the evening sky rippled like sand at low tide, its western rim touched by the long, fiery fingers of the dying sun.

"For a while, perhaps," shrugged Henry. "But not for long. The Dauphin won't aid him."

Thomas Beaufort nodded in the direction of the castle, a flat, paper shape against the darkening sky, but still grim and menacing.

"Odd," he said, "to think that our ancestor was born there; William the Bastard, son of a tanner's daughter."

"William the Conqueror," Henry answered, "son of Duke Robert of Normandy."

Exeter glanced at his half-nephew, but could discern only his hatchet-like profile silhouetted against the fading light. No tremor of emotion disturbed its calm, but the Duke divined the intensity of feeling which burned behind that high, white forehead. He had first sensed it on that day when Clarence and Warwick had let the victorious English troops run amok in Caen, killing and raping, murdering and looting with a bestiality that had shocked even a war-hardened veteran such as himself. He had looked to Henry to prevent the sack, but hours had passed before the King had finally issued his orders that women and priests were to be spared. And during those hours, Thomas Beaufort had recognised the darker side of Henry's nature; that suppressed savagery of which Henry Beaufort and Sir John Oldcastle had always been aware.

He scented danger now in Henry's tone: the King was not to be reminded of his lowly origins. Henry's heavy chin had lifted a little, jutting crag-like from beneath the long, straight nose with its flaring nostrils. He made Thomas Beaufort think of a war-horse, stamping and snorting into battle.

"When I was a child," Henry said, this rare reference to his childhood startling his half-uncle, "I was very fond of Richard." Another shock, this mention of the dead and deposed King. "My father didn't like him." The King bared his teeth in a sudden and mirthless grin. "It was jealousy, I fancy. My father never forgave Richard for the central part he played in the revolt of the peasants. It never suited Henry of Bolingbroke to take a secondary role."

It occurred to Thomas Beaufort that this half-nephew of his was more percipient than he had imagined. He would have liked to hear more of Henry's thoughts concerning his father, but the King went on: "As I said, I was fond of Richard, but he was a fool. I shall be remembered because I gave the English Agincourt and the mastery of France. Richard will be remembered—for what? The handkerchief?" And the King gave his unexpected neigh of laughter, startling a sentry into a position of stiff alarm.

But as they made their way back through the noise and bustle of the camp to the largest of the huts which served as the King's headquarters, Thomas Beaufort was horrified to find himself wondering if, perhaps, in that foggy, damp little island which Englishmen called home, the handkerchief might not prove a more lasting memorial than any battle. The conquest of France could well be as fleeting and as ephemeral as a dream.

The Duke pulled himself up short. What thoughts were these, especially in the shadow of Falaise Castle? William of Normandy had proved that a country could be conquered and, in time, subdued. What he had achieved, his war-like descendant, Henry of Monmouth, could surely do in reverse.

The candles were burning in the hut and the narrow room was full of smoke. The Dukes of Clarence and Gloucester were poring over a map on the rough wooden table and the Earls of Huntingdon and Warwick were deep in earnest conversation. They all looked up, however, as the King entered on a blast of cold night air which cut through the smoky atmosphere and scattered the wine-fumes with its chill breath.

Thomas of Clarence pushed several despatches towards Henry.

"From John," he said. "The messenger from England arrived over an hour ago."

The King sat down, breaking the seals and reading rapidly in the uncertain light of the guttering candles. After a moment or two, he stopped and sat staring before him, seeing nothing. There was a forbidding look on his face; a look compounded of both approval and resentment. Thomas Beaufort could not fathom it until the King spoke.

"Sir John Oldcastle has been captured at last," Henry said abruptly. "He was burned at the stake four days ago."

19

THOMAS BEAUFORT never heard Henry mention Oldcastle again. Nor, afterwards, when he thought about it, was he able to interpret the expression which he had seen on Henry's face. The Duke suspected, with more accuracy than he gave himself credit for, that while the orthodox Churchman had applauded the death of a heretic, the old comrade-in-arms had been nauseated by his own approbation.

Henry was indeed torn by conflicting emotions at the news. The savagery of the sentence—that Oldcastle first be hanged, then roasted alive over a slow fire—revolted the man who had calmly returned Badby to the flames. But Oldcastle was different: he had fought beside Henry at Shrewsbury and had influenced, more than either man had realised, the Prince's earlier years. Yet he was a heretic, a Lollard, and deserved to die. The King was a man who liked black to be black and white to be white. When his feelings became unruly they confused him, unleashing his baser instincts.

Falaise surrendered in February and by May the English were besieging Lisieux. It was here, while Henry was holding a Council in the Earl of Salisbury's tent, that a French gunner almost killed him with a remarkably accurate sling-shot. Henry said little at the time, brushing aside the concern of his captains in grim-faced irritation; but as soon as the town capitulated, he had every one of its gunners executed.

"The one who nearly ended my life shall not escape with his," he said in icy rage as he watched the nine men die. He felt in some twisted way as though he had now purged himself of his weaker sentiments concerning Oldcastle.

176

As he moved on towards Louviers, word reached him that the Duke of Burgundy and Queen Isabeau had entered Paris, and, in vengeance for the escape of the Dauphin, were wreaking such havoc in the city that the corpses were piled knee-high in every street and the gutters ran continuously with blood. And before Louviers fell on June the twentieth, the Duke of Burgundy had sent word that the Count of Armagnac was amongst the many victims.

Henry, however, did not trust his Burgundian ally. He was of the opinion that Duke John, playing a double game, was negotiating with both himself and the Dauphin in an effort to play off one against the other and so obtain the mastery of France for Burgundy. It was an opinion greatly strengthened when, on reaching Rouen, Henry discovered that the garrison of the ancient Norman capital was largely Burgundian.

As the English looked at the heavily fortified town through a haze of July heat; at the sixty towers bristling with guns and arrows; at the wide moat, part of which was the Seine itself; at the forbidding castle and at the surrounding country-side which had been denuded of cattle and crops, they sighed. It was going to be a long and weary siege.

Henry's chief concern was his supply lines, and things might have gone badly for him had not his first cousin, the King of Portugal, come to his aid and stationed a Portuguese fleet at the mouth of the Seine. As the Earl of Warwick, besieging Caudbec, remarked to the Earl of Huntingdon, the marriages of John of Gaunt's children were finally proving their worth. John Holland, himself Gaunt's grandson, merely laughed and said that Henry would need all the help he could get for the siege of Rouen.

"I fancy it will prove to be the most difficult task that my cousin has yet faced."

He was right. The siege was to drag on for almost seven months.

The dank autumnal mists of November were succeeded by the sharp frosts and biting winds of December. The sun, glimmering every now and then with a pallid radiance, illumined scenes of unbelievable carnage. This was war to the death, as the grim rows of gibbets, both within and without the town, testified. Each side hanged its prisoners in full view of the other with a kind of unholy glee. Corpses choked the fosse and the stench of corruption from rotting bones and decaying flesh caused as many deaths as boiling tar and burning pitch.

Food was not a problem for the English. The fall of Caudbec to the Earl of Warwick in September, had ensured free passage between Rouen and Harfleur. But within the city, the inhabitants were dying like flies from starvation, and even rats and mice were fast becoming unheard-of luxuries. No man would think twice of murdering another for a slice of black, weevily bread and it was rumoured amongst the besiegers that not a virgin was left in the city : every woman would sell herself for a leaf of cabbage or a mangy cat.

The capitulation of Cherbourg had enabled the Duke of Gloucester to rejoin his brother at Rouen and his reinforcements had been implemented by the arrival of Thomas Butler with nearly two thousand of his "wild Irish". These men from the bogs and backwoods of Ireland had at first incited the English to derision.

"They've got no breeches," screamed Thomas Tunbrigge to fellow Yeoman Robert Spore.

"And only one shoe apiece," Thomas Westerdale, Scullery Labourer, guffawed.

"And what do they 'ope to do with them 'orrible knives an' little roun' shields?" remanded John Waterton, Bowman, of his mate, William Foster.

But the laughter had dwindled to shamefaced sniggers and then died into silent respect as the kernes had proved their fighting skill. Their bravery, too, was such that when news was brought to the King of a relief force marching to Rouen's aid, the Irish were stationed at the point of greatest danger.

But there was no relief after all for the beleaguered citizens, and as Christmas approached, the Burgundian captain, Guy le Bouteiller, turned out of the starving city over twelve thousand old men, women and children, together with the wounded and dying; anyone, in short, who could no longer contribute to Rouen's defence.

"No work, no food," he said, as his soldiers inexorably carried out his commands.

Henry by this time was in a white-hot rage. Normandy was *his* duchy; Rouen *his* capital city. Everyone who resisted was guilty of high treason.

"Those people," he said, indicating the steadily increasing stream of refugees, "are not to be allowed into the English lines."

He turned abruptly on his heel and strode back into his tent where Archbishop Chichele and the Earl of Salisbury awaited him. Both these gentlemen had recently been negotiating on Henry's behalf; Salisbury with the Dauphinists at Alencon, Chicele with the Burgundians at Pont de l'Arche.

For the Duke of Burgundy was not the only man who could play a double game, and Henry, military strategist that he was, believed devoutly in the axiom, Divide and Conquer. While the two warring French factions dallied with the prospect of an English alliance, neither John the Fearless nor the Dauphin, Charles, would make any serious attempt to relieve Rouen. Henry's instructions, therefore, to both Salisbury and the Archbishop had been to keep the diplomatic pot simmering, but to ensure that it never came to the boil.

"It was a simple matter," smiled Chicele. "The Burgundians insisted on the official language being French, so we insisted on Latin." He paused, raising a mazer of wine to his lips, then dabbing at them with the hem of his flowing sleeve. A finicky man, thought Salisbury. The Archbishop continued: "And by the time that difference was resolved, there were others. The order of precedence on entering a room, who should sit where around the table; nothing was achieved."

A faint wind had sprung up, moaning through the encampment and wafting the stench of rotting flesh and unwashed bodies between the cracks and crevices. A light rain drummed with insistent fingers against the roof.

"God help those poor wretches in the fosse," said Chicele, crossing himself.

Henry, however, had no time to waste on the plight of the refugees. "And you, Thomas?" he queried briefly.

Thomas Montagu, Earl of Salisbury, nodded. "It was the same at Alençon. We argued about everything and decided nothing."

Henry smiled. He was well pleased. Somewhere a cannon boomed; somebody screamed; someone else shouted an order. Horses neighing, muffled voices, tramping feet; these were the sounds that Henry loved above all others; the sounds of war.

"You brought Cardinal Orsini with you?" he asked the Archbishop, and Chicele rose, inclining his head.

"He has something for Your Grace. If I might fetch him?"

Cardinal Orsini came into the cabin, his cloak spangled with raindrops which shimmered in a myriad rainbows as he bowed over Henry's hand. From his sleeve he produced a miniature portrait and handed it to the King.

"The Princess Katherine," he explained unnecessarily, for the painted face bore a strong resemblance to the girl's dead sister, Isabella.

A pretty enough face, thought Henry, and certainly more to his taste than Anne of Burgundy. Katherine had the de Valois nose, it was true; not prominent as yet, but likely to be so as she grew older. That was nothing; but did she have the taint of her father's madness? That was important. The King peered closer, straining his eyes in the uncertain light. The girlish face, docile and prim, gave him no answer.

On the other hand, he needed the alliance with Burgundy. It would strengthen his hand in any future dealings with either the Dauphinists (the former Armagnac party) or the Burgundians themselves.

An idea flickered in his mind. Why not marry his brother John to Anne of Burgundy? He recalled that once, long ago, Bedford had admired the girl and commended her kindly face. Well, John should have her, and the more he considered the idea, the more excellent the plan seemed to him. Sober

John of Bedford and pious Anne of Burgundy would be well suited to one another.

But that was for the future. In the meantime, he must not appear too eager for this French alliance, and, if the truth were told, he was not too eager. Always, at the back of his mind, there remained the picture of Isabella, spitting at his father and himself on that morning when he had visited London to consult with his father about Owen Glendower. Glendower was dead now, nobody quite knew how or when; but rumours of his death had gradually filtered through to the outside world, reaching Henry as he had approached Rouen last July.

The King turned to Orsini. "A charming girl," he said harshly. "But even more charming with a dowry of a million crowns, plus the lands of Ponthieu, Aquitaine, Maine and Guienne."

The Cardinal was nonplussed as he stared at that cold de Bohun face, smiling mirthlessly into his.

"I . . . I will take your request to King Charles and Queen Isabeau," he faltered.

Henry nodded briskly. He rose from the table feeling well pleased with the turn of events. His God was doing great things for Henry Plantagenet and, in gratitude, he gave food and drink on Christmas Day to the twelve thousand refugees rotting in the no-man's land of the fosse.

Rouen finally surrendered on the nineteenth of January, 1419, but its occupation by the English forces was both orderly and quiet. The scenes at Caen and Falaise were not repeated and Guy le Bouteiller was allowed to depart with the full honours of war, after swearing an oath of allegiance to Henry. And the citizens were graciously permitted to pay in instalments the fine of three thousand crowns which Henry imposed upon them. Moreover, every man was compensated for the loss of any property in the south-western corner of the city where the King immediately began the erection of a fortified palace.

Men like the Earl of Warwick and the Duke of Exeter

cocked knowing eyebrows at each other : it was obvious to them that Henry was becoming reconciled to the idea of the French marriage. The Burgundian forces had held Henry to a long and wasteful siege, but he treated them well. The Duke of Burgundy was Queen Isabeau's ally; Queen Isabeau was the mother and guardian of the Princess Katherine.

"It looks," said Gloucester to Clarence, "as though we shall have a French sister-in-law, after all." Humphrey's eyes gleamed. "I wouldn't mind cementing the alliance with Burgundy—now that Jacqueline of Hainault is a widow."

Clarence snorted. "John of Burgundy will marry her to one of his own family, you may be sure of that. She is a very wealthy young woman." Thomas grinned maliciously. "Perhaps Philip of Charolais will get her."

The Duke of Clarence was both right and wrong. John the Fearless forced his unwilling niece into marriage, not with his son, but with his kinsman, John of Brabant. He was making certain that she did not fall into the hands of the Dauphinists. Nevertheless, he continued to negotiate with young Charles as well as with King Henry, sniggering over his duplicity with Queen Isabeau.

Their mirth turned to rage, however, when they learned that Henry was also in contact with the Dauphin; that, indeed, a meeting had already been arranged between the two men near Evreux at the end of March.

Queen Isabeau, angrily biting begrimed and beringed fingers, sent messengers splashing through the thin March rain from Paris to Pontoise, threatening her "dearest son" with the direst of consequences should he go to the meeting with Henry Plantagenet. The last thing that Madame Isabeau wanted was an alliance between her enemies.

The Dauphin, lolling his big head on his shoulders and shuffling his spindly body inside his ill-fitting clothes, was upset by his mother's letter. All Isabeau's children had been brought up to fear her, and as the little black words danced on the paper before his bulbous eyes, old memories of verbal scourgings and more physical chastisements haunted his terrified mind. He was now sixteen years of age, but the thought

182

of his mother transported him back into his hideous childhood; a little boy, whimpering in the dark.

He did not go to Evreux, and the humiliated English, having waited in vain, withdrew to Rouen.

"Bloody French," spat John Canterbury, Officer of the Scullery, "wouldn't trust them no farther than I could throw 'em."

"Carrying on with the Burgundians behind our backs," opined Nicholas Brewster, Yeoman of the Bakehouse.

But a coldly furious Henry, fulminating against the treachery of the Dauphin, was playing precisely the same game and negotiating with Duke John the Fearless. His stepbrother, the Duke of Brittany, was even then arranging a meeting between the two men near Mantes.

Mantes was now in English hands and its proximity to Paris was felt by the Dauphinists to be a very real threat to the French capital. La Hire, Tanguey du Chastel and Pothon de Xantraille, their troops at Pontoise reinforced by six thousand Scots under the command of Sir William Douglas and the Earls of Buchan and Wigtown, harassed the English forces as much as they were able; but their urgent need was for a united France instead of this endless, internal bickering which was slowly bringing them all under the heel of the invader. But as the year dragged on, the divisions in their ranks became ever deeper and wider.

The Champ de la Chatte was a field just outside Meulan and on the last day of May, 1419, it blazed with colour; silver, amber, purple and yellow; bronze, amethyst, scarlet and gold. Silken tents rippled in a fine summer breeze; tables laden with food groaned beneath trees whose leaves were like daubs of emerald painted on a saffron-coloured sky.

Halfway between the English and French encampments a great pavilion of crimson silk crouched like some garish beast of prey. And in and out of its gaping jaws hurried high-ranking gentlemen of both sides in a frenzy of anxiety to ensure that no hitch marred the day's proceedings. For today, Henry of England was to meet Katherine of France.

Henry was the most unruffled person present with the exception of his brother Humphrey, who, with his capacity for wringing the maximum enjoyment from any situation, was in the sunniest of tempers.

"My jewelled belt to your new stallion," he hissed in the Earl of Warwick's ear, "that she squints."

But Richard Beauchamp was in charge of the arrangements and already sweating slightly. He was, therefore, in no mood for the Duke of Gloucester's nonsense.

The trumpets sounded; the packed bodies in the pavilion swayed as one; and every head turned in the direction of the opening. The Earl of Warwick hastened forward, his wand of office clutched stickily in his hand.

Queen Isabeau entered with her daughter, Katherine's hand laid lightly upon her arm. No greater contrast could have been imagined than between those two. The older woman was raddled, her thin, wrinkled neck rising out of a velvet gown whose purple folds only accentuated the sallow complexion of her skin. Her mouth, once described as the most voluptuous in Europe, was now a scarlet gash in her face. Only her eyes, darting voraciously hither and thither as though she would take in every detail at a glance, retained the old hypnotic quality which had sent men mad with desire for her.

By comparison, her daughter was like a May morning remembered in darkest December. At eighteen, Katherine de Valois created an illusion of beauty which only time would dispel, and in which only the most discerning of observers could detect those similarities of feature which proclaimed her Isabeau's child.

Certainly King Henry was not so perceptive. As he raised Katherine from her curtsy and kissed her blushing cheeks, he felt well satisfied that this girl might become his wife.

20

HENRY did not fall in love with Katherine; it was not in his nature to do so. Moreover, Humphrey's remarks that girls grew more like their mothers as they grew older, plus Thomas Beaufort's hints that Katherine might, in time, become more like her father, were bound to have their effect, even if Henry temporarily dismissed them from his mind.

Nevertheless, of all the eligible and nubile princesses of Europe, he considered Katherine to be the prettiest. He wanted her because he did not relish going to bed with a plain girl like Anne of Burgundy, and because he saw in Katherine a means of binding her parents more closely to his cause and of alienating Isabeau still further from her detested son, the Dauphin.

With all these considerations rolling around in his head, it was hardly surprising that Henry found neither the time nor the inclination to fall in love—which, as it turned out, was just as well, for the negotiations petered out in a welter of mutual recriminations. During a long, hot month, when the trees stood like funnels of smoke against the clouded green of the hills, the English and Burgundians haggled inside the crimson tent; dogs snarling over a bone. The air hung in a red mist all about them, the light lying in splotches of scarlet and flame, or in pools the colour of spilt wine.

Henry, in a moment of weakness, intimated that he would be willing to give up his title to the throne of France; "provided," he declared, "that I retain full sovereignty over Normandy, Anjou, Maine and Poitou. To be precise, all the land which belonged to my forefathers."

Isabeau grimaced at John of Burgundy, but she neither declined nor accepted what the English considered to be an over-generous offer. She turned, instead, to the vexed question of her daughter's dowry.

"Eight hundred thousand crowns was agreed upon," stated the Earl of Warwick.

Isabeau spread her gnarled fingers. "Admittedly," she answered. Her vividly painted mouth was pulled into a travesty of her once-seductive smile. "But as you still owe France six hundred thousand crowns—the amount of my daughter Isabella's dowry, which was never returned after King Richard's death—that reduces the amount to two hundred thousand crowns."

"Rubbish!" Thomas Beaufort broke in. "My late half-brother was not responsible for his predecessor's debts." But even as he spoke, he realised the fallacy of his statement.

Isabeau's teeth curled back from her blackened teeth. "Most certainly it was King Henry's responsibility," she retorted, "for if he had not taken what wasn't his, my child might even now be alive—she undoubtedly died of a broken heart—and Queen of England." She shrugged her shoulders. "However, I say nothing of that. One of the fortunes, or misfortunes, of war in these unsettled modern times. But Isabella's dowry should have been repaid. And then there were her jewels!"

"A few paltry trinkets," sneered the Duke of Clarence, and now Isabeau was really stung on the raw.

"My daughter went to England as befitted a Child of France," she snapped. "Her jewels were worth all of five hundred thousand crowns, so you have already had money in excess of the Princess Katherine's dowry and can expect no more."

The meeting broke up in disorder and it was the beginning of the end. Information brought to Henry by his spies that John the Fearless was once again in touch with the Dauphinist leader, Tanguey du Chastel, did nothing to further the negotiations and, towards the end of June, Henry and the Duke exchanged words which were openly hostile.

"If my suit is rejected," the King said coldly, "I shall drive both you and your mad King out of France."

His icy control infuriated the choleric Burgundian. "So you say!" he shouted with his blustering laugh. "But before you can do so, my King and I will give you such a run for your money that you will be heartily tired of us both."

After that, there was little more to be said; and the subsequent news that, on July the eleventh, Burgundy's representatives had signed a treaty with the Dauphin, had the effect of bringing the meeting to its foregone conclusion. The tents were packed, the horses saddled; the Queen and Princess withdrew to Paris, Henry to Mantes and the Duke of Burgundy to Pontoise.

Le Champ de la Chatte lay bleached and bare under the relentless glare of the sun.

The Duke of Burgundy's stay at Pontoise was short.

It was a beautiful August morning. The whole world was a crystal bowl, full of light; a sparkling, jagged brilliance that splintered here into a shower of glittering stars and diffused there into the spectral shimmer of butterflies' wings. And into this brittle glory, cracking its shining surface, came the thundering hooves and the unharmonious clashing of swords. Pontoise had been attacked.

By ten o'clock the Duke was in flight and the city had fallen to the Earl of Huntingdon and his ally, Gaston de Foix.

King Henry was triumphant, for his army was now within twenty miles of Paris. More than that, he had taught Duke John the lesson that it did not pay to be at odds with the chosen Soldier of God. But the Duke of Burgundy was about to be taught his last and most salutary lesson by someone other than Henry Plantagenet. He would learn, much too late, never to trust a former enemy.

No one could say, afterwards, what had prompted the Dauphin to the rashest act of his life. John the Fearless, smarting from his humiliation at Pontoise, was ready to be Charles's staunchest ally, and there was no doubt that the

Dauphinists needed the might of Burgundy if they were to drive the English from French soil.

A meeting was arranged between the Duke and the Dauphin for September the tenth on the bridge at Monthéreau, some forty miles south-east of Paris. An enclosure had been built in the middle of the bridge, where the two men could meet and talk.

The morning of the tenth dawned bright and clear, but towards mid-day, a wind sprang up, driving before it clouds whose shadows rippled like water across the grass and trees, and cascaded over the hills in waterfalls of purple and amethyst. Something ominous, it was afterwards recalled, lingered in the very air.

Shortly before noon, the Duke and Dauphin approached, each from his own side of the bridge, escorted by a limited number of attendants whose cloaks were whipped into the air, making them look like a crowd of strutting peacocks. Red and green, blue and silver spun out on the autumn breeze in a floating island of colour.

The Duke and the Dauphin entered the enclosure with two or three of their most trusted retainers.

"Your Highness!" The Duke bowed arrogantly. He knew that he held the best bargaining position, for, unlike Charles, he could always treat again with the English, holding as he did the trump card of the Princess Katherine.

The Dauphin returned the bow, his ugly de Valois face screwed up against the rays of the sun.

"I am certain that Your Highness realises," the Duke was beginning; but what it was that he hoped the Dauphin understood was destined never to be known.

As he spoke, Charles half-turned, with a tiny nod of his head, to Tanguey du Chastel, who stood just behind him. Instantly, du Chastel stepped forward, the crimson satin sleeve of his upraised arm now black, now scarlet under the running light. The edge of his battle-axe gleamed evilly, momentarily touched with fire, then hurtled downwards, cleaving through Burgundy's skull. The Duke fell to his knees, drops of blood and brain spattering his incredulous attendants.

And they, too, before they could really assimilate what was happening, were set upon and killed.

At the far end of the bridge, the rest of the Burgundians turned and fled for their lives.

The twenty-three-year-old Philip, now Duke of Burgundy in his murdered father's place, rode into the victorious English camp; victorious because during the past two months, Gisors and Meulan had surrendered, and recently, at the beginning of December, the "impregnable" Chateau Gaillard had fallen.

Philip's white face, set in lines of implacable hatred above the black of his clothes, told its own tale. He was consumed with the desire for revenge, his passion shaking the whole of his long, slender body.

"We will fight together," he told Henry, "until every Dauphinist has met the same fate as my father."

Henry inclined his head. He had been expecting this visit and had already been in touch with Isabeau. That astute politician, realising that Burgundy was now irrevocably committed to the English cause, had renewed her overtures of friendship within a week of Duke John's murder. No more had been said about the late Isabella's dowry.

On Christmas Eve, a treaty was signed between England and Burgundy, appointing Henry as Regent for the insane Charles the sixth, and the Princess Katherine was named as Henry's affianced bride.

Not everything, however ran quite so smoothly. In January, the Spanish gained a naval victory over the English just off La Rochelle; while the ever-growing antipathy between Humphrey of Gloucester and Philip of Burgundy resulted in the former being sent home to England as Regent and the Duke of Bedford being summoned to France in his brother's place.

Good-natured John was inclined to laugh about the feud, but Henry saw it quite otherwise.

"Trouble could easily have come of it," he said brusquely, "had Humphrey been allowed to remain. And I want nothing now to impede my negotiations with Charles and Isabeau.

189

I shall do better with Burgundy's support, although I have no doubt that I could manage alone if needs be."

Bedford had no doubt of it, either. He had always admired Henry, giving him the uncritical love which, although the King did not realise it, had always been so necessary to him. John would have liked to have made some demonstration of affection—he and Henry had seen little enough of each other in the six years since the coronation—but he knew that Henry would dislike it. So he merely laughed and said: "Humphrey will have his hands full. Talbot is back from Ireland greatly in debt and making the inevitable fuss about lack of funds."

The King, however, was totally disinterested in Ireland and its problems. One day, perhaps, he would find the time to subdue it once and for all, but at present it was as remote from him as the back of the moon. The most important moment of his whole life was approaching and he had no thoughts to spare for anything else.

March of the year 1420 was cold with wild winds that flung the branches of the trees into frenzied shapes and sent the clouds scudding in great banks of steel-grey wool across the forbidding sky. The unrelenting winds blew into the English camp at Meulan messengers from Duke Philip, who, marching from Arras, had now joined King Charles and Queen Isabeau in the city of Troyes.

Henry received the messengers in state and, afterwards, discussed the terms that they had brought, with his captains and advisers.

"The Princess Katherine in marriage," he said, "with a dowry of forty-thousand crowns a year."

"A reasonable offer," commented Thomas Beaufort, leaning forward a little in his seat and resting his elbows on the table.

There was a general murmur of agreement. But everyone present felt that the marriage had become of secondary importance. The faint traces of colour on Henry's high cheekbones and the gleam of emotion in his deep-blue eyes, suggested an offer of more moment than had been made hitherto. And the King's next words revealed just how momentous an offer it was.

"Secondly, King Charles and Queen Isabeau are to remain sovereigns of France until King Charles's death." Henry paused. A draught whistled under the door of the lodging-house, lifting the rushes on the floor and bringing with it a smell of the open drain which served the town as a sewer. "On King Charles's death," Henry continued, "the crown of France will pass to me and to my heirs for ever. The Dauphin will be formally disinherited."

The Earl of Huntingdon, Henry's cousin, John Holland, clapped his hands, while Thomas Beaufort and the Duke of Bedford embraced each other in delight. All around the table there was a buzz of barely suppressed excitement and Thomas of Clarence was thumping the arms of his chair.

The King's face immediately became congested with blood, his whole body rigid with anger.

"This is no piece of news, my lords," he said, outraged, "to be gloated over as if we had won a bargain at a fair. This is what God had already ordained when He sent me to France." The heavy chin came up; the eyes sparkled like frost on a sunny day. "No other outcome could have been possible. Your self-congratulation is as unseemly as it is blasphemous."

An embarrassed silence ensued. There was no man in the room sufficiently in advance of his time to be incredulous of Divine intervention in the affairs of men; but there were a few—the Duke of Exeter and the Earl of Warwick amongst them—who were sufficiently cynical in their approach to life to be alarmed by Henry's increased fanaticism. Not so the Duke of Bedford, who was unsubtle enough to believe devoutly in his eldest brother's burning conviction that he was the Elect of God. And it was from this moment that there stemmed the whole of John's future dedication to the preservation of Henry's French empire.

The King resumed: "The Princess Katherine and I will be married in Troyes as soon as the treaty between King Charles and myself has been concluded."

"You will go to Troyes?" The Duke of Clarence demanded.

Henry raised his eyebrows, two thin question-marks above his rather prominent eyes. "Why not?"

"The Dauphinist forces are reported as being extremely active in that district," the Earl of Warwick remarked uneasily. He doubted the wisdom of trying to deter Henry on that head, but felt that he must try.

"God will protect us," the King replied, adding: "How many more times do I have to tell you that we are under His especial protection? The Dauphin is the cold-blooded murderer of his own kinsman, the Duke of Burgundy. Do you think that God would allow such a man to wear the sacred crown of France?" He glanced about him. "We start for Troyes as soon as the final arrangements have been made. Probably within a day or two."

Henry did not in fact set out for Troyes until May the eighth, but his safe journey through hostile territory proved yet again that his confidence in the Almighty had not been misplaced.

Henry contemptuously by-passed Paris, but marched his all-conquering army within sight and sound of its walls. So thankful were the Parisians for this avoidance that they sent him four cart-loads of wine.

The King knew his troops and had no mind to enter Troyes at the head of a disorderly rabble, so he appropriated most of the liquor for his own use. At the same time, he issued instructions that the notoriously strong wine of Champagne was not to be drunk unless well diluted with water.

"Spoilsport!" grunted William Topnel of the Wardrobe, but his scrupulous observance of the edict demonstrated the extent of his respect for Henry; a respect shared by every man in the English army.

At Brie, the Dauphinist forces tried conclusions with the English King, only to be severely repulsed.

"Them Frenchies are gluttons for punishment," remarked John Breton, Clerk of the Hall, to Jacob Mendy, Yeoman of Napery. "You'd think they'd have learned a lesson by now."

At Nogent, Philip of Burgundy was waiting to escort his royal cousin into Troyes.

"King Charles," he informed Henry in a low voice, "would have come himself, but . . . unfortunately . . . his illness. . . ."

He shrugged his narrow shoulders in their sable velvet and although the late May day was pleasantly warm, a thin chill seemed to settle about Henry, stroking his spine with its clammy hand. Charles, he reflected, shuddering, would be his father-in-law; the grandfather of any children that he and Katherine might have.

But his fears were lost in the pleasure of his enthusiastic reception in Troyes, where a deputation of clergy and chief citizens came out to meet him.

At the Hôtel de Ville, Queen Isabeau, more raddled than ever in a gown of bright orange satin, welcomed her "dear son-in-law" with a coy smile and a vulgarly knowing wink. The talon-like hand which she extended for him to kiss was filthy beneath its magnificent glitter of rings. She reminded John of Bedford, whose first glimpse of her this was, of a brilliant bedizened bird of prey, quiescent for the moment upon her perch, but ready to fly out, clawing and pecking, at the slightest provocation.

It was with relief that John saw the fresh-faced young girl whom his eldest brother stooped to kiss and, unlike his brother, Humphrey, wondered how she could possibly be the daughter of Madame Isabeau.

Nevertheless, during the days of pageantry and feasting that followed; throughout the elaborate ceremonial of the signing of the treaty and the betrothal of Henry and Katherine; during the banquets and the balls, John of Bedford felt a growing uneasiness about his future sister-in-law. He divined a certain carnality in the girl's make-up which augured badly for her marriage with Henry. For if there was one thing which the days of roistering in Cheapside had taught him, it was that his eldest brother was essentially a sexually cold man. Drinking and womanising had been for Henry but substitutes for his real love, war.

There was nothing that John or indeed anyone else could do about it now. On June the second, in Troyes Cathedral, amidst great pomp and rejoicing, Henry, King of England and Regent of France, married the Princess Katherine.

G

PART THREE

THE END OF THE RAINBOW, 1420–1422

21

JOHN had been right about Henry. The King found love-
making a poor substitute for the rigours of war. The morning
after his wedding-night, he realised clearly that Katherine
would never mean much to him except as the mother of his
sons. As their sons would be the heirs of a united England
and France, he would do his duty by his wife; but he could
not help making it plain that it was a duty and not a pleasure.
His body might lie beside hers, but his mind was elsewhere;
among his men and the ballistas and the guns.

Katherine was sufficiently Isabeau's daughter to be desperately affronted by his attitude. More than that, she had,
like all her brothers and sisters, spent a lonely and terrifying
childhood in a country perpetually at war, with a mad father
and a mother whose love-affairs were the scandal of Europe.
Throughout her short life, she had looked upon marriage as
an escape; had longed with all an adolescent's dreams for the
perfect man, the *preux chevalier*, who would lap her about
with tenderness and affection; protect her with his love from
a harsh and disgusting world.

When she had first known that she was to marry Henry
the fifth of England, she had thought that her prayers were
answered. When she had first seen him at the Field of the
Cat, she had decided that dreams did come true. Handsome,
brave, the greatest soldier in Christendom, what more could
any woman ask? She had thought pityingly of her sisters and
sisters-in-law, with their weak, plain husbands. She had even
pitied her dead sister, Isabella, whose devotion to King
Richard had survived her second marriage to Charles of

Orleans and followed her into the grave. This golden hero, Henry, would never be snatched from Katherine's side as his cousin had been from Isabella's. Katherine had been, on her wedding morning, the happiest woman in Europe.

The brief period of her honeymoon came, therefore, as a severe shock to a romantic girl of nineteen. She could not complain of Henry as a lover, but as a husband and companion he did not exist. She realised, after the very first night, that to him she was simply one more acquisition in his life-long struggle to obtain the French crown. She had probably never meant anything more to him than a means to this end.

It was a bitter realisation for a young girl who craved affection and who longed for the quiet of a domestic life she had never known. There was no one in whom she could confide, for her mother, still dancing attendance upon her daughter and keeping her new son-in-law and ally under her eagle eye, would be unlikely to understand. Isabeau's great and abiding love was power, and even her lust had been subordinated to this over-riding passion. She would have found the girl's complaint trivial in the light of Katherine's elevation to the English throne.

But even Isabeau was startled by Henry's decision to set out on the hazardous journey to Paris only two days after the wedding.

"I could have held him by me for longer than that," she said scornfully to Katherine.

All her children had been a disappointment to her; her daughters pining for love and domesticity—she spat vigorously at the thought of it—and her sons effete, ugly creatures with twisted minds. She had disliked Louis and Jean, but she loathed Charles, with his big head and spindly body. Yet what else could one expect with such a father as they had? Her good Bavarian blood had done something physically for the girls, but the boys were pure de Valois. One day, perhaps, she would break away from all these encumbrances to her life and reign alone, supreme.

Meantime, Isabeau had plenty with which to occupy herself, overseeing the packing of her daughter's clothes and jewels

198

and maintaining her pleasant relationship with that priggish young lecher, Philip of Burgundy. Duke John the Fearless might have been as treacherous as a snake, but he was twice the man in Isabeau's estimation that his sanctimonious young son was. The Queen gritted her teeth. She hated Philip nearly as much as she had hated her son, the Dauphin.

"Little hypocrite," she said, speaking her thoughts aloud and frightening the scurrying maids.

The "little hypocrite" sat his horse beside Henry of England, his eyes glittering vengefully.

Sens had fallen to the joint British and Burgundian armies a week before, but this was Monthéreau, the scene of his father's murder. The town had been carried by assault yesterday, the twenty-fourth of June, but the castle, with all the garrison and a large proportion of the citizens inside, still held out.

Philip had just come from the exhumation of his father's body, rotting now after nearly a year in its humble grave, but with the signs of violence still visible upon it. The fact that he felt sick, that the palms of his hands sweated and that the decaying corpse had been an object of horror to him, only made Philip of Burgundy cry out the louder for revenge against Monthéreau.

Henry, too, was filled with a quiet rage. That morning, messengers from Humphrey in London had informed him of a plot to take his life by witchcraft; a plot that had been revealed only just in time. He need not worry, Humphrey had been at pains to assure his brother: the culprits would be speedily dealt with.

Nevertheless, Henry was terrified by the thought of witchcraft. It was all the worse in that it was the second such plot to be unconvered within a year. Last September, during John's Regency, there had been a witch-hunt involving the Dowager Queen, Joanna. She had violently protested her innocence, but Henry had not wished to believe her. He had at last discovered the means of appeasing his resentment at his father's second marriage. He had ordered her Confessor to be burned as a warlock, Joanna herself put under house-arrest at Rotherhithe and all her property and revenues to be confiscated by the crown. (The money had proved extremely useful.) The King had always borne his step-mother a grudge, though why, he could not have explained. It was a wild, un-reasoning emotion belonging to that other, vicious Henry, who lurked constantly just below the surface of his rational mind.

And it was that same, bitter creature, using Henry's voice, who, on this clear June day, was quietly ordering the execution of eleven unfortunate men who had been captured during the assault on the town. He had informed the prisoners that they would be hanged unless they could persuade the Captain of the garrison to capitulate immediately. Their pleas had been, however, in vain and so they had begged for a last sight of their wives and children.

These came; pathetic, tearful ghosts crowding the battle-ments of the castle, watching in vain for some sign of mercy on the part of the English King. Henry's eyes gleamed with cold self-righteousness; Philip's with a terrible satisfaction, and, by evening, the dying sun touched with blood-red fingers the gallows-tree and its hideous burden of fruit.

Two days later, the castle was formally surrendered.

"A few years ago, I told my half-uncle, your brother Henry, that the King of Scots might one day be of strategic importance to me." The King turned a little towards Thomas Beaufort, who, deafened by the hammering of the guns and the crash of falling masonry, was forced to bend closer to catch his half-nephew's words.

Henry gestured towards the walls of Melun. "Half of the garrison, at least, are Scots. I want James brought to me now." The King laughed. "And our dear Bishop of Win-chester would have had him back in Scotland, married to your niece, Joanna."

The September sun beat its way through the whirling smoke and dust which covered everyone and everything like a dirty gauze. The distant hills were flat as dishes against a dun-coloured sky.

James the first of Scotland, a man now of twenty-six and a captive of the English since the age of twelve, had been brought from England for Henry's wedding, but common sense told him that there was something behind this sudden desire of Henry's to honour his neglected royal prisoner. And when he was summoned to the English King's side before the walls of stubborn Melun, intuition whispered that the real reason was about to be revealed.

Coughing a little from the congested air, Henry drew James into the comparative quiet of his tent.

"In a moment," he said pleasantly, "the trumpets will sound for a parley. Then, my dear cousin, I want you, in your capacity as King of Scotland, to call upon your fellow-countrymen to surrender."

James eyed him uncertainly. "I cannot force them to surrender," he protested.

"No! Of course not!" Henry smile was unusually bland. "It's just that they might obey you. Nothing lost if they don't, but much gained if they do."

The King of Scots hesitated. He felt in his bones that this was a trap, but in Henry Plantagenet lay his only hope of freedom and marriage to his beloved Joanna Beaufort.

"Very well," he agreed at last, but his uncertainty increased.

The Scots did not surrender, neither did the French, and the siege of Melun dragged on into November. Then, when starvation had become a greater enemy than either the English or the Burgundians, the Captain of the garrison, Arnaud Guillaume, Lord of Barbazon, capitulated.

As Henry rode into the devasted city, his lips were touched with a smile of triumph—and every Scotsman in the garrison was hanged as a traitor who had refused to obey his lawful King.

Scottish enthusiasm for the war waned. As long as James remained in the English camp, the fate of the Melun garrison served as a warning and deterred Scotsmen everywhere from helping too overtly their French allies.

Paris, that Christmas of 1420, was bitterly cold. Little

flurries of sleet and hail stung the lips and cheeks, and the clouds hung in sullen formations against a lowering sky. The snow, which, in the open countryside, feather-edged leaf and twig with a rim of sparkling white, here clung about the streets like wisps of dirty rag. Starving children with frost-bitten limbs, scavenged in the ever-growing piles of rubbish near the Louvre, where the King and Queen of England kept their lavish court, and in the smaller piles near the Hôtel St Pol, where the King and Queen of France lived in compara-tive poverty. Since the arrival of the conqueror, Henry, bread had doubled in price.

The day before Christmas Eve, John of Bedford and Thomas of Clarence sat together in the main hall of the Hôtel St Pol, while their eldest brother and the mad King Charles presided over a trial of absent Dauphinists. These included not only the Dauphin himself, but also Tanguey du Chastel and Guy le Bouteiller.

On Bedford's right hand sat the black-clad Duke of Bur-gundy, and John could sense the near-hysteria which vibrated that slender frame as Henry read out the hideous sentences to be perpetrated upon the absent Dauphinists if ever they were caught.

John averted his eyes from Philip, suddenly sickened, and he realised as he did so that his distaste was directed not so much against his neighbour as against his brother. The realisation was like a physical blow, but having at last dragged the thought into the open, he was too honest to flinch from it. He was also too much a man of his time to be horrified by the barbarities involved in the execution of traitors, nor did it worry him that no evidence had been offered against the accused. These were the more sombre threads in the pattern of his age and he accepted them naturally as part of life's fabric. What did strike him as obscene, however, was that chief amongst the accused was that poor, mad, old man's son, and although King Charles sat staring vacantly into space, his mouth slack, his eyes glazed, who could tell how much he understood? And how terrible, thought John, to hear one's own flesh and blood condemned to the tortures of

202

the damned; to be trapped inside one's own mind, a prisoner, unable to escape, even to help those one loved.

But this was not the main cause of John's distress. His real concern was the pleasure which sounded so blatantly in Henry's voice as he read aloud the sentences. John was becoming daily more frightened at Henry's growing callousness. A few months ago, at Monthéreau, both John and Thomas had pleaded for the life of the King's Captain, Bertrand du Chaumont, a man who had fought valiantly for Henry at Agincourt and since, and who had been accused on the flimsiest of evidence of helping to their freedom certain men implicated in the murder of Duke John of Burgundy.

"My judgement would be the same if one of you were implicated," Henry had said with a vindictiveness that the insouciant Thomas, as well as John, had found disturbing. And du Chaumont had been executed.

John wondered why this should worry him. Henry was renowned for his justice, for his subservience to the Law: but he had no humanity any more. John of Bedford was unable to realise that what he scented was the decay of the spirit; that the object of his adoration was nothing now but a hard, bright, empty shell, glittering, but corroded from within.

Henry himself was unaware of anything except his burning dedication to the cause of God; his God, the God of Wrath and the Flaming Sword. He saw nothing incongruous in celebrating Christmas in state at the Louvre while his parents-in-law and their subjects kept the festival in near starvation. The Almighty had sent him to punish and humiliate these people and he was the humble instrument of that God.

He now pursued his way through life with that ruthlessness which had always been his most dominant characteristic, but which, in the past, had been alleviated by flashes of softer emotions. The Henry of today would never have tried to save Oldcastle nor been ashamed of approving of his death.

Although he bore his part in the Christmas festivities, clapping the mummers and jugglers, leading his bride into the dance and attending with devoted regularity the many Masses and sermons, Henry's mind was elsewhere. The administration of his newly-acquired French dominions occupied the greater part of his thoughts, and although his soldiers were everywhere waiting, if necessary, to endorse his decrees with displays of martial force, the King knew that wherever possible he must move with caution. French laws and customs must remain the basis of all government; English ways and ideas adapted to them. Particularly was this so in the case of the Church, who dignitaries were more disposed in Henry's favour than Frenchmen of the other two Estates.

It was, therefore, rather embarrassing, on Christmas Day, to be faced with an irate Duke Philip who demanded that his Burgundian nominee be immediately appointed to the vacant See of Paris.

Henry hedged. He was in a cleft stick, having himself seconded the Burgundian nomination.

"The Canons, as Your Grace knows, have made their own choice; King Charles's almoner, Jean Courtcuisse."

Through closed doors, the music of fife, rebec, tabor and drum provided a light, faint background to Henry's words, reminding the world that it was the season of Peace and Goodwill.

Duke Philip was not impressed. His young face was taut with anger; an anger the more intense because Fate and circumstances had pushed him into being this man's ally. Deep in his heart, Philip was a Frenchman first and last, and one of the few great regrets of his life was that his father had not fought by King Charles's side at Agincourt. He looked at the long, heavily jowled face opposite, and in that moment he hated Henry Plantagenet. It was an evanescent emotion, but its effects remained and was, in later years, to have its consequences for Henry's son.

"You promised to support my candidate," Philip said. "You gave me your word."

Henry hesitated. He had pledged his support and because of his rigid sense of honour, disliked breaking his word. On the other hand, he did not wish to risk antagonising the

Chapter of Nôtre Dame, whose backing was a welcome buttress to his authority.

"I will see the Canons tomorrow," he answered, "and discover what, if anything, can be done."

But that evening, in the safety of his private solar, he confided to John: "I doubt if anything can be done. Once the Chapter has decided. . . . Short of commanding them. . . ." He broke off, biting his lip, then turned towards his prie-dieu. "I shall pray," he said, "for deliverance from an awkward situation."

John thought it the most human thing that he had heard Henry say for many months, and as if God, too, was pleased by that glimmer of humanity, that acknowledgement of human frailty, Henry's prayer was promptly answered.

Two days later, messengers arrived from England demanding Henry's urgent return.

22

BEYOND the windows of Westminster Hall, over a city whose day of pageantry was ending, as usual, in riots and drunken brawls, the short February twilight was drawing to its close. The last glimmers of light showed pale green and amber between swathes of purple-edged cloud, and the houses melted into the encroaching darkness until they were no more than faint stains on an inky cloth.

Inside Westminster Hall itself, the torches were lit, their flames licking over the scene in ripples of orange and gold. Occasionally, one would splutter and die in a shower of clouded blue sparks.

The King was absent, as protocol demanded from this, the Queen's coronation banquet. Katherine reigned supreme at the high table with Gloucester and Bedford and the young King of Scots for escort. Her third brother-in-law, Thomas of Clarence, had been left in France as Regent.

This latter arrangement had been very much against Henry's inclination, for he did not trust Thomas in the same way that he trusted John or, if it came to that, Humphrey. There was a certain rashness in Clarence, aggravated by the fact that he had been absent from Agincourt. John had had his own victory at sea and it seemed to Thomas that life had not dealt fairly with him. Moreover, both his younger brothers had, at one time and another, been Regent of England: why, therefore, should he not be Regent of France?

Henry had acknowledged the argument but still would not have yielded had he not been afraid of provoking an open breach between his heir-presumptive and himself. For years he and Thomas had disliked each other, but it had been a private disagreement, not a public one. The King might cut Clarence out of his will and Thomas might annoy Henry whenever and wherever he could, but there had been nothing substantial for the court gossips to whisper about in their corners or giggle over in the long, draughty corridors of Westminster or the Louvre. The very thought of airing their mutual grievances before the world was repugnant to Henry's reserved nature, and when he had realised that Thomas was ripe for a public quarrel if he failed to get his own way, the King had appointed Clarence Regent of France and said good-bye to him, with much misgiving, at Rouen.

The welcome home given by the English to their King and his bride had been even more emotional than that accorded to Henry after Agincourt. This time there was no great victory to celebrate, but the King had brought his subjects something far more important; English domination in France. Although no one in all that vast, cheering concourse from Dover to London had put the thought into so many words, there was, nevertheless, a feeling abroad that the battle of Hastings had at last been avenged. Yet the Englishman's instinctive hatred of the French, which had been one of the fruits of Senlac Field, was only aggravated by the knowledge that Anglo-Saxon superiority had finally triumphed.

This palpable dislike of all things French had been one of the contributory factors to Katherine's growing unhappiness. She had felt, almost from the moment of stepping ashore, her isolation. The mechanical marvels—the nodding giants, the fire-snorting dragons, the eye-rolling lions—which had greeted her on every stage of her journey to the capital, had seemed expressly designed to impress her with the fertility of English invention. She had soon realised that it was not enough for her simply to wonder at these sights; she must say that she had never seen anything to rival them in France.

And now, at her coronation banquet, as throughout the entire day, her loneliness engulfed her. She turned to James of Scotland on her left as a fellow stranger in a hostile land, but found him abstracted, almost silent. The reason for his apparent discourtesy was not hard to find: a little further along the board, the beautiful Joanna Beaufort (almost as lovely as her grandmother, Lady Swynford, had once been) sat beside her uncle, the Bishop of Winchester.

At the sight of Henry Beaufort's long, clever profile, Katherine turned away. She was afraid, as were so many others, of this man whose mocking glance seemed to pry into the secret places of her soul. She infinitely preferred the gentle Archbishop Chicele who had, that morning, crowned her and who now sat on her right-hand side. But even he was uncommunicative, pushing the endless courses of fish—being Lent, no meat was allowed—around a succession of gold, gem-encrusted plates.

"I loathe fish," he confided to Katherine, his nose wrinkled distastefully above his button of a mouth. He laughed. "A very unfortunate circumstance for a cleric."

But other than that, his contribution to the general babel of conversation was negligible, and in that room of deafening chatter, Katherine was enclosed in a cocoon of silence.

Bedford and Gloucester knelt before her, bare-headed; two young men whom she hardly knew; one, conscientious, upright, who treated her with the chilling deference due to his Queen and his brother's wife; the other, a wild youth with an eye for the opposite sex, who made it devastatingly plain that as a woman she held no attractions for him whatsoever.

All around Katherine, on either side and stretching away into the smoky distance of the hall, sat everyone who was anyone; dukes, earls, lords, princes of the Church, the Mayor of London and his Aldermen, ex-Mayors, petty officials, officers of the royal household; and every one of them, thought Katherine, as proud as the Devil, with that infuriating arrogance that made the English pour scorn and pity on anyone who was not of their race.

She clenched her hands in her lap in an agony of despair. Hers was a nature that needed the love of which life had so far starved her. Her marriage was a bitter disappointment; the more bitter in that others assumed her deliriously happy.

Even her own Frenchwomen envied her, but what good was a man's body without his mind?

Her restless eyes wandered about the hall. A young man was standing by the wall at one side. He wore the King's livery and was leaning forward, listening respectfully to something Thomas Beaufort was saying in his ear. Through the smoke and the constant passing and re-passing of servers and pages, his eyes met Katherine's and he smiled. In spite of herself, she smiled in return—and the contact was made. It was the first sight that Katherine de Valois and Owen Tudor had of each other.

Katherine's mind whirled with the places she had seen, the people she had met. She would have found this country-wide progress to such places at St Albans and Shrewsbury, Bristol and Nottingham, Norwich and Pontefract, trying even in normal circumstances, but the early stages of pregnancy had added to her discomfort. She was glad to rest for a day or two at York, inimical as she found this northern half of England, with its gaunt hills and crags and its taciturn, uncompromising men who reminded her so much of her husband.

Henry was walking in the gardens of the Augustinian Friary with his half-uncle, Henry Beaufort, staring unseeingly into the soft, white distances of the April day. The King felt that all was going well with him. This progress had yielded more in money and goodwill than even he had thought possible, and in eight months' time there would be an heir for the English throne. Only one small cloud shadowed his horizon and of that he never spoke to anyone; indeed, hardly admitted it to himself. Nevertheless, his intelligence told him that there was something wrong physically; something seriously amiss with his health. The feeling of lassitude which from time to time held him in its grip, seemed causeless in a man of thirty-four. And when he thought of his father and the heap of putrified flesh that he had become in his early forties, Henry was frightened. But then he consoled himself with the assurance that God would not—could not—let him die : there was still too much work to be done in France.

This northern air did him good; braced him against fatigue, although it did not make him more convivial. The bawdy joke which Walter Hungerford had just this moment told to Edmund Mortimer, and the Earl's answering shout of laughter, drew no smile from Henry. Even the Bishop was permitting himself a discreet grin, but the King, with his eye upon the Earl of March, reflected that there was always some cause for concern in a life which, for him, was continuously grim and earnest. Edmund Mortimer had given no more trouble since the days of the Southampton plot and had fought well and faithfully for Henry. But his very existence was a menace to the House of Lancaster, and now that there was to be a child. . . .

Henry turned to his half-uncle, speaking in an undertone. "Next time your sister comes to court, I should like her to bring the little Duke of York with her."

Henry Beaufort was surprised. Since placing the child in the Neville household, the King had evinced no further interest in March's nephew. Richard Plantagenet was now eleven years old, a sturdy, stolid boy given to occasional rash impulses; nothing at all like the calculating, decadent Cambridge. In fact, looking now and then at the short, sometimes pugnacious little figure, Henry Beaufort wondered if Anne Mortimer had not played her husband false. But it was not a serious thought.

A door of the Friary opened and Humphrey of Gloucester appeared, resplendent in crimson velvet, the inevitable silk-bound folio clutched under one arm. And again, the Bishop was moved to reflect upon the perversity of human nature. Of the four sons of Henry the fourth, the volatile Humphrey had always seemed the least likely to be bookish, yet from a precociously early age he had read anything and everything that came his way and loved literature in all its forms. It was, thought the Bishop, the only thing to be said in his youngest half-nephew's favour.

It was obvious now, to anyone who knew him well, that Humphrey was labouring under great excitement. His eyes glittered in his handsome face and his upper lip quivered as it always did under any emotional stress. But his voice was perfectly calm as he addressed his eldest brother.

"A messenger has arrived from London. Jacqueline of Hainault has landed at Dover."

"Jacqueline of . . ." Henry stared at his brother uncomprehendingly.

"She has run away from her husband and throws herself on your mercy. She looks to us to protect her from Duke Philip's anger."

Henry's busy brain strove to assimilate this new fact; to assess its implications and its added complication to the political scene. He turned towards his half-uncle, but Henry Beaufort's mouth had already shut in an uncompromising line of disapproval.

Duke Philip was their ally: England could not jeopardise his goodwill by sheltering one of his rebellious subjects, particularly his own cousin. The Bishop recognised in Jacqueline potential trouble, and the thought of her in conjunction with Humphrey made his senses boggle.

"Your Grace must refuse her sanctuary," he said bluntly, but for once the King ignored his half-uncle's advice.

Jacqueline was a woman in distress and she had appealed to the King of England for aid. Henry's strict adherence to the fast-vanishing laws of chivalry allowed him no alternative but to render the lady every assistance in his power. He therefore granted Humphrey leave to go south immediately and to welcome Jacqueline in his brother's name.

Nevertheless, he knew that his action would place strain on his relationship with the Duke of Burgundy and he was still mulling over the problem as the royal cavalcade approached Beverley a few days later. But the news which awaited him within the ancient city was such as to put every other consideration from his mind.

Thomas of Clarence was dead, killed in a disastrous action near Beaugé.

The messenger who brought the news was rocking on his feet with fatigue. He had ridden almost non-stop from Paris

211

to Calais, crossed on one of the roughest seas he could remember, and then, after a brief pause in London, had been directed by Archbishop Chicele to carry his tidings north into Yorkshire. He thought resentfully that, in the circumstances, someone else might have been detailed for the second half of an extremely unpleasant journey.

"Tell me exactly how it happened," the King commanded in a cold, tight voice which made the messenger think that perhaps it was just as well for the Duke of Clarence that he had been killed at Beaugé. The man swallowed and rubbed his sweating palms against the sides of his legs.

"It was before Easter, Your Grace. The Dauphin and his troops were raiding around Tours . . ."

"Tours!" exclaimed Henry. "You mean that my brother had left Paris to look for an army a hundred miles to the south?"

"He . . . he hoped to wipe out the Dauphinist forces, Your Highness. He wanted . . ."

"I know what he wanted," fumed Henry.

Thomas had wanted his Agincourt; his hour of glory that would rival his brothers'. Henry had always said that Clarence's absence from Agincourt would one day have its results.

He nodded briefly to the messenger, who scratched his nose and continued : "We marched to Angers. The Duke, I think, intended to besiege the town but found it too heavily fortified" —Henry snorted—"and so we retired to the east, on Beaufort."

"Go on," the King commanded harshly as the man hesitated.

"On Easter Saturday we took some prisoners—Scots mostly. They told us that the Dauphin was at Beaugé. The news was taken to the Duke." Again the messenger paused, but with Henry's gimlet eye upon him, found himself unable to prevaricate. "Sir Gilbert Umfraville and the Earl of Huntingdon both tried to dissuade His Grace from engaging the enemy, but he insisted. . . . We had no archers with us. . . ."

Henry's wrath now exploded into bestial rage. Words

which even the messenger had never heard before—oaths and imprecations straight from the stews of Cheapside—were flung like sling-shots into the silence of the room and a faint line of froth whitened the King's lips. Not until the paroxysm was over could the man continue with his story.

There was little more to tell. It had been utter disaster for the English army. Clarence, Lord Roos and Umfraville were all dead, the Earls of Somerset and Huntingdon prisoners. That was catastrophe enough; but the real damage, as Henry had already realised, was to the morale of the English troops. For the first time since the landing at Harfleur, six years earlier, they had been decisively beaten in battle. The Dauphinists were jubilant; the myth of English invincibility had been laid.

For a whole day Henry said nothing to anyone. The situation was too serious to clutter his mind with other people's advice or regrets. The only counsel he needed at present was his own. He had not intended returning to France until the end of the year, after the birth of his child; but he knew now that he must go back as soon as was humanly possible.

When he had broken the news to a stunned court and condoled briefly with his half-uncles on their nephew, Somerset's capture, he issued his orders for departure to London, sending messengers ahead to convene Parliament at the end of May. Other messengers went pell-mell for the Border with Henry's proposals for the Regent, Albany. No more Scottish aid for France, and within three months of Henry's return from this present expedition, James would be returned to Scotland with Joanna Beaufort as his wife.

The rains that washed out April and ushered in a fitful May saw the completion of a treaty with Genoa, thus cutting the Dauphin off from the naval genius of that sea-faring people. At Westminster, a deputation was received from Henry's cousin of Portugal and negotiations opened with Aragon.

"The man's not human," groaned an overworked Archbishop Chicele.

"He's burning himself out," thought a concerned Henry Beaufort, contemplating an England without Henry of Monmouth and finding the picture so distressing that he pushed it hurriedly to the back of his mind.

As the King made preparations to sail from Dover at the beginning of June, other problems beset him. He had given Jacqueline of Hainault a home and a pension and, in consequence, his first meeting with Philip of Burgundy was likely to be full of tension. He knew himself at fault here, but although Burgundy's support was now more vital to him than ever, he would not withdraw his protection from a lady in need. His neglected wife found it ironic.

In addition, his step-brother, the Duke of Brittany, emboldened by the English reverse at Beaugé and deeply resentful of Henry's treatment of his mother, made a treaty with the Dauphin at Sablé. And, finally, as Henry set sail on June the tenth, he knew that his health was seriously impaired. He was developing bald patches as his father had done before him; he winced at the slightest, unexpected sound; and the awful feeling of lassitude was with him night and day.

23

IT WAS very cold at Windsor. Dampness seeped up from the river into the walls of the castle and the fogs of late November and early December added to the general miasma. From her window Katherine could see nothing but rising mists in which floated disembodied shapes; a phantasmagoria of ghostly trees and bushes awash on a vaporous grey tide.

The Queen shuddered and turned back into the comfort of her room. The heat was stifling, every door and window sealed, for any day now she would give birth to England's heir. The midwives, making the most of their temporary importance, issued their orders to her women and ensured that no male passed the sacred portals of the lying-in chamber.

Katherine, seating herself in a chair and leaning her aching back against a thoughtfully placed cushion, reflected that this complete absence of men was right and proper. In a world built entirely by, for and around the male of the species, it was only fair that woman should have her moment of glory. Giving birth to a child was the one thing a man could never do, never share in, never understand. And Katherine, in a rush of belligerent femininity, felt exultant that there was this solitary occasion when a wife was of greater importance than her husband.

She was growing scornful of men, a disdain which was hardly surprising considering her experience; a mad father, three sickly, unprepossessing brothers and, perhaps worst of all, a husband who treated her with the same detached respect that he bestowed on any other valuable trophy of war.

Then she thought of Owen Tudor and relented. The Queen

had seen very little of him since the night of her coronation banquet, but what she had seen she had liked. She had also garnered odd scraps of information; that he was Welsh; that his father's family claimed a kinship of sorts with the great rebel, Owen Glendower; that, like all his race, he loved music and sang well; that he was kind, but had, as did all the Tudors, a streak of obstinacy in his make-up tantamount at times to downright pig-headedness.

This man, whom she seldom saw and rarely spoke to, had become for Katherine the object of all her latent adolescent adoration. Although nearly twenty, she was like a schoolgirl caught in the first delicious coils of a forbidden affection, and she and her cousin, Jacqueline of Hainault, would withdraw whenever possible from the society of the other women and sigh romantically together over their secret and hopeless attachments.

For Jacqueline, who, at Katherine's request, had been allowed to join the Queen's household at Windsor, considered herself in love with Humphrey of Gloucester. But whereas Katherine was resigned to the impossibility of her affection for Owen Tudor, Jacqueline was ruthlessly determined to have the Duke at any cost. Jacqueline had been married to two most unsatisfactory husbands; Katherine's brother, Jean, who had been Dauphin for so short a time after Louis's death, and now John of Brabant, an ugly, uncouth man whom she hated. She was far more self-aware than Katherine; knew her own needs and had long ago recognised that only a man of urgent sexual requirements—a man such as Humphrey of Gloucester—could satisfy her. By fair means or foul she would be rid of John of Brabant and marry the King of England's brother.

"Does he love you?" Katherine asked now, shifting in her chair to ease her discomfort and lowering her voice so that her ladies, sewing or playing games by the fire, could not hear.

Jacqueline shrugged, the contours of her shoulders showing a seductive plumpness beneath the velvet of her winter dress.

"He wants me. It's the same thing."

"No!" The Queen spoke with suppressed vehemence, suddenly the older and wiser of the two. "It's not the same thing at all. Henry wants me : he doesn't love me."

"Henry wants you," Jacqueline pointed out with truth, "because you are the daughter of your father. Humphrey wants me . . . for other reasons." She giggled.

"Perhaps! But you are also the daughter of your father," Katherine protested. "You inherited great lands and wealth, and it may be that my dear brother-in-law has his eye on those."

Jacqueline was riled as she always was when her physical charms were called in question.

"At least I know that he wants me, whatever the reason," she replied spiritedly. "That's more than you can say about Owen Tudor."

Katherine flushed and a lively quarrel might well have developed had she not been caught in the grip of a terrible pain. She leaned forward, gasping and clutching at her back as Jacqueline leapt to her feet, shouting for the midwives.

After that, the Queen remembered nothing very clearly except waves of pain coming at her with increasing rapidity and intensity. Sometimes, when the waves receded, she was conscious of lying on her bed, anxious faces peering at her through a red mist, voices raised in peremptory order; then the waves would come rolling in again, or hover, just out of reach, threatening to engulf her.

During those dreadful hours she was aware of nobody and nothing but herself. She was alone in the whole world with an agony which, after a while, became like a familiar friend. She got to know exactly what it would do; when it would arrive, when it would go away; when it was playful, when it was in grim earnest. Then, after a terrible moment when it swung towards her in a cloud of white light, and seemed to gather her up in its arms, preparatory to carrying her off into that halo of shining brightness, it quite suddenly dropped her and departed. And she knew that it had gone for good.

Life rushed in again; smiling faces, cries of congratulation and, over all, a thin, wailing cry that her tired brain refused for a second to recognise.

"A boy! A beautiful boy!" exulted the fat midwife with the mole on her left cheek. "A son for King Henry—and for you, of course, Madame!"

A while later, a small, soft body was put into her arms.

Henry was given the news—"a healthy boy, born on December the sixth at Windsor"—just before Christmas, while still besieging the town of Meaux.

He had landed at Calais in June, where he had received the Duke of Burgundy. It had been his first and most pressing task to placate his irate ally and that he had succeeded in doing so was due more to Philip's very precise interpretation of the laws of chivalry than from any lessening of his rancour. There was no disputing the fact that any knight appealed to by a lady in distress for assistance would be churlish to refuse; but Philip felt that had the detested Humphrey of Gloucester not encouraged Jacqueline a year or so earlier at Calais, and put all manner of discontented notions into the stupid girl's head, the present situation need never have arisen.

Nevertheless, the damage was done, and without Henry it was unlikely that Philip could ever satisfactorily avenge his father's murder. So he had arranged for the safe passage of the English army through Abbeville.

After a brief stay of four days in Paris, a joint English and Burgundian army had marched to the relief of Chartres and the Dauphinist forces had withdrawn. It had then been agreed that while Philip harassed Jacques d'Harcourt in Picardy, Henry and his English troops should attempt the reduction of a string of Dauphinist-held fortresses along the valley of the Loire.

By the middle of August, Dreux had fallen, both town and castle, but at Beaugency the castle had successfull held out. The retreating French had laid waste the countryside with the inevitable consequences of dysentry and famine amongst their enemies. When Henry captured Rougemont, therefore, he vented his anger in a display of brutality that included hanging every member of the garrison, burning the fortress and drowning all prisoners.

Salisbury, Warwick and Bedford had been alarmed, not so much by the savagery of Henry's revenge as by the obvious ill-health that prompted it, and they sent secretly to England for more doctors.

By the time that the siege of Meaux began in September, the King's physical condition was the cause of gravest concern. His eyes were sunken and his flesh hung loosely about his face. There were times, indeed, when his appearance was frightening, but he drove himself on like a man who knew that he had too much to do and too little time to do it in.

The Dauphin's refusal to accept the Treaty of Troyes had become an obsession with Henry and he issued one proclamation after another naming Charles de Valois the arch-traitor of France. But worse than this, far worse because he must keep it secret, was the treachery of his own thoughts. Never in his life before had Henry questioned his actions. He had been chosen as the Scourge of France to vent God's wrath upon an evil and decadent people. Now, he found himself wondering if it were not all an illusion; whether his French empire was not built upon the sand of his own desires; desires bolstered by his Councillors because they saw in foreign wars the means of keeping the peace at home and suppressing the troubles which his father's usurpation of the throne had created.

He thrust the thoughts violently from him. The throne of England had been his father's by right of inheritance from Edmund Crouchback and God had given him, Henry of Monmouth, victory over the French because he had been chosen as the instrument of Divine retribution. Nevertheless, the mental conflict added to the King's bodily weakness.

Only his brother, Bedford, guessed at the misgivings gnawing at the King's mind and only to Bedford did Henry ever give glimpses of his carefully guarded soul. And from those glimpses, John, slow, steady, but highly intelligent, learned a lesson which would one day prove of value to him in his struggle against a young girl from Lorraine. Once Henry began to doubt his divine inspiration, his will-power and his efficacy as a leader of men started to ebb away.

219

To his new Master of the Household, Sir John Fastolfe, the Duke of Bedford remarked with apparent irrelevancy: "It's better to be a plain soldier, John, relying on your own conviction of right and wrong, than to believe your destiny guided by anyone, even God."

Fastolfe smiled with affectionate cynicism. For if any man was going to live out his life on the precepts and principles of another, he reflected, that man was John of Bedford. The Duke's devotion to, and adoration of, his eldest brother made that certain.

The arrival of the messenger with the news of Prince Henry's birth—for the Queen had presumed it to be the wish of her lord that the baby should be christened with his own and his father's name—was the medicine the King had been needing. Here, in the birth of a son, was the proof of God's continuing care for his servant, Henry Plantagenet. The King was immediately contrite and, while his army rejoiced and drank itself into a stupor at the glad tidings, he spent hours upon his knees begging forgiveness for his doubts.

As soon as the Christmas truce was over, Henry bent all his energies towards reducing Meaux. The information that the Duke of Suffolk had retaken Avranches also put new heart into troops who were beginning to be thoroughly sick of the war.

"Taking Normandy was one thing," grumbled George Bennet, Cordwainer, to John Flete, Wheelwright. "It's ours by rights. But conquering the whole of bloody France, that's another story. I've got a wife and two boys, and God alone knows what's happening to me business while I'm away. . . . My God! What's that? Look there! Look there!"

This last injunction had been startled from him by a most unusual sight and sound, and he and his friend were not the only two to stare open-mouthed at the ramparts of the town.

There had been a lull of some hours in the fighting and now a French horn-blower had driven an ass on to the walls and was beating the animal until it brayed. Then, when the attention of everyone, both high and low, in the English camp had been arrested, the Frenchman yelled: "Come and rescue your King, Englishmen! Can't you hear him crying out for help?"

"God's toe-nails and little fingers!" gulped Flete. "I wouldn't give anything to be in 'is shoes if the town surrenders. If there's one thing our King—God bless 'im—ain't got, it's a sense of 'umour."

The wheelwright was perfectly correct and it was a rash man who even mentioned the incident within Henry's hearing.

But the siege was really no laughing matter on either side. The Captain of the French garrison, the Bastard of Vaurus, was committing the most brutal atrocities on all his English prisoners. Instead of this disheartening the enemy troops, however, as was his intention, it merely engendered in them a burning determination to force the city's surrender whatever the cost. They stopped grumbling and fought like demons, with the result that at the end of May, the English marched into Meaux as conquerors.

And although it was felt that the execution of the hornblower was, if inevitable, not a spectacle which they really cared to witness, the English watched with greedy, bloodthirsty pleasure the death of the Bastard of Vaurus.

On May the twenty-sixth, Henry was joined by Katherine in Paris. They took up residence, as before, in the Louvre, with King Charles and Queen Isabeau at the Hôtel St Pol.

Katherine had left little Henry behind in England, not wishing to expose the child to the rigours of a Channel crossing in the chill of an early spring. There would be plenty of time in the future for father and son to meet.

But when she set eyes on Henry, she was not so sure. She had not seen him for almost a year and his looks appalled her. Without thinking, she said: "You are ill. You must rest."

"Nonsense!" he answered brusquely. "It's just that I'm tired." He brushed her concern aside. "We will go to Senlis," he said, "the air there will be better for me."

Katherine acquiesced and hurried on the removal. She might not love Henry, but she knew too well the precariousness of her position in a foreign country should anything

221

happen to him. The example of her kinswoman, Queen Joanna, was constantly in her thoughts.

Hardly had the court settled at Senlis, however, than messengers arrived from Philip of Burgundy begging for Henry's help at the siege of Cosnes. And while the students of Paris University prayed for the speedy restoration of Henry's health, the invalid himself, in spite of all entreaties, made preparations to leave Senlis at once. The feeling that he owed Duke Philip reparation urged him on against his better judgement.

He took abrupt leave of his wife and parents-in-law and set out in a horse-litter in all the heat and stench of a plague-ridden July, but at Corbeil it became obvious, even to himself, that he could travel no further.

"You must go back," besought Bedford. "The doctors say it will be madness to continue."

"Not back to Senlis," Henry protested feebly. "Take me to Vincennes. It's cooler there. But you and our uncle of Exeter must go to Cosnes. There may be a battle. You must. . . ."

John, seeing his brother becoming agitated, soothed him with the promise that he and Thomas Beaufort would depart within the hour. If there was to be a pitched battle, the English would be there to add their weight and experience to the Burgundian side.

But there was no battle, for the Dauphinists raised the siege and melted away into the hot August sunshine. Hardly had they done so, when messengers arrived to summon Bedford and Exeter back to Vincennes. There was no doubt now that the King was dying.

It took Henry three weeks to die. His once-splendid body refused to yield up his spirit without a struggle.

"It's the death-curse of all the Plantagenets," he said with a weak smile to his half-uncle, Thomas Beaufort. "Our constitutions are too strong to let our souls go with ease."

The Duke turned away, gasping with emotion. He could not credit that Henry was going to die. He thought of him as he had been on his coronation day, full of health and vigour.

No one could really believe it except the King. He knew that he was dying; could feel the strength slipping away from him day by day and made preparations accordingly. Bedford was to carry on Henry's work as Regent of France, while Humphrey was to be Regent of England, but always subordinate to Bedford. Henry Beaufort and his brother Thomas were to be the little King's governors. Of Katherine, there was no mention : Bedford doubted if Henry thought of her at all.

The end came on the night of August the thirty-first after a day of almost incandescent heat. Henry had just dozed off in the arms of his Confessor, Thomas Netter, when he was jerked awake with a terrible cry.

"You lie! You lie!" His voice rose to a frenzy. "My portion is with the Lord Jesus Christ!"

He saw them all around him, the mangled bodies of the dead; the Scots archers, the prisoners of Monthéreau, the horn-blower of Meaux. Their faces, with the withered skin and empty eye-sockets, leered at him through the darkness; their broken bodies moved slowly about his bed in the Dance of Death.

After this rebuke, however, they slunk away into the night and he saw that their faces were really those of his friends; brother Bedford, his half-uncle, Thomas Beaufort, his Confessor, Thomas Netter. But he knew that the time had come.

As Netter raised him in his arms, a great calm came over the King and he uttered the time-honoured words: "In manus tuas Domine . . ." in a steady voice. There was a brilliant flash of light. . . .

The crucifix slipped from his hands.